Evanescence

Evanescence

STORIES 1950's–2000

AUDREY BORENSTEIN

Copyright © Audrey Borenstein.

All rights reserved. No part of this book may be reproduced in any form or by any electronic or mechanical means, including information storage and retrieval systems, without permission in writing from the publisher, except by reviewers, who may quote brief passages in a review.

ISBN: 978-1-64713-517-1   (Paperback Edition)
ISBN: 978-1-64713-518-8   (Hardcover Edition)
ISBN: 978-1-64713-515-7   (E-book Edition)

Some characters and events in this book are fictitious. Any similarity to real persons, living or dead, is coincidental and not intended by the author.

Book Ordering Information

Phone Number: 347-901-4929 or 347-901-4920
Email: info@globalsummithouse.com
Global Summit House
www.globalsummithouse.com

Printed in the United States of America

Evanescence: Stories, 1950s-2000 is a collection of twelve stories by Audrey Borenstein portraying life in the United States during the second half of "the American century" followed by her Afterword. Although public events in this work are part of the historical record, the characters portrayed herein are fictional, composites drawn from several individuals combined with the literary imagination. No reference to any living person is intended or should be inferred.

"The Visions" was published in *Kansas Quarterly*, Volume 5, No. 3 (Summer 1973), pp. 53-58, and selected as one of the Distinctive Short Stories, 1973" in *The Best American Short Stories 1974*, edited by Martha Foley.

"The Natural History of a Friendship" was published in *Nimrod*, Vol. 11, No. 2 (Winter 1966), pp. 5-27.

"A Time for Good-bye Forevers" was published in *Ascent*, Vol. 1, No. 1 (Summer 1975), pp. 24-36.

"A Fragment of Glass" was published in *The Arlington Quarterly*, Vol. 1, No. 1 (Fall 1967), pp. 75-83, and received the Award for Excellence in Fiction, Fiction Prize for New York State, in The National League of American Pen Women's annual competition in published or unpublished fiction and poetry, April 1988.)

"Tide of the Unborn" was published in *Ais-Eiri, the Magazine of Irish-America*, Vol. 2, No. 3 (June 1978), pp. 36-41.

"Rites of Separation" was published in *Womanblood: Portraits of Women In Poetry and Prose*, edited by Aline O'Brien, Chrys Rasmussen and Catherine Costello (San Francisco, California: Continuing SAGA Press, 1981), pp. 148-156, and was nominated by the editors for a Pushcart Prize in Fiction.

"In a Brief Space" was published in *North Dakota Quarterly*, Vol. 52, No. 1 (June 1984), pp. 34-53, and was nominated by the editor for a Pushcart Prize in Fiction.

"Evanescence" was published in *Kansas Quarterly/Arkansas Review*, Vol. 26, Nos. 1-4, Transition Issue (Spring 1996), pp. 374-385.

"The Cameo." Fifty copies of this story were privately printed by the author for distribution to friends of her literary estate.

Books by Audrey Borenstein

Custom: An Essay on Social Codes, a translation of *Die Sitte* by Ferdinand Tönnies (New York: The Free Press, 1961)

Redeeming the Sin: Social Science and Literature (New York: Columbia University Press, 1978)

Older Women in Twentieth-Century America: A Selected Annotated Bibliography (New York: Garland Publishing, Inc., 1982)

Chimes of Change and Hours: Views of Older Women in Twentieth-Century America (New Jersey: Fairleigh Dickinson University Press/ Associated University Presses, 1983)

Through the Years: A Chronicle of Congregation Ahavath Achim, 5725-5750 by Walter and Audrey Borenstein (New Paltz, New York: Franklin Printing, 1989)

Simurgh, a novel-in-the-round (Fifty copies, privately printed by Audrey Borenstein, and donated to Judaica Collections of Special Libraries throughout the U.S. and to friends of her literary estate, 1991)

One Journal's Life: A Meditation on Journal-Keeping (Seattle: Impassio Press, 2002)

The Kingdom Where Nobody Dies (Xlibris Corporation, 2009)

Evanescence: Stories, 1950s-2000

Contents

1950s

The Visions 3
The Natural History of a Friendship 12

1960s

A Time For Good-bye Forevers 41
A Fragment of Glass 55

1970s

Tide of the Unborn 65
Rites of Separation 80

1980s

In a Brief Space 93
Evanescence 118
The Cameo 135

1990s

After Many Days, a story of coming-of-age 175
Brief Gallantry 193

2000

Hart Strings 213

Afterword 229

for my beloved children and grandchildren

1950S

The Visions

The two physicians strolled over the grounds back of the Meyer estate. Thaddeus was nearly a foot taller than his friend. He kept his hands locked behind his back, his shaggy head bent, his stride slow. Carl—always animated, always on the edge of irritability—whacked at the trees with the stick Billie Joe had given him. The child was forever digging, digging pits and holes of various sizes with a rapt intensity, though he'd been scolded for it often by his mother and by the yard man. Last week, he had made a gift of his favorite stick to his father.

Carl's whacks were playful at first. Then, as they approached the green slopes leading down to the bayou, he smacked at the trunks with an energy that was more like anger.

"Did I ever tell you that the fellow who landscaped this place died before the house was finished? Frances and I decided to let the plans go through anyway. I remember, we were both superstitious about fooling with them."

"Whoever he was, he had the soul of an artist."

"You leave your mark," Carl mused, "where you least expect to."

Thaddeus's heart pounded painfully.

THWACK!

Thaddeus winced at the pounding his friend gave the sweet gum at the edge of the slope. Not that the tree couldn't take the battering—it was Carl he fretted about.

"I'm gratified you're not aiming that thing at me."

"Too decent for that. You're unarmed."

They stood for a moment before making their descent, drawing in the silence of early evening. The land flowed down to the swamp, a lush green river of grass banked on either side with bridal wreath and azalea, boxwood and crape myrtle. At the foot of the hill, where the soil was over-rich, Carl had planted a half-grown Chinese elm over Ellen's protest that it couldn't possibly survive the transplant. "Even if it *does* live," she fretted, vexed at Carl's mulishness, "who on *earth* would ever come down there to admire it? Besides, I don't think it's *any*thing to look at!" Ruth had been over at the house during this exchange. Embarrassed by the fuss, she had wandered out to the yard and taken a swing with Billie Joe on the glider. But their voices had carried out there—Ellen's accent growing thicker with her exasperation, Carl's tone more and more belligerent. "*Good*ness," Ruth had said, reporting it all to Thaddeus, "how two grown people can feel so passionately about a *tree!*" Carl had won his case, of course ("That tree's for me! For me, you hear! Not for your ladyfriends at the Garden Club!") and he'd been vindicated too, for the tree had flourished.

A tender drift of twilight wind, mixing swampscent and flowers, brushed the slender limbs; they lifted and fell, and the pale green hearts of their leaves shimmered in the humid air.

The sun was just falling beyond the swamp. Its fire drove upward through the trees. *Like a serpent's tongue*, Thaddeus thought, remembering the theophany of his boyhood. *A hidden serpent, with golden coils that lock in the cosmic rhythms.* The milky flesh of the sky was veined with rose and violet, and pure pale blue. A moist wind, the breath of the bayou sweet and decaying, lifted the braids of Spanish moss and wound them lightly around the trunks of the ancient cypresses. Birds were swooping, diving, spinning through the heavy wood of oak and birch and pine. Branches threaded through one another, their leaves swimming like green minnows in a river of shifting lights.

Carl shouldered his stick and began the descent. Thaddeus called to him. Without turning, he shouted back, "I don't need your nostrums!" He held his head high going down, Thaddeus saw with love and pity, doomed and knowing he was doomed, striding through that marshy grass with a courage so flamboyant, one who was not his friend would have called it by another name.

Stopping under his tree, Carl poked thoughtfully through the branches with his new toy.

"Look up there!" he called, waiting impatiently for Thaddeus to catch up with him. "See that patch of scorched branches? Tent caterpillars did that." He grinned. "I've been comin' out here early in the morning lately. First thing I knew, I felt a presence. Like you do when there's a snake around. You know what it's like that time of day—hummingbirds everywhere, dew heavy on the grass and bushes, every manner of spider out after his business, that wet mist around the trees . . . well, sir, somethin' made me look up there in the branches. And I thought I saw some kind of fowl up there. Starin' at me. That's the shape it took—a fowl—this place the caterpillars ate away. Transparent, of course, but all the same, I felt it starin' at me. Sitting up there in the branches like Pride itself."

"I thought twilight was the hour for visions. Not dawn."

"You don't go out seekin' after 'em like you're frog giggin' or somethin', you know. They come to *you*."

"Haven't any come to me yet."

"If you weren't such a hard-shell nonbeliever, you'd see somethin'."

"You and your fowl come to any understanding?"

"You might call it that. I got up there with an oil rag wrapped around my weapon here, and burned him out. Before those cannibals could eat up my tree entirely. Come on. Let's go down."

Thaddeus followed his friend into the wood. Just when he had assumed they were in for a good hike, Carl stopped, drew a circle in the grass with his stick, whacked the pine cones out of the way, and sat down, leaning on it now, his chin resting on his knuckles, staring ahead into his fate. Thaddeus came up in back of him and paused to read the sky and his mood. Both, he decided, were inscrutable. Shrugging, he stretched out across from Carl and leaned back on his elbows.

"Bet this grass has just the right feel for bare toes."

"Look at this." Carl plucked up one of the toadstools that studded the thick, wet turf. He pressed it, his thumb pleasuring in its spongy feel. The surface of the umbrella cap was salted with small, brown nodules; turning it over, he pondered the symmetry of the filaments on the underside. "Couple drove down from the Midwest a few weeks back, stopped along the road to pick mushrooms for their supper. Both dead. Damn fools." In a sudden disgust, he threw it toward the darkening water. Then he took his pipe out of his shirt pocket and closed his teeth over the cold stem.

Thaddeus grunted, pulled up his knees, and clasped them with his hands. "You want a light, or is that thing just for pacifyin' purposes?"

"Pacifyin'. Think I'll just suck a while."

Waiting for a sign, Thaddeus studied his friend frankly now that Carl had turned his face away. The illness had turned his hair completely white. But his body had not given up its youthfulness. *Never would*, Thaddeus thought, *even at sixty. If he had till sixty.* Carl's face was swollen from the edema—his cheeks puffy, his eyes strangely smaller now; and his lips stretched almost in a grimace. As though smiles cost him pain. "*Ridi, Pagliacci*" . . . one of the many arias he sang with genuine self-mockery. He'd treated them to it on his last birthday-he'd turned forty-seven then. First, the four of them had gone over to New Orleans for a dinner of Lobster Thermidor. They'd toasted his future, his many happy returns, with champagne. That was a few weeks before Carl's attack. His vision had been affected for a while. That was the hypertension. Then the swelling began. *He's going out fast*, old Hallowell had told Thaddeus. *Bright's disease. He never told you it was in the family?* No, Thaddeus hadn't known, nor Ellen, nor, probably, Frances before her. None of them had the courage Carl had, to look the beast in the face. *The wonder of it is*, Carl had marveled, shaken but still in control, *Papa's symptoms didn't even appear until after he was sixty. Thought I had time.* He'd chuckled then, with the clinician's sense of the ironic. Up in the solarium Ellen had only said, *It can't be. No. It can't*, first to Thaddeus, then to Ruth, then to Thaddeus again.

"*Ridi, Pagliacci.*" That night, when they were riding back from the restaurant, Ellen had leaned her head on her husband's shoulder as he steered the car through a heavy downpour. The rains brought on reminiscing about the floods in Magnolia City; more than once, Carl said, he'd gone over to the hospital by pirogue. Like his father before him. He'd been singing in the car, some damnfool song, "*There Ain't No Flies on the Lamb of God.*" Ruth was wearing a new perfume that minded Thaddeus of gardenias and damp moss and a young girl's hair long and silky and bright under the moonlight. Ellen was dressed in white lace, he remembered. And the straps gleamed on her dark, smooth shoulders. And she'd sprinkled some kind of sparkle-dust on her hair. *Feeling faintly festive*, she'd said drolly. And Carl had smacked her behind as she got into the car. And she'd screamed. *Downright wicked in white*, Carl had said, to justify himself. Or something like that. It was when they'd come back to the house that he'd treated them to the aria.

Carl twirled the end of his stick in the soft earth. "She won't have it, Dee. No, sir, she just won't have it." He spoke softly, never once looking up.

"What did you expect, Carl?"

"Know what that girl wants?" Now Carl *did* look up, his face all fury. "Another baby. Yessir, she wants another baby!"

Thaddeus shook his head.

"And I'm gonna tell you why. At first, I thought, that's just like a woman-chile, she doesn't want to lose all of me. Though Lord knows Billie Joe's enough to keep her mindful. But then I thought again. She doesn't believe it, Dee, she has no understanding of it."

"She needs time, Carl."

"Time!" Carl took his pipe out of his mouth and pointed the stem of it at Thaddeus. "Dee, time's just what I haven't got!"

"I know."

"Now, hear me out. After all, you're the faith healer, you're the one with the license to hear confessions. Damn!" He smacked at a mosquito on his neck.

The light was just now beginning to fade. Deep in the wood a water thrush called. Both men waited, and smiled at one another when they heard, after a moment, the answer of its mate.

"You will remember how wild I was for her. Yes, sir, you will well remember. I had to have that woman-chile. Had to have her all for myself. Drove Frances and my girls out of that house up there. Tore up my life when I was nearer forty than I'd care to acknowledge. For those dark good looks, those big brown eyes. It came like a fever. And it burned like a fever. Now, Dee, in God's truth, I can't go *near* her. And I don't want her anywhere near me."

"Since when is all this, now? Last week? Last night?"

"Since old Hallowell passed sentence on me."

"Just like that? Like lightning struck?"

"Just like that. It struck the day I first set eyes on her. And now it's struck again, the other way."

"Have you tried to tell her?"

"Dee, what man can tell a woman-chile anything?"

"Carl." His friend's eyes, as death approached, seemed to burn with an astral light. Thaddeus couldn't look at him anymore without hurting. "How do you know what she's made of? Maybe . . . maybe you ought to give her a chance."

"She's playmate, Dee. A silly, beautiful playmate. Made out of no more stuff than this evenin' wind. I tell you, I loathe the sight of her now—"

"Good God!"

"You cut into your patients like that?"

"You're not my patient. Never were."

"Well, I've just appointed you my confessor. Every man has to have one when he's goin'. It's your hard luck. I've sinned, I've sinned mightily, Dee, against Frances, against my daughters—"

Against Ellen, Thaddeus thought. *Plus there's Billie Joe*. But he kept his peace, a peace aching from Carl's cruelty.

"First thing that goes is wanting a woman. Dee, I can't even recollect the fire that burned me. I can't even *believe* in it!" He pulled up a fistful of grass and threw it over his shoulder. Then another. And another.

"Easy. Easy."

"Got to work this out, once for all. *Got* to, Dee!"

The two men could no longer make out one another's features. The dusk had sunk into a darkening that shaded the trees first a deep blue, then black. The chanting of the crickets rose from the edge of the bayou, persistent, keening, like Indian music—a thin, high utterance of exquisite pathos.

"Woman doesn't believe in death. No, sir. I learned that twenty years ago, when I did OB. She thinks she's got some kind of *claim* on immortality. That's why she wants to get pregnant, keep *gettin'* pregnant. She's fierce, then, when she's got that seed planted in her.

Knows Nature'll protect her. Knows her life's safe. *Sacred*, maybe. She's got a sense that death won't touch her then. Frances was the same. The very same."

"Maybe that's the design of it."

"Way I read your design, she wants some kind of sign that she'll go on, part way to forever."

"That's only human, Carl, only human. You want it too. So do I, so do we all. But there's another way to read it, try to be more generous." Thaddeus was aware his tone was pleading. But he no longer cared about things like that. "Just turn it, a little turn. Another child . . . it might seem to her to be a way of keeping *you*—part way to forever."

Carl thumped the stick in and out of the grass—short, savage strokes. "I don't want to hear that sweet talk, Dee! I know what she's made of! Didn't you tell me yourself, eight years ago? Didn't you try to warn me off?"

Indeed I did, Thaddeus thought, *I did indeed*. Maybe he'd spoken more out of a sense of duty than out of the hope of being listened to. *You're just like any shaman*, Carl had laughed, *you're all such sanctimonious bastards!* Yes, he'd been bewitched all right, by Ellen's Latin beauty. The sort of beauty, Thaddeus had thought then, that blooms and blooms—and then fades all at once, completely. Yes, she'd quickened something in Carl—the mad dream of immortality, maybe, eternal youth . . . the very dream that fired her now, that caused him to turn away like this. No, he'd spoken gently, just once, not so much for Frances's sake, nor even for Carl's, but for the sake of their friendship. More than anything, Thaddeus had wanted it to survive, as few friendships do, the ruptures of divorce, remarriage.

"Carl, no one stays the same. Not even from one week to the next. That's the devil of it."

"Well, *I* do! *I* do!"

"Damn your hide, you always want to *think* you do! You always insist on yourself! You won't let any of us in!"

The night that had gathered itself in seemed to both of them alive, aswarm with their emotions. A frog had joined the chorus of the crickets; the cloying wind searched out the trees to make its music; the swamp murmured of its secrets.

"Tell you what, Dee. Hallowell wants me to go up to that clinic. Thinks they can do something for me I know better. But I've had second thoughts. I intend to go."

"I was hoping you would."

"I won't come back. You know that."

"I know nothin'."

"Dee, I want you, you and Ruth, to keep Ellen down here with Billie Joe. I don't care what manner of lie you tell her. Just keep her down here. That woman won't let me die my own death. And every man's entitled to that. I want my own death, hear?"

Thaddeus sighed. He reached for Carl's fist, grasped it, held it for a moment. "All right. It's as good as done."

It was so dark now that he could see only Carl's hair, a wraith floating above the pale torso. He imagined he could see his eyes too, though, and that they were fixed on a point above the trees.

Carl raised his stick—his weapon, his cane, his wand, his divining rod, his baton of command. "Let's get out of here. My britches are soaked through."

Thaddeus got to his feet and reached for his friend's arm. Carl gave the proffered hand a shove.

"I know this land better than anyone," he said. Then he swore.

They walked abreast of one another toward the slope. They passed Carl's tree, and now Thaddeus too felt its presence in back of him, felt the eyes of the visitant Carl had immolated, on his back. The tree, the fowl, the vision, he wondered, what did it all come to? Was it that recognition comes at the same moment as loss—faith in the power to heal, awareness of what youth means . . . like Aeneas recognizing his mother just as she turned away? There was a light, he thought, a radiance, buried in the pit of the skull. So placed that the eye might never behold the face of truth.

They began the climb slowly. They used to race up; and Carl always won. Thaddeus remembered more keenly than he cared to how Carl had taught Billie Joe to somersault and do handsprings and stand on his head at the very top of the slope. Now that they were almost there, he remembered too how many years ago, before Billie Joe, before Ellen even, Carl had decided to give a midnight concert out in the yard. He'd been standing in the glider, one leg thrust out in front, singing for all the world to hear, while Frances tried to shush him. Finally, finally, Frances had learned too that there was a price for sharing in his light, his *mana*—that magic he gave off like electric waves. What he wanted, he spoke for and he put claim to and he took. His was a breed that never knew refusal or failure, a breed that never had to compromise. Such a man would never turn up in Thaddeus's chambers. Though often their wives did. And even more often, their children.

Why, why did he have to go and marry a playmate? Some men, Thaddeus thought, were twice-born in religion. And some in art. And some in sex.

Now, at the top of the slope, he remembered the party evenings, and they became one evening—the lawn a cool, dark green . . . the Japanese lanterns blossoming in the trees . . . the magnolias gleaming like asphodels . . . the laughter and the teasing . . . the ambrosia of the women's perfumes, the potion of their love-magic . . . the glasses lifted to the lips, the ice in the glasses tinkling . . . the deep tones of the baby grand in the room beyond the veranda, and Carl's voice, mellow and strong . . . Ellen in pale green chiffon, fluttering like a great luna moth under the mimosa . . . the descant of the night insects, the fragrances and voices and Southernsweet air commingling in an incense heady with romance and pleasure and concupiscence . . . the lovely masquerade ball each one of them imagined as unending.

As they came nearer the house, they saw the lights spill through the glass doors onto the veranda. The women were inside. Waiting. "A kidney," Carl marveled. "To be undone by a kidney!"

They put their heads together, colleagues now, losing themselves in the old fascination. But then, as they turned onto the flagstone path, Thaddeus happened to glance up; and the vision Carl had promised he'd one day see hovered over the glass doors: It was a silhouette rimmed in gold, his, unmistakably his—the head, the shoulders, the elbows bent now, the familiar pipe in his lips, the hands lighting the pipe. The shadows of the mimosa tree fluttered across the image imprinted on the glass. It seemed to deepen, to grow, to take in the grace and the vigor of this man at his side . . . this man he loved, and was therefore powerless to heal.

The Natural History of a Friendship

We became friends in our student days because, George said, of common circumstance, not character. I accepted his judgment, although then as now I can find no precise distinction between the two. Our bonds, whatever their name, were formed on that campus—under the elms in all their seasons, in the bicycle lot back of the library, at the open stalls in front of the bookshop, and across the table of a certain booth in a certain drugstore, where we idled away many a Sunday morning after a breakfast of waffles or eggs . . . . These places, and those strange, bright years of my awakening have endowed me with souvenirs, with sentiments; and many of them have the impress of my friend.

We contradicted one another in appearance. George used to remark: "No one would ever take you for a Jew. You're too tall, and your nose is too straight. Now, *I*—" slapping at his heavy middle—"I am a perfect stereotype of the Semite." This would irritate me—not only because I reject stereotypes, but because he was so derisive about our common ancestry that he provoked me to defend it at a time when I was struggling with my own spiritual crisis.

In temperament, George was restive. His vocabulary was rich with curses and superlatives; he had a nervous brilliance and a remarkable memory for facts. I am more phlegmatic. My speech is dispassionate, and in matters of aesthetics and morals I have always tended toward balance and harmony. Our friendship, then, had to depend on other similarities-our love of argument, our idealization of an ascetic life, our habits (we were both confirmed *voyeurs*.) As in all close associations, we inspired the worst and best in one another, and sometimes our intimacy brought us to grief. At these times we would exchange insults which were all the more wounding because we knew where to aim. After that we would avoid one another for days, even weeks at a time. The truth is, we both had the great moral flaw of youth—we were more anxious to be understood than to understand. We fell out, but we fell in again: we had given each other knowledge about ourselves that could not be redeemed.

George confided his personal history to me with great pride. He was born in Czechoslovakia of very well-to-do parents, and had been given an excellent education. During the war he was deported to a concentration camp with his father and older sister; his mother, who was not Jewish, remained at their home in Prague. After the war had ended, the family was brought to the United States by relatives. George's sister had since married, and his parents were living in Chicago. His father had once been a successful lawyer; now, both his health and spirit were broken.

"My parents torment me," George told me when we first met. "I have no ambition; I don't believe in anything. I am a demoralized person. Yet they want me to go to Law School. My father, who could not practice here even if he were able, wants to be born again in me. I can't even go home anymore without getting into a fight. Their situation is tragic, yes; but so is mine. I have no more interest in systems of any kind. You'd think the old man would learn to live with his despair, as I do."

I told him that I thought the despair of the old was a bit more difficult to cope with than the despair of someone twenty-one years old.

"You can talk, Martin, you can talk! What do you know of exile? What do you know of the loss of paradise?"

At times, his insinuations angered me. Once I shouted at him, "Do I have to apologize for having been born here? Don't you think the good life can mean as much to me as it does to you? Is experience the only measure of truth? If so, I can talk about certain truths you have never encountered—about poverty, about active combat—" George shook his head and smiled in a way that exasperated me.

He told me with a pomposity that I thought outrageous: "To me, you are more European than American. It is the European in you that I admire."

The remark was ridiculous, but it had its sting. I envied George, then; I suppose I still do. He seemed to have a larger measure of spiritual integrity than I; his life seemed marked by the force of dramatic decisions, while mine has always moved, dreamlike, along the parallel of natural inclination. Yet it was George who insisted, "Choice is pure illusion," and I was fond of saying, "We are our own architects."

George had to take up a major subject sooner or later, and it was anthropology. He was a good craftsman, and he enjoyed making replicas of some of the objects of his study—pottery, amulets, kachina dolls, figures of chiefs and shamans in authentic costume. He worked with clay and stone, but wood was by far his best medium. He lived in the basement apartment of an old frame house near the campus, and the place was filled with his work. We used to take a bottle of chianti down there, and sit and talk until long after midnight. George fascinated me with his descriptions of Eskimo art, of the philosophy of the Balinese and the religion of the Hopi Indians, of the rites of establishing legitimacy, of taboos and myths and ceremonies. We found in all these rules of life beautiful metaphors of the human condition; yet we could apply little of what we had learned to our own existence. George delighted in quoting a line from Edna St. Vincent Millay's *Aria da Capo*: "I love Humanity, but I hate people." The words displeased me. I used to tell him that his intellect was far more developed than his feeling, and that this might one day prove to be his undoing.

Although I have always been less passionate about ideas and people than George, I had many friends; he had only me. Partly this was because, though I never would have admitted it then, George was more of a stranger in the university world than I was. Partly it was because I am a musician, and musicians generally fraternize with one another; we have our own universe of discourse. George was jealous of my friends, and criticized them incessantly. He claimed that he despised a specialist of any sort, that anyone in the twentieth century who was moving toward a goal was either a fool or a knave.

I argued with him: "You have to move toward something. You take a direction in any study, and you build on what you've learned. No one can stand still—not even you."

"You're wrong, my friend. I am an encyclopedia of facts, largely useless, which I collect for my own amusement. I am only marking time. I'm no philosopher of history; I have no magic formula. Let the great Toynbees spin their webs. Sooner or later, they'll only ensnare themselves."

"Do you think you can be a student forever?"

"Why couldn't I? The truth is, some day I'll get bored with this life and go back to my country. I don't belong anywhere, but here least of all." In those years I still cherished certain illusions about my talents. I am a violinist, and I wanted to eventually play in a major symphony orchestra. It came to me, very gradually, that I was good but not good enough. I suppose I always suspected that I would end by teaching music, and become in time a permanent attachment to some university. When I spoke of this to George, he protested vigorously against what he chose to call "false humility" and "selling out to the system." "So," he would say, "you will one day marry and have children and teach, and reduce yourself, in short, to a middle-class cipher."

I had little to answer to his challenge. I knew I could never have his passion and acumen in political matters. As my future became all the more imminent, I would draw our discussion away from it—for the sake of preserving my dignity as well as our friendship. In the meantime, George learned something of aesthetics and philosophy from me, and continued in his impetuous, brilliant way to instruct me in the varieties of human experience.

We went on this way, meeting outside the library and in the Commons of the Union Building for supper. We used to make the rounds of the campus afterwards, browsing at the magazine rack in the drugstore, walking past the girls' dormitories later at night (always seeing less than we hoped to see) and, still later, walking each other home three and four and five times, creating and destroying and recreating our vision of the Good Life. In the spring of the last year I spent on that campus, George met Lorraine and introduced her to me. From that time till I married her, the three of us were inseparable companions—George and I abreast of one another, and at my left side the woman who was to become my wife. Lorraine was active in the campus theatre guild; she worked for pure pleasure and said she had no ambitions. With her perspicacity and zest for things, she added a new dimension to my relationship with George, but both he and I knew that her advent marked an unalterable change in the way we had shared our time, our ideas, our habits and our anxieties. We were married just as I completed the work for my Master's degree, and I accepted a teaching job in the South. When we left, George was just beginning to become involved with a beautiful girl in the Department of Zoology; during our first year away, they were married. I remember how they stood in front of the lilac bushes that last afternoon, waving goodbye to us—George short and stocky, the white sleeves of his shirt rolled back to the elbows, his large moonface sulky and unhappy, the bright sun flashing across his spectacles and hiding his eyes, one arm around Jean, the other lifted in farewell . . . and Jean regal and poised, slender but very womanly in her belted laboratory coat, her glossy pompadour perhaps an inch above George's head—Jean smiling, in love, serene.

2

A few years later, after an erratic correspondence, I wrote George and Jean that Lorraine and I wanted to come through the Midwest in late summer to visit them. They sent us an enthusiastic telegram of welcome.

They had a small apartment near the campus, and Lorraine and I had a feeling of coming home—a return to lighthearted youth—when we walked up the steps and found George at the door, his arms outstretched, blaspheming and laughing and calling to us in an excess of pleasure.

We sat and talked in that cramped living room waiting for Jean to come home with some goodies for supper. The heavy flowered drapes were drawn; the air was thick with that summer heat that we have come to associate with them both. In front of the long window was a desk that George had built himself, and it had taken in his character.

At the far end was his typewriter with a thin yellow sheet in its roller. George told us that he had been composing another of his vituperative letters to the editor. Books were stacked in a dozen towers with note-cards and papers sticking out of the pages. There was a folder full of drawings that George had made of masks that he said he hoped to reproduce. He had spread a huge linguistic map of North America over one side of the desk, and he was doing some intricate diagrams in an open notebook based on the information contained on the map. Under the map there were little boxes filled with carefully sorted bones; he called this his "paleontology section" of the desk. The drawers were filled with envelopes and miniature burlap bags, all neatly tied and clipped together and labeled according to the geological and cultural oddments they contained. That desk was the room. It filled and overflowed into everything else—the threadbare sofa where we sat, the table and chairs stacked against the far wall next to the kitchenette; the ottoman around which George would pace, occasionally lifting one leg to straighten his sock (he never rested); the cheap lamps and tables that had been furnished by his landlord. That desk was the theme of the room, and the shelves took up the theme. The place resounded with George's energy and George's preoccupations. He told us that Jean had a laboratory where she kept all her properties, and that except for some clothes in the bedroom closet and a pink shower cap in the bathroom, no one would know of her presence in the apartment.

Lorraine couldn't resist asking him, "How long will you stay here?"

George shrugged. "I suppose we can go on working this way indefinitely. Jean likes her situation and, as for me, this place is as good as any."

"Are you working toward a degree now?" she asked him carefully. "Why should I? I enjoy doing just what I'm doing. As long as Jean doesn't get it into her head to commit me to anything, I can keep my freedom and my anonymity. That's all that matters—to be left alone to do as one likes. What else is there?"

"Responsibility," Lorraine said softly. "Children."

George laughed. "That's for madmen, children and responsibility. Life is so short. You don't want that, do you, Martin?"

Lorraine didn't say anything, so I told him, "Eventually."

He looked at me keenly. "Isn't your work enough for you? Why should someone like you look for involvement? It never made any sense to me."

"We're all involved, whether we like it or not," Lorraine said, in the old tone of chiding humor we used to adopt toward one another.

He frowned, but then he laughed again. "You're right. I don't like what you say, but it's true. I have to accept it."

"For yourself?" I asked him.

"You're looking for my soul again, eh? How do I know for myself? I've still got conflicts; I still get angry at things, as you can see from my letters—even if I say I don't give a damn."

There it was. During the first hours of our reunion, the old question came up—What will become of George? He looked at me shrewdly, as if to say: "Go ahead, I dare you to decide. I still don't know myself."

Sometimes I have, even now, a keen nostalgia for the moments of that visit—for George, holding the ladle over the soup tureen, announcing that we were about to taste "the dish of dishes, judiciously spiced and steaming like the left nostril of a dragon" . . . for the delightful sounds of Jean's toilette beyond the bathroom door, her heels clicking back and forth, the spring of the medicine cabinet as she opened and closed it half a dozen times, taking down her powders and creams and fragrances, her soft contralto always rendering the same art song, "The Sleep That Flits On Baby's Eyes" . . . Lorraine leaning against cushions stacked on the floor at George's feet, drowsy and drunk, composing limericks about Eisenhower and kitsch culture and the Southern Way of Life . . . . After supper, George sat with a jar of Spanish olives on his lap and devoured them all, announcing, "Whatever I love I love to excess, so Jean, beware."

Late that evening we read a one-act play, recorded our reading, and played back the tape. Then we sang the quartet from *Rigoletto*, George and I in falsetto and the women assuming the roles of the males. George then read us an essay by Henry Miller on bread, and then a poem about Señor Dildo from a large volume of *Poetica*

Erotica, after which he proposed with great solemnity that we have a "Chinese gang-bang." Our wives were sleepy, so George and I retreated to the bedroom window with his binoculars, and watched the girls in the sorority house across the street. It was "rush week" and we watched three of the nubile maidens combing one another's hair, smoking, reading to one another, exchanging whispers and giggles, and finally undressing—but chastely, half inside the closet. At one point, squinting through the binoculars, George claimed that he "saw all," but I suspect that his enthusiasm had the better of him. My portion was a glimpse of a supple back and some lacy, well-filled briefs which I foolishly offered to describe to George. For my pains I lost the binoculars to him, and a few minutes later our subjects turned out the lights.

George and Jean insisted that we take their bed, and they slept on the couch in the living room. When we walked out there the next morning, they had prepared an elaborate breakfast of several courses, during which we analyzed our lives, concluded that none of us had a genuine sense of direction, congratulated ourselves on that, and began to argue all over again. George's short-wave radio wasn't functioning, so he and I worked on it for a while. There was the gentle, competent way he always handled things. No object was alien to him. He respected the purpose and need of each, and its relation to the whole. I commented on this, and he laughed and said, "I am only impatient with people. Besides, I am an animist. In this little circuit there might be a living form of some of my great-grandfather's spirit. Did you ever hear of the tribe of North American Indians who never killed a bear without first apologizing to it? They had more sense and more feeling than most of our so-called 'civilized' modern men."

They drove us to the train depot in an old car that Jean had bought for herself (George still kept his bicycle, disdaining the use of all other vehicles.) On our way there, George taught Lorraine an old and very filthy Russian song in which scatological curses are heaped on the heads of the celebrant's family with special mention made of the mother. "This," he said, "should become the anthem of our quartet." When we boarded the train, after a round of warm embraces, we promised to see one another "again and again, very soon." But we all knew better than that. I had, as George would put it, "made a commitment to society." I had found a place for Lorraine and myself—at least for the moment. George was still true to his gods of freedom and anonymity, and it didn't look as though he would ever renounce them.

3

When something that happened on the national or international level excited him, George would sit down at the typewriter and compose a long essay for us. These were his letters. Lorraine and I saved every one of them, often saying they should be bound and sent to a publisher. We keep them in a cardboard box on our closet shelf, and sometimes we still take them down and read them aloud to one another. Because of the imposed need for concentration in writing, George's written word always surpassed the spoken. I often felt mortified to answer these witty and sage chronicles with my own organized and uninspired comments. He wrote about Russia's sputnik and the United States's *spätnik*; he had a great deal to say about elections in this country and elsewhere, and about Indochina and Formosa and Nasser. I thought I could tell from the way he wrote that his personal political destiny was beginning to crystallize. He related all things to himself in an ironic way. Once in a great while he would say, entirely out of context, "You know, I am really in exile." Of all these missives, one was vastly personal—

> "My good friends, it is well past midnight, and I have been chipping away at flint for half the evening. Lucky me! Even though we all live in caves, at least I have the awareness of where I am. And I can try to find something to celebrate in here . . . maybe a scratch of primitive art on the dark wall—or is it only the mark that sets off this corner as the sacred pissing-ground? Today was our anniversary, and I made Jean cry by asking her why I married her. She is a true woman, which explains why she wept, and which also answers

my question. She has a lot of things I had in the old life in Prague—a genteel tradition, leisure, breeding, indulgent parents. And all this she rejects! She *wants* to live this wretchedly empty life. She says she needs nothing but me and her laboratory. Foolish girl! Who wouldn't want to surround himself in luxury if he had the chance? I was reading another one of Dorothy Sayers's novels about Lord Peter Wimsey and his man Bunter. I think everybody should have a Bunter, to lay out his clothes and taste his tea and make his reservations at the London station. Things are closing in on us. Some day soon Jean will have a Ph.D., and then she will look for a job. They have already offered her one here. Commitment. Permanence. Enough money for a bountiful table and for the movies every Sunday. And my esteemed professors tell me there is no point in taking one course after another. I have to build toward something, they say. Everybody is building his house. I can lay bricks, too—but I prefer women. Next we will have an age-old tale to tell of an accident, then an heir who must eat and sleep and be educated. I think I ought to leave her. It's her only chance for salvation. Her parents love her, which makes everything more difficult for her. They want to 'help' us. They want to buy us a house or a car or a trip to Europe—to launch us in some way. They will never understand why she chose to live with me, but their love for her is even stronger than their disapproval. I wish I could have that gift—of selfless love. I am warning Jean in many ways, but she doesn't hear me. When a man is drowning, he wants to drown alone. Or does he?

"She is so beautiful. You know. She has two costumes. By day she is the Efficient Scientist in her white cotton coats with the buttons missing, and her black skirts and blouses underneath, and her heavy shoes. Then she braids her hair around her head. When I look at her long, slender fingers and her brilliant eyes with that fever, that terrible fever in them, I think of one of the few poems in English I have ever understood—that one by Frost where he says: 'The woods are lovely, dark and deep/But I have promises to keep,/And miles to go before I sleep.'

"And by night, she can't resist. She takes down her hair, and she has all her lovely rituals in the bath, and she is so much a woman that I forget there are tomorrows. She is a poem, an epic of muliebrity, in those satin slippers and light gowns, and rustling dresses, and with jewels in her ears. She has a pair of red silk Oriental pajamas with a mandarin collar, and with great embroidered buttons. And when she wears them I can't think at all. Her parents still send her a generous allowance with which she buys these things, and if she refused it I would never forgive her. Only someone without a sense of beauty would make a moral issue out of this.

"All next year, Jean will be at work on her dissertation. So we still have time; we can still procrastinate. By the way, we are going to come and see you. In August."

4

One of the first things George said to me when they came into our apartment was, "I'm glad you don't have any children. None of this would be possible anymore if you did. Friendship today depends on circumstance. This should not be. Just because people are thrown together and share certain experiences doesn't mean they should cultivate one another. But this is the way things are."

I told him that soon we would all be put to the test. Lorraine was in the third month of pregnancy.

He looked at me reproachfully. "How could you? A beautiful, wild girl like Lorraine . . . everything that I admired about her will be taken away. Now she'll think of nothing but wash-machines and nurses, and she'll regiment your life; you won't recognize yourself anymore."

He was driving too hard, and I asked him what made him such an expert. He laughed in embarrassment at his speech, and said he had only been teasing me: "I've made you into my other self long ago, Martin. And myself into yours."

I went off to my building to practice in the mornings, and George insisted on walking with me. He said that the place where we lived had all sorts of possibilities for a dedicated anthropologist. For the first time since I had met him, his company depressed me. He talked until my head ached about, among other things, the origins of the idea of carnival, the agricultural rites of the Natchez Indians, the architectural concepts of the Eskimo, the migration of peoples in the Americas. I confided to Lorraine, "In his letters you can take him at your own pace, but in his company you're on a marathon."

She gave me an answer of unerring insight: "You're a little irritable lately, Martin. You're worried because our lives are changing, and George's hasn't. You're using his life as a measure for your own. That's a mistake, don't you see? We can't allow ourselves to envy each other. That would be the death of any relationship."

Jean spent the whole day with Lorraine, every day; George went off on private expeditions. I was happy to be able to keep some of my privacy; I think George felt the same way. I told him God only knew what the women could talk about so much. Their temperament suits them to explore matters that will forever be an enigma to the male. George answered in the silly way he had sometimes, by saying that they were probably discussing him.

On the third night of their visit, one of my students was scheduled to give a recital. George knew almost nothing about music, but he wanted us all to attend; after the program we decided to go to a bar. It was there that I made a chance remark about my job in the South; our discussion of the future began afresh.

"Where will you go then?" George asked me.

"Where is there to go?" I asked him (I was really asking myself.)

"You're right. You can't spend your life running from one bad situation to another. Why change at all, if it doesn't make any difference? I don't know what problems you have in music, but I imagine they'll be much the same wherever you find yourself. Not only in this country, but anywhere. This isn't an age for music. Or for much else that matters."

I asked him, smiling, if it was really so desperate as all that. I told him that, whatever the age was, it was ours.

He looked at me with a profound unhappiness. Perhaps he had never really stopped struggling, I thought; perhaps he never would.

"I know. And no matter what I've said before, I think we have to make choices. I'm coming to one. I can feel it. It's taken me one hell of a long time."

"What are the alternatives?" I asked him.

"What they've always been—to go or to stay."

"But to go, George—what kind of life would it be for you?"

"Maybe the only kind, however miserable it might be. I'm thirty-one years old now, think of that. Half my life's over. And I'm like a kid who's having such a good time in the playground, he won't go home. But you can't just stay there on the swing forever, having a good time."

"What about your work?"

"You know the answer. The work is the playground. Indulgence, self-indulgence. I tell you, Martin, I don't belong here. I don't know where I belong, but I know it's not here. I don't understand this life, full of imitation of idiots, full of things, things, things. If there's more substance to it, it escapes me."

"If you go to Prague, for how long would it be?"

He stared at me. "Do you think that if I went back there would ever be any chance of leaving again?"

"What about Jean?"

"Yes, what about Jean. She says she'd go too, but that's impossible. Impossible. These are matters you can't involve anyone else in."

"Maybe there's some third alternative—"

"In any other century but ours, Martin. Don't you know the highways are closed?"

He took out his wallet, fondled it, then he opened it and showed me an old photograph, one he had shown me years before. It was a snapshot of a young girl, seventeen perhaps, standing in front of a large, flowering tree. She was frowning, probably because of the strong sunlight. Her hair was blowing around her face, and I couldn't make out her features very clearly. Her eyes seemed small, her nose prominent. Her lips were drawn together—petulantly, I thought; and her hands were on her hips. She was wearing a white peasant blouse, gathered in a drawstring at her throat, and her breasts were very large and full.

"Remember? This is the end of the highway—my childhood sweetheart, in a Prague that will always be lost to me. Sometimes I have the feeling she still waits."

George's sentiment sounded fraudulent to me. I was angry—that he kept the photograph, that he had brought it out just now, in front of Jean, who was sitting across the table talking with Lorraine, innocent of her husband's words.

"Why don't you grow up?" I asked him, with a deliberate desire to hurt him.

"You don't understand, Martin."

"Oh, but I do. Is this your chief weapon against your wife? I thought you had more ingenuity."

To my surprise he didn't take offense. He was silent for a moment. He picked up his glass and drank steadily until he'd drained it. Then, holding it in his hand, he turned sideways and talked to me, looking directly and intently into my face.

"I don't use that photograph for Jean, but for myself. It is a symbol of a riddle I've never been able to solve. When I took that picture, I was someone else. Who was I? Maybe the only genuine George was back there. Please keep in mind, Martin, I didn't forsake my home voluntarily. If certain events had not come about, I would not be here; I would have had no problem."

"But they have. And you're here. And in the whole problem, there is one aspect that really troubles me."

"What's that?"

"The way you take your work so lightly. Look how many years you've been at it—studying, digging up facts and artifacts . . . . You can't convince me that it means so little to you. Why don't you begin with your work and try to find a way through it? You can't just throw it away."

"What makes you think that this side of the world needs my services any more than the other? Is someone looking for me? If I apply for a job, will someone open his arms and say, 'I've been waiting for someone like you all my life'?"

I told him that, in the first place, one's work was more a question of his own needs than of society's, and that, in the second place, there are damned few of us who are wanted badly—anywhere, by anyone. I told him, a little brutally, "You haven't matured in some respects; you're still a child... narcissistic, megalomaniac... Everyone wants applause, George; everyone wants to be appreciated, not only you. Do you think you're alone in feeling alienated? You've got to do what all of us must do—use the talents you have in the best way you can." I quoted a Biblical passage I remembered from childhood: "Whatsoever thy right hand does, do with thy might."

He listened very attentively. Then he answered me:

"I agree with you in almost every respect. But you left out a few elements. Remember, I have to believe in what I'm doing."

"In other words, you're not as disengaged as you pretend to be?"

"Disengaged... that's for a lion in the jungle!"

"All right, then. And you mean to say you honestly don't see any value in your work?"

He set his glass down carefully. "Not enough, Martin. Not nearly enough."

"But, George, maybe that's your portion. Maybe that's all there *is*, for you... for me. We'd all like to be Caesars—"

This time he did get angry. "I wouldn't be any more of a Caesar in Prague than I would be in this country."

"Then why go back?"

"Because, as you yourself insist, none of us lives in a vacuum. Our work must have some relationship to... the rest of it. At least, it does for me. And, damn it, I can't accept the rest of it!"

"What is the rest of it, George? Can you define it?"

"The rest of it is society—the people, the way they're going, the things they think are important, the future they're building. Listen, you think I run away from responsibility. All right, how can you help but think so? Haven't I admitted as much myself? The truth is, I want to have sons and daughters like anyone else. I'd like to see what kind of contribution I might make to the race; I'd like to fill up the world with variations of Jean and me. But what world? Everything I create I have a responsibility to—my work, my supposed family, my very supposed future . . . ."

"You're not God," I said.

His eyes flashed, and he took hold of my arm. "That's where you're wrong, Martin. I *am* God! We who think and struggle with our destinies, we are all God! God can't exist without us."

I told him that when I'd first met him, I'd felt compassion for him, because I'd thought then that he had no convictions. But as it turned out, I said, I was jealous—because he had more convictions than I probably ever would.

The week-end came, and we put it to good use, driving to some of the historical sites in the state. Jean had brought a camera with her, and she took several snapshots. She was interested in perfecting her photographic techniques, and she made some very intelligent comments about art films. Her enthusiasm carried her away, and we all learned a great deal from her.

Lorraine and I saw the landscape once more, through their eyes—the old plantations, the bayous, the majestic trees with their long, gray webs of Spanish moss, the melancholy ugliness of the Mississippi River . . . it conveyed a poetic vision to us, a romantic decadent sense of what might have been. Once George said, a little reluctantly, "I can see certain values in living here." But he amended that by adding, "In comparison, that is, with the industrial cesspools of the North."

Lorraine surprised me with her vehemence when she answered: "I doubt that anyone can really understand this country unless he was born here, or spent his youth here. And even then, there's a great deal beneath the surface."

"Have you been angry with my criticism?" George asked her, smiling.

"Maybe not angry, but a little impatient. There's nothing so glib as anti-Americanism for its own sake. I can't take any criticism too seriously unless it's been thought out deeply and related to experience."

"I think your wife is finally telling me off, Martin, my friend."
"We're both defending ourselves against you," I answered. "In a sense, we have the same spiritual problems that you have. But we've made a decision or two since the old days; we've taken a direction, slight as it may be. And that means we've exposed ourselves to judgment. You haven't, because you haven't moved. You haven't changed." George seemed exasperated by Jean's silence, and asked her:

"Why don't you say what *you* think? Have I changed?"

Jean told him with a droll smile, "I think you're an incorrigible egotist. You always manage to twist conversation around to yourself. In *that* respect, at least, you haven't changed."

George scowled. I changed the subject quickly, wondering if this was more than a lovers' quarrel. I think it came to all of us that afternoon that Lorraine, with her swelling breasts and loosened skirts, had unwittingly illumined a threshold we would never cross again. George put it into words; he observed, morosely, "We're not kids anymore."

Could a man's life be wholly anarchic? Could it lack discipline in all fundamental matters? Believing in and apprehending a sense of intelligible order, could a man refuse to submit his spirit to it? More concretely, could a man work with ideas and materials wholly for the sake of the moment's fulfillment? Was it possible not to move from lower to higher forms? Was George a tragic waste, or a buffoon, or a keen but insubstantial thinker, an imposter to the life of the mind? Was it possible for a man to live always in doubt, always questioning, rebelling, always on the outside? "I'm not really an activist," George had told me. "I'm not an adventurer. But a generation ago, I would have involved myself in the Spanish Civil War. Maybe I'd have been killed. The idea of a heroic death has a certain appeal. But what would I take up arms for today? The truth is, I don't believe in anything, because no one else does. Damn it, Martin, give me good and evil, give me something to chew on; get me off the grandstand at this baseball game with its 'your team' and 'our team.' I used to believe in the idea of a third force. Now I know there aren't any forces at all."

"Maybe the only answer is to work within the small circle of your own private life, George."

"Listen. If I stay with Jean the circle will soon be wider. And then where will I be?"

"With the rest of us. Not fighting or dying, maybe, but trying to make a difference."

"In Eisenhower's America?"

"In anybody's America. In the world."

The day before they left, George disclosed himself to me in a new and strangely consummate way. We were lolling around the living room together, drinking his favorite summer beverage of vermouth and quinine water. Our wives were out walking, and in their absence both of us felt a vague and troubling sense of the friendship and intimacy of the past. We talked lazily about anything that came to mind—national lotteries, Southern literary figures, automobiles. We had each taken one of the sectional sofas to stretch out on; George was on his side, with his arm supporting his head, and I lay on my belly with my drink set on the floor just in reach of my hand. The window fan across the room was whirling at a high speed; venetian blinds rattled against the windows, and there was a stirring in the room of loose papers and cloths and the edges of the marquisette curtains. I felt as though I were a minnow swimming in a glass bubble filled with water; the summer heat had been interminable—humid and tedious, studded with academic tasks and new, mundane domestic preoccupations. I had come to realize that I was losing whatever small creative gifts had been mine. My limitations were clear to me, and my awareness of them still raw; I had yet to really accept my falling sky. All my introspection, and the difficult summer, had left me exhausted and depressed. I was envious of Lorraine, too, and through her of all women, who could, I thought, justify their lives through an act of biological nature. There, bursting from their wombs, was the startling, irrevocable beginning and end of all creativity. With whatever pride or shame they might one day behold what they had wrought, at least it was tangible; at least it would have its season. My thoughts turned this way, and I quoted Yeats to George: "We long to tread a way none trod before,/But find the excellent old way through love/And through the care of children to the hour/For bidding Fate and Time and Change goodbye."

As I might have expected, George began to relate these words to himself—to his life and to his future. Whenever he liked something very much—whether it was poetry or music or a good anecdote—he would say, "I should have written that myself." It was the highest approbation he could bestow on anything. He said it again after hearing Yeats's lines, and then he added:

"Is the old way excellent just because it's old? Well, Martin, I suppose you'll be buying a house of your own soon. Most Americans seem to want a lot of room. They dream of big, airy places with a set of four walls for each function, a throne room apiece, and a huge compound for their kids and their dogs. I think they're trying to make their private worlds as large as possible, because the one outside it has shrunk so much, and a man's so insignificant in it. I like compact, small rooms, preferably in apartments, where nothing can be out of my sight. When I was a kid I used to put my toys and books and things into boxes with lids. I used to open the boxes and count everything, to make sure nobody had stolen anything from me. When I travel, I make lists of my possessions, even down to my underwear and pencils. You'll say I'm still that kid. In a way, this is my whole problem. I'd like to make my private life as neat and small as possible, and walk out of it into something big and meaningful. I can't believe that a man can make a difference in his private life alone. It's only in that other life that he can find real identity, really *be* someone."

"I'm no sociologist," I told him. "But it looks to me as if it's just not structured that way anymore. Everything meaningful is being spoken in muted tones, in closed little drawing-rooms, to very small gatherings."

"That's the rub, Martin—no ceremony, no ritual, no sacred grounds.... We're not moving forward in time; we're not even moving backwards. I'd give anything to have a star to follow—or a pirate."

"Do you think there are stars or pirates in Prague?"

He gave me the old answer: "I don't know. I only know there aren't any here."

"Maybe there aren't any at all."

"That would be my mistake. But I've got to find out."

Under the whirring of that fan, in that dim living room with the sun shut out and the vague fluttering of things forever inanimate around us, I listened to George. And I supposed that he was at last putting into words a choice he must have made a long time ago, a decision that had finally crystallized: he would go back to Czechoslovakia.

On that last day of their visit, George and Jean opened a bottle of Liebfraumilch they had brought for us. We ate a loaf of freshly baked bread and drank the wine together. We stood around the kitchen table saying very little, looking at one another in a fugitive way. Through trying to understand ourselves, we had reached some understanding of one another. I felt that we had enjoyed perhaps the richest, highest form of friendship this sort of existence could afford anyone. I felt too that we might never see one another again. And even if we would, we could never come together again so openly, with such warmth and spontaneity.

5

During the year after their visit, George was awarded a Master's degree in anthropology. He wrote—

> "For the first time in my life, I have finished something. But it was not an act of my will. It was pure inertia. Jean is working steadily. She is incorruptible. Some day she will unlock all the mysteries of the genes, and then none of us will be tormented by questions anymore. Believe it or not, I have made a friend—an actual friend. By that I mean, we can talk at any time in any place and really communicate. He is a professor in the department here, imported from Mexico, and he has seduced me into working with him on three or four projects. He has me running to the library and filling little black boxes with notes and references. I am actually working *toward* something—but I don't know what it is. He wants me to go to Mexico with a group of his students next summer. He talks as though

I have already given my consent. I am given to feel that others are responsible for my life—this man and Jean, who want between them to save me from my nihilism, from the demon who sits on my left shoulder tempting me to folly, to any action so long as it *is* action, a deed, a move of some kind. And I? I prefer to be responsible for myself. Well, we will see who is victorious in the struggle for George's soul."

By the time this letter was written, George's *angst* and Jean's quiet unhappiness had begun to seem to have less bearing on our lives. In fact, with the birth of our daughter, my entire relationship with Lorraine was transformed. Under the signature of my answer to George, Lorraine wrote:

"Right now, we are all feeling, nothing else. You wouldn't recognize us—exhausted, inside out... letters unopened and books, too, and our spiritual selves in a cycle of thesis and antithesis... the hands on the clock and the days of the week have lost the conventional meanings. This creature, less than four weeks old, has challenged everything. Who were we before she came? What is her heritage? All the questions we've asked each other seem to converge over her cradle. I feel, in some elemental way, as though Martin and I were beginning at the beginning. And I am afraid."

Then we had a message from Jean, along with a gift for the baby. In her letter, she told us that George was going to Mexico in the summer, but that she wanted to come anyway, to see Rachel for herself. She ended by saying, "Be happy. Rejoice in your good fortune. Give Rachel love... simple, native love. Sometimes I think that must be all that matters."

The summer came. Rachel was fat and sociable. She had her little rituals to which Lorraine surrendered with a grace I thought very touching. I felt that in some ways I had lost my wife—that at the cold, white bedside of birth the messengers of Eros had borne away certain qualities she might never recapture, qualities that seemed immiscible, yet taken together contained her selfhood: the delicacy and coquetry that were souvenirs of her adolescence, and her glorious imperatives when we used to make love in a universe where we were only lovers. She was someone else now, but was I? I wondered what George would have to say about this. But these were matters I couldn't take up with him by correspondence. I began to wonder if only woman evolved, if only woman had a history, a purpose, and an achievement, and if man was simply a pawn of certain forces of nature which, although she had not devised, she had come to master. I would watch her nursing our child, with the beautiful slope of her naked shoulders, and below them the full, white breasts that once were mine, now filled with the thin, bluish wine of life.... Lorraine in profile, her hair smoothed back from her face and gathered in a dark wing at the nape of her neck, with one foot tucked under her skirts and the other touching the floor, giving a rhythmic movement to the rocking chair ... where, George, in this most sacred, most primitive rite, was there a place for me? And I had wanted a son—would it be the same if this infant had been my son? And where was my wife? I sat in the library one afternoon, reading a book of stories by Isaac Bashevis Singer; in one of them, he said that the woman who never bears children is still a virgin.

That summer there was a drought. The grass was burned by the sun, and when I walked on it barefoot, as I like to do, it felt crisp and stinging. There were patches where it was singed, and the black runners lay exposed on the ground; here and there, clumps of weeds sprang up with points like those of a star, sharp and slender; some of them were tall enough to brush my knees. The roots of the younger trees broke through the ground; the few flowers that had bloomed, withered and died on the dry, dusty leaves of rose and gardenia bushes, and in the hard ground where Lorraine had planted daisies and gladioli. I walked back and forth to my classes, my practice rooms, my office, through the dark, cool hallways of the music building, uninspired, depressed, thinking how small my portion was, and how alone each of us is. I even suspected that I had made no choices, ever. But the thought of absolution from responsibility gave me no solace. I realized that I was becoming more and more involved with academic tasks, that my life was circumscribed by things I had once thought alien to myself. I said little to Lorraine about these things, but once she observed, "We're still growing, still changing. Believe it or not, you still have certain discoveries that are yet to be made." How banal she could be! When I thought of George now, it was with anger and jealousy; I could imagine how severely he would judge us. Because of the silence between him and me, I imagined he was having certain adventures which he thought I could not hope to understand. I had an idea, which filled me with bitterness, that his life was a romance into which I had trespassed, mistaking myself for him. In this way I poisoned my memory of our friendship.

6

In August, when I met Jean at the train depot, she told me in her direct way that she was four months pregnant. I asked her if George knew, and she said that she was afraid to write him.

Lorraine's prompt response was, "This is really madness." I agreed with her.

"He has a right to know," I said to Jean.

"Don't you think I thought about these things? I don't know what to do . . . obviously, I can't take a job next year. And I can't turn to my parents. I have too much pride for that."

"When will George be back?" Lorraine asked her.

We were sitting in the kitchen, Lorraine cross-legged on the Step-stool, chopping some vegetables for supper, I with Rachel on my lap, and Jean looking very forlorn, leaning against the edge of the table.

"I don't think he is coming back. Gómez left Mexico last week; the work is finished, and the group has already come back to the campus. George wasn't with them. I didn't think he would be."

Our eyes met; I looked away. Lorraine asked for me:

"Do you mean that you did this deliberately? That you wanted the child? Even though you knew George wouldn't be coming back?"

"Yes, I suppose that's true. If an impulse can ever be true." Jean stayed with us during our brief vacation; we had no funds to travel, and no place to go with a small baby. We had rented a house, and Jean offered to take care of Rachel while we moved in. We made the move with a lot of confusion, but during it some of our old gaiety came back, some of the lighthearted abandon we had known on that last visit.

On our second evening in the house, Lorraine was storing books away and dropped an album of photographs. They lay strewn over the floor—faces of people who were dead . . . Lorraine's father, my parents, Lorraine as a baby, me in my army uniform, high school graduation pictures, our wedding photographs, some snapshots Jean had taken on the last visit. Jean helped Lorraine sort them, and at one point she looked up and said:

"This is a beautiful commentary on life . . . all the ages mixed up with one another. I'm sure it's very instructive, but I don't know what it means."

She held up a snapshot of George that we had taken in the kitchen of the apartment where he was preparing us a supper of meat and dumplings. He had tied a bath towel around his middle and put an old painter's cap on his head. George the Chef. There was flour and grease all over the stove and the counter near the sink. He hadn't expected the picture; that was the best part of it. I looked at his round eyes in the black frames of his glasses, his heavy mouth still closed (there wasn't time to smile); I thought, *You bastard.*

Jean was still sitting on the floor, holding the snapshot absently. She told us, "The last time I heard from him, he asked me to be patient."

Lorraine asked her if she knew positively that George would not be coming back.

"How could I know when George wasn't even sure himself? He told me to pack for him. Imagine! Even that responsibility had to be someone else's. But you know—" She looked up at us with a brilliant smile. "If this is the end, I haven't any bitterness. Maybe you can't understand that. You aren't married to him; you don't love him as I do; how can you know? George never led me to believe that he could accept my world, and he never asked me to take his. I wanted to, God knows I wanted to. You know how women can be—women in love. His people my people . . . but to George, all that was nonsense.

He believed that each of us is separate and free. That's why he never wanted a child. He is essentially a very moral man."

"You're making it sound as though *you* did the immoral thing," Lorraine chided her.

"In a sense I did. How can George be responsible for something that wasn't an act of his will?"

I was grateful that it was late and everyone wanted to go to bed. I felt I couldn't listen to them talking like this without saying something I might later regret.

But the next afternoon they went on again, about responsibility and authenticity, about deeds and consequences. I left Rachel with them and went outside. Our clippers were on the window sill, and I took them over to the nandina bushes and began to trim them, without any system or skill. The moment the blades closed over a stem, a host of gnats swarmed out and flew upward into the hot bright air. While I worked I composed a letter, to George and to myself. The women, I said in it, are at least eight years behind us, mouthing phrases we used to like to think were of the greatest profundity. When they talk like this, they make me sick, reminding me of how absurd both of us were. Well, George, we created them, didn't we? We gave them life, eh? Told them what to read and how to think? And how will we be with our children? Will they give us this kind of homage, too? Maybe not; we've already unveiled ourselves; it won't be long before we can't deceive anymore. Sickness of will, that's what it is, George . . . loving the world on our own terms. When does a man mature? Will we ever know? Maybe this is a beginning, though—when he covets nobody's empire but his own. Tell me, George: what trophies will they bury with the likes of us?

I pared the bushes down to half their height, cursing, furious, extending my soliloquy. Lorraine called me in for supper three times before I heard her.

George did come back from Mexico, less than a month after Jean's visit to us—came back, Jean wrote us, an errant but not humbled knight. Their son was born this last winter. Jean is teaching at a college in the East now, and George commutes to a university near their town where he intends to complete his studies. Jean wrote that he is working in earnest now, and that he may go to the Near East next year with a study group: "I think that travel will redeem him; it's best he goes alone."

Now the women correspond. And the letters chronicle certain events that once might have seemed momentous and full of implication—the death of George's father, the birth of our son . . . . Between the script on the crisp stationery and the images on the glossy photographs, I can find no reconciliation with the past—at least not yet. Perhaps the *telos* of our friendship has at last been realized. It was over a decade ago that George first said, "Modern friendship can't be based on similarity of persons anymore, but only on similarity of circumstance." In the occasion of friendship, then, the dialectic is born; and they vanish together.

Still, we made a difference to one another, though not in the ways we expected. Once I wrote something for him. I keep it in the cardboard box where we have stored his letters. In it I say: "I hear fragments of conversation from students in the dining hall. They talk of despair and heroism, of the tragic sense of life, of nihilism and early love. The elements of biography re-arrange themselves. The gods, wanting in imagination, weave dreams in which we can only reveal ourselves as we must be."

1960S

A Time For Good-bye Forevers

Bernie's Mama waved and smiled and wept a little, the mama-heart overflowing at the foot of the ramp. Her hair was blue this season, and she wore a wine-colored pants suit splashed with black roses. Her dentures bedazzled—at seventy-five, she could enter herself for the Mrs. Universe of South Miami Beach. Her friend this season was Mrs. Friedman, who was stuffed into a yellow dashiki and—though it was nearly midnight—was wearing big dark sunglasses in yellow plastic frames. He pretended to hurry into the arms of the two widows opening to embrace him.

They kissed and hugged and scolded him, and interrogated him, not waiting for answers. They'd call a cab, it was easiest. How come the plane was so late, couldn't he stay for more than a week-end this time, why didn't he watch his weight better, how long since he ate, see how his hair thinned at the top, just like his father's, in a year, two at most he'd be bald altogether, and how was Deborah, and what did he hear from the children?

They made negotiations with the cab driver: he should turn on the air-condition, he should put the boy's valise in the trunk, the trip should run no more than five, absolutely six dollars at the most. Knowing better than to interrupt, he inhaled the summersoft night air into lungs that, for all he knew, were already spotted up with tropical fungi. One whiff of Miami and his head turned into date-nut bread, his insides into a pulpy mass of mango meat.

They pressed him between them like a flower in a memory book; his Mama lay siege:

"Remember Resnick?"

"Resnick? When was Resnick? 1945? 1940?"

"What's twenty-five years?" She gave him a smack on the arm. "Everything you live you should remember. Myself, it's clear like a piece of glass all that happened in my sad life. The further back you go the clearer it gets. Isn't, Minnie?"

Minnie shrugged, taking his shoulder with hers in the rise and fall. "Who wants to live in the past? Who wants to feel sorry for myself? When you see your husband drop dead in front of you, what's left to think?"

Now his Mama sighed, and he shook with *her* vibrations. Mrs. Friedman was smelling of gardenias and she of some spice—was it thyme, or rosemary, or chives? Whatever it was, he'd be dead of suffocation before they got to the apartment if they didn't open a window.

"How my poor husband, your father, suffered. He should only have dropped dead, it took from me ten, maybe fifteen years, to watch it."

"What do you know?" Minnie sing-songed. "Don't talk what you don't know."

"Mama, please, can you open the window a little?"

"Not on your life. I'm paying for the air condition. So tell me, what's with Deborah, she's so busy she can never come to Florida anymore? I haven't seen my daughter-in-law for almost three years now. What's she so busy with?" Her pants-leg pressed into his, and he gave an Oedipal shudder.

"Maybe next year," Bernie lied, thinking already, *Briskin, help me. Help me, Briskin.*

"And Sandra, is she too busy too, to visit her old grandmother? They used to all come every summer, Minnie, you should have seen. It was a beautiful family."

Briskin, I'm drowning.

"Harold it's no use to talk altogether. I didn't have a letter for two years. Does they keep 'em that busy, the Peace Corps? What does Deborah think about it, she has a boy they turned him into a farmer? What does he say in his letters?"

"He's fine, Mama. Fine. He works hard there. Studies at night. He's learning the language."

"Language! He could never learn a word of Yiddish, but he can learn Indian, Hindu? Some boy! A good heart, a good head, but too much conscience. You and Deborah, I warned you, you taught him too much conscience for the world. There is trouble right here at home. Plenty."

"Well, it was partly the war. And you have to go where they send you."

"*My* grandson," Minnie began, "got a deferment because of his ears, he didn't have to bother with a Peace Corps. It was my daughter-in-law's fault those ears, of course I don't blame her, she did it out of ignorance, bathing him in alcohol when he had the measles. But maybe it saved him from the draft. Now he's a big success, they say people come from all over New York, New Jersey, even from as far as New England, to have him look at their feet. There never was a better podiatrist. He loves his work, doesn't care for the money, but all the same he's a millionaire."

By the time they arrived at South Beach and deposited Minnie at her hotel (she'd be by for dinner tomorrow night, she was too tired to stay up and visit now, she had a Yoga lesson today), the two of them had filled the cab with people he didn't know, he didn't want to know, he didn't need them: material for a dozen soap operas, a few television plays, a couple of books, at least one movie. Martin was held up in his butcher shop. Ruth was in a kidney machine. Sylvia's brother's boy they put in jail for a conscientious objector. Mrs. Cohen had no luck with any of her children—Ben married a *shiksa,* and Herman ran around with other women so his wife divorced him and took away his house, his cabin cruiser, and the twins. Norma went in a sanitarium after her daughter ran away to California for a hippie. Fannie had a heart attack while she was already packing for her trip to Israel. Feivel was being operated on for cataracts in both eyes. Myron's wife was a big success as an occupational therapist, between the two of them they made thirty-five, maybe forty thousand a year. Lenny Gerber, almost ready for his bar mitzvah, still wet the bed at night. Irwin opened a music store in Chicago with the money his father left him. His sister still didn't find a husband, all she could think to do was go to the beauty parlor every day and play cards and take dancing lessons. Maybe she'll end up with an *alter* you-should-excuse-the-expression *kakker*, he'll take her fortune away and make her wait on him.

Before she could start a fight with the cab driver, Bernie tapped his shoulder, asked him the fare, and paid it. Then and only then did he come around to let them out.

I just barely creep around anymore, she wrote in her letters. *I'm a broken person, in very bad health and spirits. Not much time left.* This last spring, she scribbled on his fiftieth birthday card, *If you think you're old, look at your poor mother, G-d forbid some day you'll know what real age is.*

Under the street light, he searched her face for the signs of the suffering she poured out in her letters. Twice a year he came to see her, to pray at his father's grave. And every time he came she looked younger. Whereas Deborah's face, even by candlelight, was ravaged.

Go! she had shrieked, this stranger who stomped from room to room, stripping the windows, the floors, this human demolition squad who was taking their house, their life down, *Go see your Mama! Go read your damned* Forward, *go talk to your old man, what's-his-name again, maybe he'll tell you your fortune!*

Briskin, he had said, gentle in the face of such harshness. *Briskin was my friend's name. Last year he died.*

"What does Deborah say about the woman's liberationists?" his mother wanted to know, pouring tea, setting out a plate of cakes, guessing close enough to give him a good scare. He used his ancient art, evading as far as he could evade, then lying. He thought with rue that he wouldn't have to juggle these two women anymore. If he didn't go to Miami Beach, he used to remind Deborah, Miami Beach would come to visit *them.* The threat had always worked. Now there wouldn't be any place for Mama to visit. He thought fast: how to explain the change of address? *Later,* he promised himself, *later, maybe in a letter, explain how Deborah had decided to go back to school. With Sandra. How they'd agreed it would be cheaper to live in an apartment.*

"For breakfast you want an egg? No? You're right, too much cholesterol, also egg has no taste without salt. The doctors say no more salt for *me*. You'll like coffee? I'll make it with the freeze dried, the flavor's just as good. We'll have farmer cheese and the fruit compote I make."

The mention of her stewed fruit set his bowels on fire.

"When you get up, you'll shave, you'll take a shower, then you'll go bathing. After lunch, you'll dress nice. We'll go to see Mr. Perlman, he told me to bring the boy over for a visit. You'll wear a nice shirt, and make sure your hair is neat. Why should you be getting so bald at your age, you're only fifty. Your father still had all his hair until he was sixty, maybe sixty-five. Wait till you see the dinner I'll make for your Shabbos, a regular traditional meal, I know Deborah doesn't cook for you such a meal, the modern women don't have the patience. You'll tell me what you hear from Harold, what Sandra's doing, what she's taking up to study, if she's got a steady yet. Make sure she don't start in with a *goy*, once they get started it's hard to break 'em up. When do you make, usually, in the morning or at night, I forgot . . . ."

He lay in his underwear, too tired to unpack at one a.m., lay listening to the venetian blinds clack against the window, listening to his mother's steady snore. He felt the drift of the moon; its light fell in a pale rain through the warm, fragrant air. Then he felt the old desire, the old hunger for his wife, plump and *knaidel*-soft. And a hunger for the time that had fled into eternity, the time they lay together listening to the untroubled breathing of the two little ones in the room next to their own.

Briskin, he prayed, *tell me why life is so long.*

At the corner of Washington Avenue and Thirteenth Street he saw the owner of the fruit and vegetable store run out in a fury to yell at a woman for squeezing the peaches. He stopped at the news stand to buy his *Forward,* keeping one ear to the talk of the old as they went from the butcher to the bakery to the produce stands to pick out the makings of their Sabbath meal. When he passed the barber's his knees melted. The old owner had always come out to watch him and Deborah shepherd Harold and Sandra down the street; always, his greeting had been the same:

"May they be with you a hundred years."

Briskin. Now that he was almost on Ocean Drive, Bernie couldn't wait anymore; he started to run, his beach chair folded under one arm, his newspaper under the other. At the corner he stopped, shaded his eyes, and looked toward the empty chair at the end of the row on the veranda of the Biscayne Shores. Then he started to run again, across the broad avenue, over the grassy patch of park, and onto the sands. He had an appointment with his friend, his confessor.

There was a strong wind this morning—not too many people were out. He counted only five heads in the water. He set up his chair under the thatched roof of the beach umbrella where they always used to meet, and sank into it, knocking off his thongs and burrowing his toes in the cool sand. The brisk winds set his father's old shirt flapping against his skin. It even set the hair on his bare legs stirring. He closed his eyes.

Harold had sent him a photograph. His head was wrapped in a turban pinned in the middle with a dark jewel. Who was this Brahman with the deep, reproving gaze, his lips sealed in renunciation? What was this accusing look that came into his eyes in the dark winter of his boyhood? When he was fifteen, the silence began between them. Then, when he talked again it was in harsh words, about the war machine, the death machine, the filthy system. In his last letter, the son gave counsel to the father: "Read *Siddhartha.* Learn to pronounce the holy *Om.*"

Listen, he had tried to reason with Deborah, *you and I, our generation, we're right in the middle. The first to have the old live on in such numbers, the first to believe we owed our lives to our children. The old on one side, the kids on the other, they're eating us alive, they're drinking our blood. We need each other, you and I, we need to help each other—*

Go to hell! she had shouted, *I lost my son, he'll never come back, he's on the other side of the world and you talk that he's drinking my blood! Did you ever think how your mother drank up yours? How you never had enough left for your own family? When did you ever put your children or your wife first? This is* your *doing,* yours! *It's your doing that I lost him! You, you failed as a father. Because all you ever knew was how to be a son!*

A son's duty . . . he wore it for a frontlet between his eyes. His old father drifted across the beach, strolled down Washington Avenue. He was singing to himself, twiddling his fingers that he always kept behind his back. His cap was pulled down over his eyes; his pants were shiny, he wore them like a sack on his bony backside. The tall, hulking figure was coming and going through all the back doors of the world. Now somebody else was floating in the darkness—his father's father, rocking, *dahvening,* in the basement of the apartment house, growing into the furnace, black on black, the eyes in his gray face coals themselves. *Ki haym chayaynu vyorech yamaynu.* He was a religious man. If you gave him a million dollars, he wouldn't work on a Saturday.

Briskin, Bernie wept, squeezing his eyes shut tighter than ever, *what is this crooked line that goes from man to man, this line we hang onto like the fat ladies hanging onto the rope in the water so the tide won't pull 'em away, holding fast just to stay where we are, the water is getting higher, Briskin—*

"For I have loved thee with an everlasting love"—Jeremiah . . . was that from Jeremiah? *Briskin, Briskin, what does a man leave his son? Do you leave him what your father left you? When I came back to the apartment after he died, I went through his things, so few, so pitiful you could pack them all in a cigar box and they'd still rattle around. What was I looking for, the papers to his burial society, some clue to his life, the* yarooshah? *And I found in the pocket of his baggy pants a piece of candy wrapped in cellophane.*

So great was his need for Briskin that Briskin appeared at last. He was stooping over a circle he kept drawing in the sand. He was working with the handle of the shovel that Harold broke and cried over. Now Deborah had the children in the water, they were riding the waves. The sun was so bright you could only see three balloons, one big, two little, bobbing up and down, you could hear their happy shrieks, or maybe it was only your own crying. And Briskin looked up, and his smile lit up the whole world, his sweet old-man's smile. And he asked, gently:

"You expected maybe you'd find a map to Treasure Island in his pockets?"

"Briskin," Bernie whispered. "At last I dreamed you back."

"If you open your eyes," Briskin sing-songed, "I have to go away. Me and those three out there in the water."

"My eyes stay closed," Bernie muttered fiercely, with joy.

But the guard blew his shrill whistle, and Bernie's eyes opened. Two men were running out to the ocean, one of them with a life preserver under his arm.

"What did I tell you?" he heard behind him. He looked around, and saw a couple getting up from their beach chairs, shading their eyes with their hands. The man was skinny like a *cheder* boy, pale, but withered, with hair sprouting like white fibers from his pink skull. He was scolding, *Ah, ah,* as he directed the rescue of some daredevil swimmer out there in the punishing waves. The woman's head was swathed in a plastic shower cap. Her face was like dough except for the dark jewels of her eyes and her purple lipsticked mouth. Her useless, heavy breasts were cleft by a thick brown line; her stomach bulged against her flowered bathing suit with used-up womb. Her legs, like sandstone pillars, were ribbed with the thick blue twine of old age.

"They always think they're in shape, those dummies!" she yelled into the wind. Then she saw Bernie looking, and called to him: "They still didn't find the body of that boy that went in on Tuesday. From Long Island he came here with two friends, I suppose in a jalopy, they thought they'd have a holiday."

Bernie shook his head and turned around again. The one with the life preserver had just reached the gambler . . . he grabbed at it and caught it . . . now the two rescuers started to tow him in . . . .

The water was thick, viscous, green—deep, bitter green. The waves rushed over one another, throwing up waterfalls of crystal. The whole ocean was moving, pulsing. Gulls soared toward the sun—

"Papa," Harold was asking, crouching at Bernie's feet, pointing to the horizon, "what's on the other side?"

"Africa. Morocco, maybe."

And now, to find him he would have to cross the whole continent, and then the Arabian Sea, and then journey half a continent more. And would Harold be there? How would they recognize each other?

"Briskin, I've got a grief inside me like a ball of hot wax under my ribs."

"What can a man expect unless he dies young?"

"It isn't only that I lost my son. Now my wife and daughter I lost too."

Briskin closed the circle he was drawing. He waited.

"Deborah. She's decided she wants to start life all over again. No, not what you think, not with another man, *that* I could try to understand. She's going to school with Sandra this fall. She's decided she wants to be a sociologist."

"For this she has to leave you? You can't learn about society with a husband around?"

"She says she doesn't need me anymore. She says we made a life, it didn't work out, it's finished. Also she blames me that Harold went away. Also that my mother won't die, she blames me that I keep coming back to visit. And she's in the change—I think it drove her crazy. Briskin, do you know what my family portrait would look like now? A costume party. Harold in a turban—a Hindu, a peasant. Sandra like an orphan, a scarecrow, her hair hanging down over her face, her face still with pimples, in blue jeans they sell in stores already torn and with bleach stains. And Deborah in a pants suit that looks like pajamas, her hair all cut off—"

"It's still a family."

"Blown by the four winds! I could laugh, if I wasn't crying."

"I learned," Briskin sing-songed, "you make the same face, the same sounds for either one."

Bernie dozed. He saw himself standing in the ocean on a day of peace—no wind, no undertow. Briskin was splashing water up on his sides, his arms, taking a bath in the milk of the ocean. He had his hat on in the water, the old Panama. *I miss my son sometimes* he was saying to Bernie. Deborah was kneeling under the beach umbrella, rubbing suntan lotion on Harold's back. Her face was dark with anger over an argument she'd just had with her mother-in-law.

"You'll come. You'll go. You'll call. You'll say hello. You'll do. You'll be. She's got the whole program set up for us! You're thirty-six years old and she's still bossing you! When will you ever be free?"

"What do you do with women?" he asked Briskin.

"Pickle them," Briskin laughed. "Then they'll crawl out of the jar, they'll eat their way back into your liver, your heart. You think *your* wife will be different? *Di vayber dergeyen di yahren.* They eat your life. Some day you'll read about your son in a mental health magazine, maybe. To hear you talk, you've got enough material to keep a dozen stand-up comedians going in the Catskills, they'll keep 'em rolling in the aisles ten seasons running."

He told Briskin the whole issue. Every summer she dared him to say *no*, just once. But if he did, who would come to visit *them* then? And Deborah said it was his fault, he made his mother feel welcome. And he asked her, did he make his mother, would she want Harold's wife to think like her? It was easy for her to talk, her parents were dead, her only sister lived in Europe. The way she collapses into a chair, Deborah used to say, the way her legs fall apart like that, you'd think she gave birth to the whole human race. Cruel, the cruelty of women! But was his mother any different—picking, criticizing, insulting, never pleased?

"Too much bitterness," Briskin had sighed. "Gotta live better." He was an orphan since the age of fifteen. And his wife was dead.

Now Bernie rode along the beach, abreast of the blue waters rolling away to forever under a buttercream sky. And sunlight fell, shimmering on the waxy red and green leaves of the sea-grape and through the wide leaves of the palms and the coconut trees. Now he went down the alley and came in the back way to his mother's apartment door. The walk was bordered with bushes of xoria. There were marigolds planted, with leaves that looked like green lace.

"Briskin," he wept, "where did I make the wrong turn?"

Briskin's eyes were blue with compassion. The two men sang together, softly:

"Vi der mentsh vert geboyrn,/Iz er zeyer kleyn,"
("When man is born,/He is very small.")
"Vi er kumt in di mitele yorn,/Iz er zeyer sheyn,"
"(In middle age,/He is very handsome,")
"Un vi er kumt in di eltere yorn,/Ruft men im aheym."
"(And when old age comes,/He is called home.")

"Harold said goodbye to me like that—" His eyes still squeezed shut, Bernie raised his arm, waved his hand, let it fall.

Briskin's head dropped down on his chest. "I said goodbye to my father . . . when you said Goodbye in those days, when you went to cross the ocean, you knew it was forever, you wouldn't see each other again, not in this life. I was a boy still. I looked back—I saw my father turn and walk away. All around him was the mud, the poverty. He went to his broken wagon. He was a broken man."

Bernie wept for Briskin's father.

"You taught him he should worry about the *woild*," Briskin said gently. "You gave him some ideas what he could do to change it. Maybe you even taught him he could save it. Maybe you thought he might be the Messiah, you generation of fathers. Everything they asked for, you ran to give 'em. When they asked the *woild* should be what they wanted, and you couldn't give, they ran away. Maybe."

"Briskin, Briskin, how does a man get wise?"

"You think I didn't have a son once? I raised him to make his way in America. He was your generation, *yours*. He got rich. And he lost his memory. Then he had a son. And his son didn't want the money, didn't want the America. To *me* he came, because I had the memory. Maybe your real son is your grandson, your own son always a stranger."

Now with his eyes full of tears, Bernie went walking on South Beach. He saw the *alte* sitting in front of the hotels on Ocean Drive. He saw some of them poking through the garbage cans in the alleys, sifting the wet bags stuffed with eggshells and cantaloupe rinds and coffee grounds—the Social Security checks didn't come till the third. He followed them up Washington Avenue, past barber shops and beauty parlors and fruit stands and novelty shops with the souvenirs, the key chains with sea horses dangling from them, the underpants for the grandchildren with "Grandma loves me" stamped on them, the tiny crates stuffed with orange gumballs . . . . He followed them past the steamy laundromats, the bakery with the Special on honey cake, the drugstore where they honored the Senior Citizens cards, the ice cream parlor, the dime stores, the travel bureau. He wandered up to the mall on Lincoln Road where there were fancy department stores and linen shops and book stalls and wig salons, where there was a trolley car with a peppermint-striped awning on it. He saw the stone around the fountain, and the tacks the merchants put on it so the old wouldn't use it to sit and visit. All the women, with their painted hair and lips and nails, with their big hats and flowered print dresses and pastel pumps, they were all his mother. All the men, with their skinny arms, with their pale legs, with their caps pulled down, they were all his father. He stopped for a sandwich; he bought a *Forward* at the news stand . . . .

He walked in South Park past the empty tennis courts and the desolate children's playground. He strolled behind the benches where the *alte* gathered. He saw an old man stand up in front of his audience and shout, *In the Old World you could work fifty years and still not have a piece of bread!* He heard the arguments of the old-style socialists and the old-style union men. Each of them carried a whole shtetl in his head. He saw the women opening their purses, taking out the photographs of the grandchildren.

"Such a skinny!"

"This one don't look Jewish."

He heard them talking about *der pressure,* about their salt-free diets . . . .

He walked down Thirteenth Street again to his mother's apartment house, hearing the ambulance siren screaming in the sunbright air, in the warm and sunny deathhouse of America's old Jews. He saw the *alte* running out of their rooms to get the mail, like crows flocking for crumbs, for letters from children, for Social Security checks . . . he smelled the cooking from the kitchens—the noodle pudding, the boiled tongue, the stuffed cabbage . . . he sat down at his mother's table and saw the challah crumbs under his dinner plate. And he saw her plump hand set down half a grapefruit in front of him, with a big red cherry in it. He saw his mother open the drawer in the side table and take out his children's letters to her, tied with a faded red ribbon. He smelled the wax of the burning Shabbos candles. He heard Mr. Perlman in the patio telling how the kids were vandalizing, they were tearing the coconuts off the trees and throwing them like baseballs. He smelled the wet grass of the cemetery where he stood at his father's grave, holding an umbrella over his mother's head while she embraced the stone. He heard her cry, *You're better off where you are, believe me.*

"Briskin. When I'm here I don't believe there's any other life that I live. It's like I stepped into one of those picture postcards in the drugstore. I don't think I can stand it anymore."

And Briskin smiled a smile that made the sands warm. And he promised him:

"It'll be all right. You'll stand it."

"If I didn't keep coming back, would I still have my son? That's what tortures me, would I still have my family?"

"You didn't make the *woild*. What should you be, like an animal that doesn't know he has ancestors? When I said Goodbye, it was for good. Now it's different. This isn't a time for goodbye forevers."

"Help me, Briskin. I come back here out of pity, pity bigger than love."

"What do you think I'm doing here now, a dead man?"

"Why won't my wife understand?"

"She doesn't want to."

"Why did I have to lose my son?"

"You think he'll make himself all over again, start from a beginning? You think he won't find out there's *tsores* in India, that people don't hurt each other there too, and starve each other, and make war?"

"Briskin," Bernie sobbed, "say he'll come back."

"I'll say it, he'll come back. Nobody goes away for good anymore. But maybe he won't come back like you expect. Maybe he'll have a little boy by the hand. And maybe the love of that boy you'll have."

The anguish of his loss flowered full in his body. In an act of self-preservation, Bernie opened his eyes. The sky was as pale white-blue as human breast milk. Strong winds still blew over the water, sending the waves tumbling over one another. The sunlight was so bright that he saw the swimmers as silhouettes, gleaming gold-framed black forms in the dazzling ocean. The gulls tipped their wings, streaming away, too far for him to hear their cries. He lay cradled in the strong woman-smell of the ocean, a homunculus in a watery womb, a mummy wrapped up in his father's old shirt. Slowly he began to heal himself, to forgive himself, to give up—his son, and the dream of his returning; his wife, and the need for her; his daughter, her hand that used to pull on his. Once—was it thirty years ago? Thirty-five?—he had found the strength to give up, give up on sharing something with his parents. He had grieved then, over the hurt. But it had been a silent grieving. A private brooding. Now you made speeches, you blew the *shofar* when you separated. Every word spoken was like written in blood on the wall.

"Learn to pronounce the holy *Om*," Harold had counseled. Meanwhile, Briskin had been drawing for him a circle in the sand—a line that curved around to meet its beginning. The design of life.

Briskin he would give up too, he would keep his eyes open now, to fold up his beach chair, to walk back to his mother waiting with his lunch. *Goodbye, Briskin. Rest in peace. G-d bless you, Briskin, thank you for saying the healing words:*

"You didn't make the *woild*." The *woild* . . . in Briskin's mouth, the word was still like a blessing.

A Fragment of Glass

He was aware that first night only of a small white glare emanating from somewhere within himself, reflected in the rectangular mirror of the bureau across his bedroom. He listened with the attentive power of the newly awakened, smoothing back phases of time as leaves, unfurling their edges, searching for the cause of the sense of doom that burned through his consciousness. In a silence hard and clear as crystal, the breathing of the woman at his side and of the children in their rooms nearby became as one—a counterpoint of rhythm close as the eyelid to the eye. But remote. Remote.

It was no sound that had awakened him. It was the light.

He turned back the blankets and the sheets. A small, steady glow illumined the center of his body. There was a fragment of glass in his navel, a souvenir of an accident that had befallen him months ago. The doctors had left it there when they had sewn the torn flesh together. It would do more harm, they said, to cut it out than to let it remain. He had laughed about it with them, saying that he suspected it was the bit of glass that would now hold his body together. Since his childhood he had made humor the harvest of his fears.

A mist rose from his body, and pollen drifted through his trunk, his groin, his limbs. His navel grew heavy and sharp and hot. It drew him to the mirror. Its light cut into the surface of glass and shaped a sun and fired it. His eyes bled with the radiance and he fell backward, certain that he was dying.

"Joseph!"

His wife flung the bedclothes aside. Her cry awakened the children. Lights were turned on; a doctor was summoned. They helped him back to bed.

The room was dense with the odors of human flesh.

His little girl, her long dark hair falling like night over her pale blue nightdress, gazed at him with her thumb against her lips. "Just a dream," he murmured, smiling. "I had a dream."

He was lying now at the threshold of their world.

Now that he had recognized the presence of the light and had come to know that it glowed only at night when he was a truly solitary being, he remembered that it had been summoning him—perhaps for weeks, perhaps for months. It was not the light that beckoned to him, but something, someone within the light. The light was a gate. He had to forbear, to feel his capacity to receive grow deeper. Without the visionary, the vision does not come into being.

Seven was his mystic number. For seven days he prepared himself. He fasted. He was silent. He abstained from the connubial joys.

He withdrew from the world. For seven nights he lay, baring his belly, lifting it, sending the light within him as an arrow into the beacon shining in the mirror. Each night it pierced the circle of light. On the seventh night, the arrow pierced its eye.

He drew close to the mirror, his body weightless. In a column of light, the axis of the circle, he saw an image—the head and shoulders of a man. The hair was dark and thick as his, but longer. The eyes were like his, too—big and mournful, glistening like obsidian. The broad bridge of the nose, the high cheekbones, the full, slack lips—they were all his. And the sallow cast of the skin. But there was no mole on the left shoulder of the image.

A voice deeper than his, more melancholy, spoke from the reaches of the pillar of light: "*Hermano.*"

"You know me!" Joseph cried in love and terror.

"We are brothers."

Joseph moved closer to the image, but the man lifted his hand in warning.

"If you touch the glass, we both will disappear."

"How shall I reach you, then?"
"It is already done."
"Where do you come from?"
"From within you."
"From here." Joseph cupped his hand over his navel. The light eclipsed; the image began to flutter.
"Don't go," he wept, "don't go."
"We will meet again," the Other said.
The light, in dying, turned silver and then a blue paler than the sea at dawn.

In the darkness the blood began to flow through his body, warming it. He knelt and bent his head. In the folds of his navel, a blue star gleamed. He heard the pigeons stirring in their nest beyond the window in the alcove.

He took leave of the world. The water he lifted to his face that morning had the warmth and weight of tears. The clothing he drew over his body lay against his skin with the insinuating intimacy of moist silk. His wife's lips were cool and new. The voices of his children, the singing of the birds hidden in the evergreens, the hiss of the bus before it gathered speed, the pulse of the hospital doors opening to admit him, the greetings of his familiars struck against him for the last time as he drew the pane around himself. The chemicals in the laboratory where he worked stank in his nostrils for the last time with an elemental fury.

At noon he left the hospital and walked to a little café. He took a booth next to the window and under the inverted letters painted on the dingy glass, he peered out at the sunless winter day. At the corner of the street was a red brick building, a rooming house for transients built more than a century ago. Next to it was the newspaper office, with its stone steps and iron railing and cellar door. Then there was the barber shop, then the bakery with its display of breads and biscuits and tarts and pies . . . . One day last spring he had stopped in there to buy a bag of doughnuts for the children. A man had entered whistling, smiling, cracking jokes with the fat old proprietress behind the counter. It was April, the sun was shining, early lilacs bloomed, the birds had come back north, the trees were budding, the air was sweet. The man could not keep his joy-in-being to himself. He was like a kid again, wanting everyone to know what he knew, feel what he felt that morning—his body light, his bones supple, his field of vision clear . . . perhaps he had awakened that morning finding himself whole for the first time in hundreds or even thousands of days. Perhaps it did not matter to him that it might never happen again. The day had achieved itself.

Now the pavement was wet and dark, and slush banked the curb, and the dismal pallor of winter justified all that he had resolved. The normal struggle had ended at last. All the thoughts and desires of his life fell into place. *I will make of Chance what it is not.* The "accident," the embedding of the glass in his navel, was anticlimactic. He had known long before his discovery that he could summon him, that José was there. And others.

Now there would be no more rages. No more shouting at his children if they played with their food. The awareness was his, not theirs; the terror was his. He could not communicate it to them.

No more speeches to his wife: "How can you go to the supermarket, walk past all those packages and cans and jars of food . . . the wrapped meats, the shelves of butter and milk, the bins full of potatoes and apples. How can you write a list of what you want, week after week, year after year, when your pen is dipped in blood?"

"You think you are keeper of the world!" she would scream. "If you stay away, will that change anything? Will it distribute?"

"It changes nothing on the outside. Nor here, either." He would lay his hand across his heart. "No, you're right, Mary. It makes no difference—thrusting the harpoon into the fish, or standing on the beach with your back to the ocean. You see? I am part of the hunting party, too."

"You must eat, Joseph."

"Mary," he would say. "Mary, there are so many who must, who don't. What in God's name shall I do?"

No, he would ask no more. Now he understood: When a man can do nothing, then that is what he must do.

"I am hungry," José told him.

"I know, I know."

"There are dreams a man has only when he is hungry," José whispered. "When the belly is full, a man cannot dream like this."

"You are dreaming me."

"*Sí.*"

"What do you feel when you dream now?" Joseph asked tenderly.

"I feel that I am warm, very warm. My belly sleeps and does not cry out. I dream that tomorrow my baby will not be dying, that nothing evil will happen. I dream that I will never be angry again."

"If I were God—" Joseph whispered.

"*Sí.* But you are only my brother."

The ring of light began to turn as a wheel set afire. Joseph's body too began to spin. He lay his limbs upon the flashing spokes and whirled over and over, faster and faster, as the shining spore in his navel drew in the force of his being.

She knocked on the door and called to him: "Joseph, come out! Joseph, why have you locked yourself away? What are you doing?"

"Praying."

Remembering the religion of his childhood, he formed his prayers as one in a confessional, praying no longer to God but to José, and through him to all his brothers: *Mea culpa,* when I was hungry, I sought food; when I was thirsty, I wet my tongue on pure water, sweet drinks and aging wines. When I was cold, I warmed myself. *Mea culpa, mea maxima culpa,* I lay beside my wife, knowing nothing but my desire. When my child was ill, I sought the aid of physicians, driving Death from my side, making It one with Evil.

As the days passed, his visions increased in intensity and purity.

On the last day he spent at home, a flame-tipped spear thrust through his navel and he fell on his back. He felt the light spread through his body and, looking up, he saw a cone of white radiance on the ceiling.

"I know you are there," José said.

"And you? Where are you?" Joseph whispered.

"Dreaming in the fields."

"How is it with your little son?"

José smiled. "How can it be? *Hermano,* he is dead."

Moaning with grief, Joseph lay his hands over his belly, extinguished the dream, and lost consciousness.

He had been in the hospital for nearly two months now. He had refused to speak, to eat, to drink; although the doctors had given him a number of tests and could find no scientific basis for it, they recognized that he was dying. They fed him nourishment through his veins, but his body rejected it. He grew emaciated. His skin shone, giving off a saffron glow. He refused to respond to the utterance of his name. He never inquired of his family. He did not recognize his visitors, nor did he acknowledge the presence of his wife sitting at his bedside, sometimes weeping, but now more often in silence.

"It is clear," the physician told her, "that your husband no longer has the will to live. He resists every effort to restore his strength. I have checked the reports concerning his accident, and it is apparent that his recovery should have been excellent."

"I'm desperate," Mary said. "Just desperate."

"What do you know about his medical history before you met him?"

"He had no major illnesses. He grew up in a very large family. They were poor. He never had enough to eat; in the winter he was always cold. He was deprived in many ways. But he left them; he went away to school, and received a good education. And since we have been married, we have been very comfortable. We've never wanted for the necessities."

"I'm mystified, then. Completely mystified."

The nurses would hear him at night, murmuring and weeping. When they went to his room they would find him curled up like a fetus, his hands clutching his belly. They would give him a shot to quiet him.

"It's hunger," one of the nurses insisted. "I worked overseas, and I've seen the symptoms many times. He's dying of starvation."

"Nobody starves anymore," another nurse said. "You know that's ridiculous."

"What about fasting?" the other challenged her.

"You see that sort of fasting in other countries. Never in this one."

"Why in other countries where people don't have enough to eat as it is?"

No one could answer.

One morning the doctors told Mary her husband was nearing the end. His room was in total darkness. He said that he found the light intolerable. The flesh was drawn tightly over his shoulders and ribs now, and gave off a phosphorescent glow.

His eyes were closed and his face composed, as though he had already died. He looked so thin, so cold, that she reached out to lift the sheet and fold it more smoothly over his body. As she drew the sheet down, she saw a silver-blue flash in the darkness, in the pit of his belly. She bent over him and saw the bit of glass that the surgeons had left in his navel. His "souvenir," he had called it.

Burning with bitterness and anger at their shattered lives, she hooked her fingers and plunged them into the folds, and plucked out the glass. At once the navel began to bleed, to weep a pale substance blue and thin as breast milk that trickled down into his groin.

Joseph opened his eyes, and moved his arms, and smiled.

She saw that he felt hunger, many hungers. And that he was restored to her.

1970S

Tide of the Unborn

Halfway through the woman's broken story of a runaway daughter, the name *Jennie* connected. "I called your daughter Kathy, and she swears she doesn't know where my Jennie went." Now the woman was giving him a voluptuous look of accusation. "I'll be honest with you, I don't believe your daughter. The girls were very close. She's in some kind of trouble; a mother can feel these things—"

She wept; he suffered the display. He asked her to give him over the weekend; he'd call her Monday morning.

He put the whole thing in his pocket for the rest of the day. When he went back to the house, he found it in the Friday condition in which Mrs. Ericson could be depended upon to leave it. Strong smell of wax and polish. A good stew simmering on the front burner. The silence and peace of the crusty bachelorhood which, his ex-wife Liz had said often enough, was his natural calling.

Still in his hat and overcoat, he called Kathy's apartment. Someone—male or female he couldn't tell—told him she was out, promised to leave the message that her father would be over Sunday afternoon, would meet her in the college library. A stupefied robot's voice. Drugs, he thought. Another of the new breed; their name was legion: glazed eyes, stringbean hair, the brain of a turnip, the sensibility of a squid. Well, he'd have to settle the thing. Back in the kitchen, he poured himself three fingers of vodka and sat down at the table, reminding himself that his brother Gerald would be coming by in a few hours and that he was to prime himself for the dress rehearsal for the show tomorrow. Two good reasons for letting his first drink be his last this evening.

Her Jennie, my Kathy, their "peers." The pack of them had turned into a tribe of zombies. It was lasting longer than anything ought to: if the old man could see them he'd have a stroke all over again. And to think of all he'd had to say the first time around. About the zoot suiters and the bobby socks and saddle shoes, the boogie beat, the fellows' duck-tail haircuts. Bellowing that the world was coming to a bitter end, that there was no respect anymore, that a man couldn't be a man, not even by half. Mass murder, that's what he'd commit if he were around now.

Well, God damn it, he, Gallagher, was out of it all for a good while now. Liz had taken the girls for herself when they were on a threshold. The older girl Frances, with her Haitian husband in a fleabag flat in the city, playing miracle worker of the slums. Her mother all over again. She'd been seventeen at the time of the break-up. All that burning intensity could have been poured into something else. Music, why not? Or languages. She was always quick with her tongue; she had an ear. Ah, no, Liz had to make a missionary nun out of her. Out of the two of them.

Kathy, Kathy . . . and what was *she* making of Liz's dogma that we're all here on this earth for a purpose and a grim one at that? She'd just turned thirteen at the time Liz had filed for divorce. She'd still been climbing up on his lap now and then for a bit of comfort. Funnyface hiding in his shoulder. She'd been studying ballet at the time, at his insistence. He had dropped by one afternoon to have a look. And he'd looked his fill. A young willow she was, in the tutu. Her glasses were put aside and *there* was the transformation. You could appreciate the high cheekbones then. And the fine eyebrows of her paternal ancestors, the good rich brown of them. She had grace all right, and beautiful balance. And a wistful air. He was thinking of a field of husked corn on a sad autumn evening . . . of a bell-shaped flower, very small. There was the fall of her thick braid on the smooth neck. He was thinking of things so fragile that the very air might bruise them. Of things not meant to last. A mere girl, and O God he was aching.

Well, Liz had taken her too. And he had let her. They had come to a pass where neither of them was fit to argue anymore.

After that, in the summers and on holidays when they came to visit, he watched them turn, he watched them change. He saw Liz's handiwork, he had a good whiff of it. Franny took on that Intellectual's Frown. She used to blink over and over while he was talking, as if an ass had been braying in her direction. Liz's blond good looks all over again in Franny. And Liz's ways. That same fake casualness when she left a good coat over the back of a chair, a leather bag drooping on the carpet. The same hardness in those green eyes. The same smile of self-absorption, the terrible triumph in it. On this earth to save it, the two of them, if they had to crush it first. Mother and Daughter Superior of some new order of the Crusades.

For all that, he could never have enough of Liz. It wasn't often that he could share the same room with her when it didn't come to mind. Maybe that was her trick: she gave you the feeling you were about to be having a nun.

The hell with it all. He'd had enough, more than enough, for a lifetime.

Kathy, now, she would take some bending. She was his, after all, a Gallagher. Skinny. Big grin. Amblyopia in one eye, far-sighted in both. He had let Liz take Kathy, too. And what had it all been about?

His drinking, her saving the world. Those were the official reasons. The truth was, they couldn't stand one another. And ought to have known that beforehand. Indeed, they had flown in the face of the premonition. And wasn't that the Irish way? She was a graduate of Smith, very bright, very articulate, very Catholic Social Action. A feminist more than a good twenty years before it became the fashion. A precursor of the banshee the old man was certain there haunts every woman, that he said you kept where it belonged by a good belt when and where it was due. To "A small café/Mam'selle" and "Red Sails In the Sunset," they had swept one another off their feet and away, in the style of the late Forties, on the Roof Garden of downtown Milwaukee. He remembered it all and he remembered it well. Her green taffeta dress. Her cameo earrings. White Shoulders cologne. Even the mixers against the ice cubes in their glasses of Seven and Seven. All that blather about the poor. That place in Lower Bohemia in Chicago where she and her redeemer-friends cranked out a weekly socialism for the saints. With the poetry in it, sometimes Liz's own, with all that fever and trembling of the long overdue sexual coming-of-age. He had been stationed at Great Lakes, he had found her in Schlitz country. And there had been dinners and drinking and dancing and opera. And beach parties, with the sort of bundling that a virginal Catholic girl could get an honorary degree in. And crash drives up Michigan Avenue, with Mad Dog Gehegen at the wheel of his convertible, and her hair whipping across this nose while he sang with happy lechery, "Please do to me/What you did to Marie/Last Saturday night...."

Her family had money, too much for the likes of a Gallagher; his father had warned him. He ought to have listened when there was still time. That pride, that independence she'd kept well hidden during the long pull through medical school.

Afterward he had brought her East, where his parents were, thinking it might tip the balance of power in his favor. Well, it had not. His mother's reign at St. Andrew's, where she played and sang every morning Mass for over thirty years, had passed with her passing, which was a year after they had moved back here. And the old man hadn't lasted long after that.

Then came the mutation of the Church. New men, and then new women. His brother Gerald was forever bemoaning the fact, saying they might all turn their collars around for all the meaning they had anymore. *Mark my words Frank, they'll turn the Holy Mass into a cabaret before the decade is out.* And so they had.

With Liz lending them a mighty hand. First in her toreador pants, beating bongo drums at benefits, dancing the Watusi. Then handing out leaflets to the parishioners as they came out of a Mass celebrated by Gerald. Then reading her anti-war poems over the local radio station. And finding her presence needed more and more at marches and demonstrations, at sit-ins and kneel-ins. He had ranted about her leaving the two little girls to look after themselves. And she had flung a potful of blather at him about the search for identity. Nor was the house his any more than it was the girls' then, what with her friends trooping in and out at all hours. And he had given up private practice for the sake of a family life! Well, Liz hadn't been satisfied until she got herself arrested. And he had roared at her, "What in hell are you after, your own crucifixion?"

In truth it was that she was after, to be burned at the stake—on television—and to have the angels swoop down to carry her soul up to heaven. All that caviling about injustice. He couldn't stomach it. That sanctimoniousness, that moral superiority. He had told her the country was full of it, everyone having himself privately canonized as the Way and the Truth and the Life. Everyone waving papers, telling you where to sign, calling you up to direct you where and when to stand up, sit down, and pray. The very thing she despised in Gerald, that holier-than-thou, it was in herself. That self-serving, pinched martyrdom, *that* was in his own wife's eyes. She was looking at him all through the Sixties with that contempt. She was casting him as a thief and a murderer, one of a lower order. No, he told her he would not turn his life into one long penance for crimes he swore he had no hand in. He had come to hate the war in Vietnam even more than she did. Because it was in his bed.

"It isn't any principle you'd die for! Not that there *is* a principle worth the hair of anyone's head!" he had raged at her. "Then tell me, great healer, what it *is* I'd give my life for?"

"It's Franny's and Kathy's and mine, our life together you're laying down for those phony Samaritans, for that pack of priests and nuns in and out of habits, for those eternal adolescents you run around with! Liz, Liz, you're not the first or the last of the women who find it hard to cope, with the same man in their beds every night and the whining of children and a house to look after. *That's* what's under all the piety and protest! *That's* what's behind those voices you hear in the night electing you to save the world! Look after your own, woman, take care of your own! Do you think it was all invented yesterday—evil, corruption, the war, the lot? Didn't you learn any history at that college of yours?"

O there'd been no end to what she had had to say then. About the Doll House he wanted her to look after. And about his *own* pack at the clinic, that coven of tin-jesus witch doctors she'd called them.

About Gerald, that pious fraud of a brother of his, pouring the soothing syrup of his sermons over the consciences of the idle rich.

"I'm not responsible for my brother!" he'd shouted.

"And *there's* the heart of the difference between us."

Once he'd all but gone on his knees before her, pleading with her to hold it together. And she'd said, *Leave me be, Frank, I need to be free of you, to find who I am.*

And the voice of the old man came out of his mouth then, when he told her she was like all the kids still wet behind the ears, that the search for the Holy Grail was a fairy tale for children.

An old grief. An old argument.

About to pour himself another, he thought better of it and took down a dinner plate to serve himself a helping of Mrs. Ericson's stew. He ate it standing up, looking out the window at the row of poplar trees along the edge of the backyard. Leafless now and regal, they curved with the wind toward the western horizon: proud priestesses attending the altar of dying light.

There was plenty of time; he took the side roads all the forty-odd miles. To catch the last of the autumn. And to meditate. The old man had taught him one lesson well: it wouldn't be long before you got it, and got it good. Expect as little as possible from anyone. Know well the devil in yourself. Had the lesson harmed him then? He used to think so. Now, no more. One thing, sure: it had kept him from making the fatal mistake of looking for his salvation in other people. Well, he had more to thank his father for than did Kathy. Somewhere along the way she'd have to learn it for herself. But probably not before she worked some dark mischief. Ah, he'd have knocked the lesson into any son of his at half her age. But a girl... well, there it was. One look from them. Ah, they could teach a man humility. That soft hair falling over the temple. The tender curve of those lips.

Kathleen? He fixed her image on the windshield with a Gallagher stare. *I've owed you this for some time now. Life isn't a game. Life isn't a Candyland. You've had your own way for too long, my girl. Every last one of that pack you run around with will have a way of disappearing. Do you hear me, girl? Before too long, you won't remember which was* which. Kathy, listen, there's not much in these few years you're living now that you can use later on. And that later on is so long, so long. Trust only yourself, girl, because that's the one you'll have to contend with. Remember you used to ask me what life is made of? Do you know what a poor thing each of us is? For more years than I care to count, I've been looking through this flesh of ours, looking at films of our insides, of our skulls. Kathy, Kathy, we're nothing but sand, we have no more substance than thistledown.

Do you hear me, girl? He was talking aloud now as he drove past the apple orchards long since harvested, their bare branches buttered with early afternoon sunlight. *It doesn't make any difference what style you have when you run up that hill. The view from the top doesn't change. We are weak, Kathy, weak when we ought to be strong. And strong when we ought to be humble. And if we ever find out what it is we ought to be doing, it's that which we never do.*

He was minutes away from the bridge now. And across it was the town, and in the town was the campus, and on the campus, somewhere, there was Kathy. He wondered if there were any young men living in the apartment. Or was she going in for lesbianism now, as probably Liz had? He parked at the shopping center half a mile from the campus and walked toward the residence halls where she ought to be staying. The state university, that was *her* decision. And a good crack at Liz, who had taken it for granted that both girls would aim for Smith. Franny had chosen Vassar. So much for Franny's rebellion.

But it hadn't been rebellion on Kathy's part to come here. There had been an April Fairweather in high school, who had talked up the state university. A girl with hair down to her bottom who burned incense and talked about "the aggressive component in Man" which, she claimed, could be bred out of the population in twenty years by abstinence from meat. Following *this* Pied Piper, Kathy had gone through a vegetarian period. Then April had drifted off—to Guatemala. Kathy, lost, had enrolled in summer school. And had met Jennie. The first friend she had brought over for her summer visit of whom he had approved. Most of them looked so raggle-tag, smelled so gamey. *This* the result of years of vitamins, orthodontics, music lessons, private rooms and telephones, and expensive summer camps. Ah, they had brought up a generation of eternal children, they had! So many of the boys refused to become men. And for so many of the girls, womanhood was a word in currency in enemy territory. And while two-thirds of the human race or better went undernourished, overworked, died before their prime, these kids, given gifts denied kings because kings had been born too soon, masqueraded as the poor, the oppressed. *And*, Liz had asked, as if it had been himself who was responsible for the edict by which the fruits of the world had been so divided, *do you think the privileged will get away with this much longer*? By some trick of logic she had halved the world into the two classes of oppressor and oppressed. And by some further trick she had placed herself on the side of the archangels. For the thousandth time he had thanked her not to be his conscience. One does the little one can in his own corner, he had told her. But there it was: Liz, sure she was at the right hand of God. And he could count on the fingers of one hand those he had met in his life who were decent enough to deserve being called human. *Save them, then*, she had mocked him, *those parasites on the human race, your patients. Fatten them up so they can go out and devour more.*

Well then, he had asked her, had her art achieved the purpose she claimed for it? Had the bombs turned into blossoms on the way down, then? For all her fasting and praying and marching, would justice and mercy and goodness prevail? Did she really believe that some people were better than others because they said the right words? *The only way*, he had told her, *you can be certain you're walking in God's grace is when you're walking alone. And even then, you ought not be too sure of yourself. Because the devil you harbor has no need of sleep.*

And she had said that his lack of faith in his fellowman had given him the excuse he craved for doing nothing.

And he had said that her playing the Redeemer had given her the excuse she craved, to tear up the family.

Well, one thing he knew that she wouldn't admit: they had both been right. He decided *that* as he let himself into the lobby of the library. Seeing nothing of Kathy there, he sat down at a reading table and folded his hands and waited. So he had waited for Liz long ago, while she browsed in a reading room. Waited with a speech in his head and a ring in his pocket. And the one he had made, and the other put on her finger, in the lobby of a residence hall where at least half a dozen couples were locked in the sort of embrace that had passed out of this world. When you made love then . . . what a sweet victory. What became of desire when the pleasures could always be had?

Kathy put her hand on top of his, and squeezed, and then took it away. She sat down across from him. They smiled at one another. Sweet God, she was so little, still! Did she eat nothing? Her hair wanted brushing. Her coat was ten sizes too big. Under it, he knew, there would be a sweatshirt. And jeans. Her face was wan. Looking at her more keenly now, he felt the old sorrow that came with his waking some mornings, when she lay like a heated stone under his ribs.

It was *his* face he was looking into, he saw himself had he been the daughter his mother had pined for: broad forehead, strong Gallagher brows, the sea-eyes. Proud, high cheekbones. An auspicious beginning for a human head. Then the bottom half of it—pushed together as if the Maker wanted to be done with the job. Clumsy nose, nostrils fleeing in different directions. Wide lips. The sharp forward thrust of the chin. On *this* cartography his daughter had rubbed in pale green eye-shadow and balanced a pair of aviator glasses.

He wanted to feed her and groom her, this little orphan of his. Did men once live, he marveled, in such a way that they were separated from their children only by death? Her Gallagher lips were still smiling. He saw a need for him in her eyes that he would never know how to answer.

He held up his index finger, a signal to wait. This was a library, after all. He took his pen and tablet from his vest pocket and wrote her a note. And folded it elaborately before passing it across the table:

"You're a sight for these sore eyes. What about some dinner?" The note came back, her spidery script asking, "How do I know if your intentions are pure?"

"Life is a risk, remember," he printed under her question. When she read it she laughed aloud, then clapped her hand over her mouth.

They went through the turnstile gravely, one by one. Then they were holding hands.

The vegetarian period seemed to be over. She had accepted his suggestion of the steak house at the shopping center. He needed the walk, and he hoped it might improve her appetite. With her at his side again, reels of film went off in his head, scenes, moments, all disconnected, rushing through his mind. Once, when he had driven her home from summer camp, they had had a fine incestuous old time, stopping halfway for fried chicken, calling up Liz to announce they'd just eloped. Liz had not been amused. In a time earlier than that, on a trip to the railroad museum, he had lifted her up to have a look into the first Pullman car, at the green plush seats inside. In the Gay Nineties shop, there had been a black velvet purse on a long gold chain that had fascinated her. And she had been sitting on his lap on the train ride around the cranberry bogs.

Since those times, and he did not know when this happened, a new sense of things had come to him, an understanding of things passing. And he had grown silent. He wondered how others took it, those born to a life of action, when they had their first taste of this sense that they were reading from a script. The more passionate, he guessed, committed suicide, or murder. Or went mad. What would happen to Liz when it came over her? She wouldn't take it gracefully, he knew. Nor was she likely to take it alone. *Well, when you couldn't make a religion out of social protest anymore, Liz, you might try making a religion out of religion. That ought to last you.* She could open a salon for the elect, she could. There would always be visionaries and prophets enough around, happy to play court to his ex-Queen Maeve.

Kathy was full of her college experiences, all the things she was *into*. And there was a *real* revolution coming, she would have him know, the *true* liberation of all humankind. It was her generation, she said, that would give the *coup de grâce* to the nuclear family. And she was reading the greatest book, *Seven Arrows*. And she was taking a course in the Counter Curriculum, and it was full of revelations.

Holding the door open for her, he almost said that one revelation every couple of thousand years used to be more than enough. But he thought better of it. And he thought better too of reminding her of what Jennie had said last summer, that all they were doing was scavenging on the ruins left by the crazies of the older generation, that the young kids coming in to college now were stuffier than her own parents.

Time passes us all by, he thought wryly, *the old and the middle-aged, and even the young, it makes fools of us all.*

Jennie. Their steaks and salads ordered, it was time to ask after Jennie.

"Jennie Corelli? Why do you want to know about Jennie?"

He told her.

"I might have known." She dug around for cigarettes in the saddle bag still slung over her shoulders. "And I thought you just wanted to see me, just to talk to *me*. See how naïve I still am? Never learn, do I?"

Well, he had *that* coming.

"Sweetheart, don't make a Greek tragedy out of everything. The full truth of it is, I think the Greeks were putting it on a little thick. And probably no one knew it better than themselves. Kathy?"

The waitress served their salads. To punish him, Kathy pushed hers aside.

"Please, Kathy. Eat your salad. You know I wish you wouldn't smoke."

That did it. She went on, now, about not knowing that he cared about her or her habits. Didn't he have his own life, after all. His clinic, his great love, and then his community theatre group and his endless rehearsals. And wasn't he always seeing Uncle Gerald too. So how could there be any time for him to be worrying about her smoking or, indeed, about anything else she might be doing.

There was so much of Liz in her just now. For one thing, she had the trick of putting her finger on the inconsequentiality of his life. This was necessary for her self-preservation, he knew. And better this than the hysterics of the old days, over how he and Liz might have divided the girls up between themselves. Over how she had deified him, and he had let her down. Over how she had dreamed and day-dreamed that he would keep her once the divorce became final. No, her anger was far better than all that. Her only chance for self-mastery was in weaning herself from him. He had made it his Eleventh Commandment some years ago, never to tell her that he loved her.

When she stopped talking to take another puff, he reached over and moved her salad bowl back in place. "There's a good ecologist," he said, "blowing cigarette smoke over fresh vegetables. And I thought you young people lived your politics."

"Very funny, Dad." All the same, she put out the cigarette and began to eat. "You could make a joke about anything, couldn't you?"

"And what else am I to make of things? Not so long ago, I was bathing you in a little basin, and carrying you around on my arm. Now you sit across from me and fill me up with blather about seven arrows and the nuclear family. Kathy, I am going to ask you again. Tell me about Jennie."

"All right, if you *must* know, though I think it's Jennie's business. And if you tell that family of hers, I'll never forgive you. Jennie had an abortion. She's still in the city. But she'll be back on campus in another week or so. I know where she is; and I know she's all right. Dad, don't you dare—"

He held up his right hand. "I won't, Kathy, I won't." He shook his head. "An abortion. Jennie Corelli. Pregnant. A virginal girl like that."

"That's just why it happened to her, don't you see? You're right, she *is* virginal . . . the most innocent girl I'll ever meet in my life. Her mother . . . that woman raised a nun, not a woman! For Jennie's sake, I hope she never finds out. But it would be real justice for her to be standing outside the hospital waving a Right to Life sign and then to have her own daughter come down the steps."

"What about the fellow?"

"That's not even worth talking about. Believe me, Dad, don't ask. It's too ridiculous."

He bet it was. Well, as long as the girl was all right.

Kathy asked, then, what he planned to tell Jennie's mother.

Leave it to him, he said. He'd figure out something.

"God, O God, what a prude that woman is! And all that whimpering over Jennie. It's disgusting."

"Kathy, Kathy, some day you'll be a mother too."

She laughed a false laugh, taking off her big round glasses to dab at her eyes. And she choked a little with the effort of it. Watching her perform, an old veteran now of the wars with Liz, he thought of the life of the monastery, that it might be second-best only to being a hermit. Gerald, of course, had known that long before he. But, then, Gerald was a eunuch. In *his* monastery, now, celibacy would be a device for protecting the monks from the women, a law honored most often in the breach, and quoted chapter and verse whenever most convenient.

Kathy was doing justice to her dinner now, and full of fire and brimstone. She would, she said, rather die than become a mother. She lectured him about world population. Did he realize that, unless something radical and immediate were done, there would be over seven billion souls crawling about on the globe before the century was out? Did he know there wasn't enough food, air, space, fuel for even half that number, which is what we've already exceeded? It was up to the women, she said, to save humanity from the worst disaster to ever befall the human race. Women, she said, must hold back the tide, the great tide of the unborn; women must seize their freedom and the responsibility this freedom involves. When women did this, we would all witness the greatest insurrection of slaves since time began. For it was the male, she said, who had been filling up women with babies, and then so running the world that they would be slaughtered when they came of age. The male, she said, is a born murderer. Men destroy; it is woman's nature to create.

"I see," he said, the two or three times she paused so he could say something. He wondered how much the divorce had entered into her fervor. Self-recrimination was second nature to him, after all. For he was the parent of grown children. And he had been in the habit of examining his conscience since the age of seven.

Kathy's was the voice of the true believer just now. He wondered what Liz might have to say about all this. Ah, well, this was one of the prices you had to pay for divorce, giving up having the other around to talk with about the children. There wasn't any substitute for *that*, not in any social arrangements he could think of. Not even in Kathy's organic gardens. But then, in Kathy's organic gardens there wouldn't be any children to talk about, if he'd heard her right.

"Shall we go anywhere?"

"No, Dad, I think I'd just like to go back to my apartment. There's some work I have to do before classes tomorrow."

She took up as little of the front seat of the car as she could. Huddling, almost, at the window. She was smoking again. *Leave her,* he thought. *Leave her alone.*

They were only a block away from the apartment when she broke the silence, in a voice very different from the one that had lectured him in the restaurant.

"Religion," she said, "gets into your bones. Your blood. I can't get rid of the feeling I helped kill someone. I didn't tell you, did I, that I was the one who helped Jennie make arrangements for the abortion."

He reached over for her hand. "Your Greek tragedies again. Be careful. If you want to feel guilty, there's no end to it."

"I tell myself a lot of things. That if it hadn't been me, it would have been someone else. That Jennie pleaded with me, and that if I waited it wouldn't have been safe anymore. That there wasn't any real life there. Certainly it would have been far from anything *human*. But I dream about it, Dad. I have these dreams."

You'll always have dreams, he thought, *may God have mercy on your soul, that much you got from your mother, to carry the sins of the world on your back.*

"God damn it!" He drew the car up to the curb, shut off the ignition and turned to her, pushing his hat back on his head. "Why does it always have to be the likes of you who feel guilty, the likes of you and Jennie? You're still children, the two of you, you haven't even started yet and you're beating your breasts already. Get rid of it, girl, before it ruins you! Don't exaggerate like that. A wick of a life not even begun, and you're calling yourself a murderer? What do you think they're doing in Ireland, both sides, all these terrible years? Is it justified just because they're out of the womb and they had water sprinkled on their heads and they've grown to full size? Weren't you telling me some grand theory about all this back in the restaurant? Or didn't you believe what you were saying?"

"I don't know what I believe. Oh, Dad, I don't know what in God's name I'm doing . . . ."

She was crying now, and she worked her way over to him, need overcoming her shame, and she leaned her head against his coat. And he held her there for the moment; it was only for the moment he could make it all right. She had made her confession. She thought he had give her absolution.

"None of us do, girl. None of us." He stroked her hair, thinking of the time after this, when she would be wanting children. The time when the ancient needs would break over the banks of ideology and she would be done playing games, done with missionaries. And the time after that, when lovers and children go their ways. Faith, like love, he thought, has its own season. Against our will, they age; they die. But hope . . . hope always dies in its infancy.

When Liz had been looking for reasons why they had failed one another, she had spoken of the son they never had. Well then, and would a boy have held them together? And was *that* what children were for?

No to both, he decided, for Liz would have left a boy alone no more than she had the girls. Nor could he have redeemed a son anymore than he could Kathy.

And whatever children were for was not revealed to their parents.

He closed his eyes, and saw first his father's face. The face of a man whose measure had never been fully taken, for he had sired only sons. And then Liz's face very close to his own, so close that he caught her perfume, her very breath. Then, opening his eyes, he saw his own face in the green lenses of Kathy's glasses, two little Rumpelstilskins leering back at him. They lay now on the floor of the car where they had fallen when she came to him for comfort. He caught the musk of her hair. She might be eight years old again, maybe six, in all the times he had offered to put her in his pocket. He looked up and out the window. It would be dusk soon. Never mind. He might be holding her there for a while yet. Neither of them had anywhere in particular to go.

Rites of Separation

My mother-in-law wants to divest herself of her things, her properties. Whenever we visit her now in her apartment on South Miami Beach, my husband and I have a ritual tussle with her. She offers, we protest, she insists; finally we pack away another piece of crystal or jewelry, another envelope of photographs. *Take, take,* she commands, pressing her treasures upon us as once, still duenna of her kitchen, she heaped another spoonful of rice pudding on our plates.

Her world has become too big for her. Her living quarters consist of a large room furnished with couches that are hideaway beds, of a walk-in kitchenette and a small bathroom. *I want a smaller place,* she tells us. She has in mind a single room in a hotel that has no more than a bed, a chair or two, a tiny refrigerator, a hot-plate she can use for a stove. She is tired of cooking; she is tired of making her bed. And besides, there is a man at the desk twenty-four hours a day whose presence (or so she claims) would make her feel safer.

She has, this woman of will, this boss of bosses, grown very fearful—of what? Of falling gravely ill, with no one nearby to hear, to care. Of being robbed at knifepoint, gunpoint. Her apartment was burglarized once when she was away for the afternoon. What if there is a next time, and she happens to be home? She confides that she remembers her dreams now, as she never used to, and that they are often dreams that someone leaps in front of her path and points a weapon at her, and demands her treasures. Someone is lying in wait for her, in ambush.

In his report of "Aging Among the Highland Maya," David Gutmann writes that the older men told him of dreams in which they were helpless before attack. The younger men have "mastery dreams," Gutmann tells us, whereas the older men are passive, even overwhelmed in their dreams. There are other differences. When the younger men spoke of the deaths of others to Gutmann, whether these were deaths by accident, illness or murder, they did not say they were caused by witchcraft. The older men did. And, in the Rorschach cards, older men often saw animals who bite and contend. And demons. In later life, Gutmann suggests, the boundary between self and other, between emotion and the object of emotion, may begin to crumble. For older people, "death is the signature of personal malice, envious thoughts, rather than natural, impersonal process."

We never came to love one another, my mother-in-law and I; we never became good friends. All that no longer matters to her. She is in need of a confessor now, of one who will listen in silence to her resentments, her angers, her regrets. She does not begin to know how much she is teaching me, and how magnificent she can sometimes be. *So much of it is in shadows*, she whispers to me. Sometimes she rages: *Old age is a curse, a hell! Better to die young!* How can I believe her? There is still that thrust toward life. She cares for herself in every affliction, with infinite tenderness. Once, she pounded her fist on the table, shouting, *No matter what you do, you can't make any of it come back!* Later, she clutched at her heart and told me, *I am afraid*. She speaks of her dreams over and over again. I remember that Robert Butler found the assassin dream is quite common among the older patients he has in psychoanalysis. I would not dare to tell her this. Nothing would make her more furious than the suggestion that her experience, her suffering is not unique. She is at the far side of life. Each, for our own reasons, reaches for the other. And we touch, we meet.

Her life, she says, is shrinking, moving inward to enclose her.

There is little she needs. When you are young, you are building, expanding, extending yourself outward. When you are old, you draw yourself in to fit the narrowing space. You comb the beaches of your reserves again and again, finding ever more vanities to cast off, to give away. Aging is a diminishing. Whatever you still cling to, *that* will bind you to life. It will not let you go, gently or defiantly, into *that good night*.

Her sister lives in an apartment building nearby. The bitter quarrel between them has its twisted roots in their childhood. They do not even speak to one another anymore. My mother-in-law lies on the couch in the evening, sighing, murmuring, as her inner eye moves across the retrospective of her life. *It was so unfair, my children, you can never believe all what she did to me. No one could believe such cruelty from a sister.*

To silence her, to turn away, to speak in platitudes, even to chide her, or worse, to tell her what I am coming to know that there is judgment . . . we withstand these temptations, my husband and I, these temptations to spare ourselves, to allay our own fears and anxieties, to reproach her. No; she has chosen to lay herself bare before us. I took his people as mine; this has fallen to my lot. We say to one another, *Let her rage, let her remember, be merciful. One day we too shall need a confessor.*

The scavengers wait, she warns us. *If they have to break down the door to find me in bed, or on the floor, or, God forbid, in the bathroom, they will loot this place, they'll look in every corner.* The birds of prey: they watch, they wait, they listen.

Look. This jewelry is for a younger woman. It is not fitting for someone in my age to wear it. These linens I'll never use. These little spoons. This coat: no one in Florida could use such a heavy coat, old or young, why do I need to leave it hanging in my closet, waiting for moths, for mold, for thieves? Take. Take.

She turns to my husband. *Tell me, what will you do with these photographs? Remember that this is the only picture anybody has left of my mother. Take it down, take it with you, you should have it, your children should have it, they should keep it for* their *children. Remember her. Remember me.*

If history had taken another course, she would be living now in a little place, in a *shtetl* in Europe, still. In her old age she would be at work tending the household gods, tending the ghosts. I dream her there. The crib where my husband slept in infancy waits under this small window for our children's children. All her properties would circulate for their season of use and be returned to her, for polishing and starching and keeping. Until the final day of divestiture, the hour of the last division, when the last will is opened to be read. In the Old World the ghosts must be appeased, their fires tended, their names and deeds committed to memory. In this very old book her grandfather breathes; in this bit of cloth her father stirs. Her mother looks out from this mirror; that is why its face is turned to the wall. I see her there more clearly than in this room of her confessional, where the couches and chairs are covered with flashy floral prints, where the venetian blinds are closed against the murderous sun, where the clacking thrum of the air-conditioner curls back the hem of the plastic tablecloth. The ancestors are displeased to find her here. Their visits are brief; they have little to say.

Take. Take. She is so eager to give her things away. What is happening inside her? There are old people who hold on fiercely: nothing must be touched or moved. There are old people who have grown fast to their properties, who refuse to leave their houses. An old Cajun woman in Champs d'Or stated the simple law to my friend: *When a person is old, she wants to be near her things.* "A man's self," William James explained, "is the sum total of all he can call his, not only his body and his psychic powers, but his clothes and his house, his wife and children, his ancestors and friends, his reputation and works, his lands and horses and yacht and bank-account. All these things give him the same emotions." A woman's self too. If she were living in her own house, would my mother-in-law have this same urge, to take things down and give them away, to come undone?

My revered professor is now past eighty. He and his wife, my beloved friend, live in the same house where they raised their children. Émigrés from a place ravaged beyond recovery, they made their home in America. There, portraits of parents and grandparents guard the beds; the ancestors make their wishes known through dreams. Years ago a porch was added to the house, and the children wrote their names in the fresh cement. Last winter, when we visited them, I read the names and dates aloud to my own children: Gerda, on the bottom step; then Peter; then Joseph. Summer, 1946. They were teen-agers, my children's ages, then. *1946!* one of my daughters echoed. *That was yesterday*, Frau Professor said. The floorboards creak and sigh with the passages of spirits. Wood and flesh, they have become as one.

My mother too has a house. She too is eighty. Her house is very small, yet it seems to me it is too big for her. Of course, she and I never speak of such matters. We play cards; we exchange recipes; we smile; we are careful during my visits. When I read about growing old in America, I learn that my mother is a statistic, that the whole country is becoming ever more thickly inhabited by widows living alone in little houses. I learn that widows have "options," that they might consider selling their houses and moving into "retirement villages" where they would pay rent instead of taxes and fuel bills and bills for house repairs.

My mother's is not a house of memories. Throughout most of her married life she was a gypsy, moving from one apartment to another in Chicago, taking along her growing family. It must have seemed to her then that we would always be with her. She did not grasp the equation: growing up is growing away. I am only beginning to understand it as my own children draw nearer the threshold. We used to gather around the kitchen table, my sisters, my mother and I, wrapping glasses and cups in newspaper and packing them in boxes. We scrubbed the floors of the places we left and the floors of the places we moved into. Ritual purifications. Then there was the limbo between the time of moving out and the time for settling in, when we belonged nowhere, when we were homeless. The stark look of the windows after the curtains had been taken down, and of the bare closets and of the pantry shelves hollowed out, made my sister's stomach hurt, made my throat tighten so that by moving day I could hardly swallow. In this, my mother's house, she lived with my father and her youngest, my little sister, for only three years before she was widowed and the last of her children married. For almost twenty years now she has been alone here. There was no time to thread the loom, to begin the weaving of a family memory here. There are no ghosts to tend.

Perhaps the house, the shell, is the final property of divestiture. I have discovered that, like my mother-in-law, my mother has been giving things away. She too has been saying, though with her own inflection, *Take, take*, to her other daughters, to my sisters. I know this because in recent visits I find things missing—books, a piece of furniture, a lamp. When I last visited her, she told me I could go up to the attic and look through the box of old photographs and take what I liked. I sat at the top of the stairs with my husband, looking at snapshots of people I once imagined I knew—my parents when they were young, my sisters and I in infancy and childhood and then, in adolescence, as "little women." I found one where they were gathered around my mother—her Meg, her Beth, her Amy. Though I took nothing, I sorted them and arranged them so that the ages followed one another. My husband asked my mother if he might have one snapshot of me when I was three or so and standing alone, in a white pinafore, looking quizzically at the photographer, my father. *Of course*, she said, and then, *Are you sure that's all you want*? She seems to have no fear of what scavengers might take; she is not haunted like my mother-in-law. But then my husband is an only child.

My friends are amused at my superstitions. I do not like to have my picture taken; I do not borrow; I do not like to lend. I used to go to auctions and stand in the back of the hall and watch, with a kind of horrified fascination, all the bidding and bargaining. Now I stand at the edge of the lawn or the back of the church at garage sales, flea markets, lawn sales, rummage sales, and watch the people wander from table to table, fingering, weighing, considering. They laugh, they gossip, they haggle; people have such a good time on market day! After a while I look away, I look down. I open a book lying on one of the tables, and read the inscription slanting across the title page: *To our dearest son Ted, on his graduation day, with all our hopes for a bright future, Love, Mom and Dad.*

The things made in America, Rilke once wrote to his Polish translator, are forms of *dummy-life*. Rilke believed that the poet is a bee of the invisible; the poet must cherish and protect the things inhabited by gods, by spirits, by ancestors. Things are relics, but also charms. Amulets. Talismans. What is the fate of those who mutilate a thing, or lose or destroy it?

To accept the proffered thing is to consent to serve as a trustee. To reject it is even more harrowing.

Please, we plead with my mother-in-law, *keep it for yourself.*

Keep it for what? she mocks us. *To put in my grave? To leave it for some thief to take and sell?*

I read of a people who believed that all things are animated by spirits. No one is an owner; the living are only caretakers. Who among these people would dare to steal fruit from the orchard of another clan, or a necklace of cowrie shells made for another, who would dare to disturb the spirits in these things? The spirit who inhabits each thing knows its rightful place and proprietor. It will haunt the thief until it is returned; it will avenge its loss or destruction. Among these people theft, like incest, would be committed only by someone mad, by someone possessed by an evil force.

In what ways will my daughters remember me? I have no power over this. We are all caught in this network of exchanging, of giving and taking away fragments of ourselves and others. Parents have secret hiding-places where they have stored a lock of hair, a string of baby teeth, a letter of apology or a pledge of undying love written in the spidery hand of a five-year-old. Estranged lovers have their ruins, the widowed their buried treasures. Such is the stuff of witchcraft; the hold one of us has over another can only be loosed by working magic through their properties. One must be wary of leaving intimate things about—a fingernail, a tooth, a curl. We are all pirates; each of us has a cache where we keep the things that must go with us in all our wanderings.

In the small box where I keep the things I shall never use, the things I dare not lose, is a cameo earring, a woman's head and neck in agate dangling from a thin gold wire. It was given to me by my aunt, my father's sister, when she was dying. The earrings belonged to her mother. They were a gift from her husband on their tenth wedding anniversary; they were his last gift to her; he died that same year. Theirs was a deep and beautiful love, my grandparents'; it became a legend in my family. The cameo earrings sang with the longing of a lover for her mate. My grandmother cherished them as she cherished nothing and no one else. My father accepted this; his sisters did not. They coveted them, these twin cameos possessed of their mother's affections.

The girls might have been green when they were born, my grandmother sighed, *that's how jealous they were from the very beginning.* When she was nursing Lily, she pleaded with Rose, who, then not quite two years old, would storm through the apartment throwing books from shelves, pulling the tablecloth off the table, peeling wallpaper, making a broth of fresh eggs and lettuce leaves in the middle of the kitchen floor. Time and again my grandmother would find Rose "doing things" to the baby. Lily had her revenge; by the time she was able to walk, she attacked Rose's possessions, tearing things down, tearing things apart. When she turned two she attacked Rose herself and, claiming the moral advantage the younger and smaller always learn to claim, she answered Rose's taunts with curses my grandmother never even knew were in the language, and Rose's pushes and light blows with deep scratches and bites. My grandmother often spoke of the years of bringing up her children as the Twenty Years War or The War of the Roses and Lilies. But there was more bitterness than humor in her remarks. My father had to share a room with one or the other of them until they were well into their teens and the family moved into a larger apartment. *The two of them,* he'd say, *the two of them,* and shake his head. *Peace, peace,* my grandmother used to plead, cry, scream, whisper, pray. But there was no peace.

In their adolescence, my aunts' rivalry came to turn on the question of who would inherit the cameo earrings. At first my grandmother was horrified at this; then she saw how she might use it to her advantage. She would promise them to whoever was behaving at the time, she said, which meant that the cameo earrings were kept in circulation. Back and forth they migrated from Lily's dresser drawer to Rose's. In their journeys they were the embodiments of grave threats, glorious promises, self-righteous smugness, and claims to virtue that were doomed to be dishonored.

Lily married and moved away to Ohio. Rose stayed on with her mother. The earrings waited in their bright red velvet box; the war waged on. Who *really* loved her mother, who was *really* taking care of her? Rose wanted to know. But Lily said it was quite clear to *her* who was taking care of whom in that apartment, and even clearer why Rose had chosen to remain an old maid. More than once, they slapped one another in my presence. When they were well past thirty, they pulled one another's hair one afternoon while my grandmother lay wasting of her long illness on the couch in the dining room. *Girls*, she wept. *Girls*.

She never forgave them; perhaps no mother forgives her children their warring. She was a long time dying; there were many opportunities for them to lay down their arms, for her sake at least. They never took one of them; there was no reconciliation. My father saw to it that her last wish was respected: she was buried wearing one of the cameo earrings. The other was to go back and forth between them, half a year to Lily, the other half to Rose, to remind them of what bound them together and at the same time divided them, to serve as a remembrance and a lesson. The cameo would go, at last, to the survivor. *You might just throw it away*, my father told them at the funeral. *She said that you might. Or one of you might take back the mate from her. She mentioned that too*. Neither of them could meet his eye, he told me. He gave it to Rose first, as she was the oldest.

Lily had two sons. I doubt that she told them about the cameo or that, if she had, the story would impress them as it did my sisters and me in its countless tellings. It was she who died first. And seven years ago, when my Aunt Rose lay in the hospital with what she knew was her last illness, she asked to see me.

Take it.

But, Aunt Rose, why me?

Take it. It was a command.

The cameo is sick with an old passion that all but only children come to know. It glows green in darkening rooms. When you hold it to your ear, it crackles and hums. How shall the questions of distributive justice—the just division of the goods of the earth, or of a mother's love—be resolved? Though I teach them the lesson of the cameo, my daughters shall not inherit it. Their quarrels are my penance. I am, like my mother, a quiet woman; I, like her, do not seem to have strong emotions. But when they suffer their envy of one another, or when I think of the burden that every gift must be, I feel such compassion for my daughters that my throat begins to tighten, I can hardly swallow.

All through the cycle of life, we divest ourselves of our things, we take our leave. At childhood's end, my children gave away and threw away, without once looking back. When they were in school I hurried to rescue drawings, poems, stuffed toys, from the trash bin. They are all in a chest in the back of my closet, where I keep the box with the cameo.

"To marry," Arnold Van Gennep says in his classic work on the rites of passage, "is to pass from the group of children or adolescents into the adult group, from a given clan to another, from one family to another, and often from one village to another. An individual's separation from these groups weakens them but strengthens those he joins." It is the same when the youth is initiated; it is the same at the hour of dying.

It is not easy to be an animist. There are stories in the newspapers of young people who prey upon the old, who break into their houses and apartments to steal, who beat and sometimes even kill their victims. There was a little town in Iowa where I once lived, where shrewd bargain-hunters kept a list of the very old and waited for the announcement of their death, when their houses and their possessions were put on the block. I try to imagine what it must be like, to live so fearlessly.

After the rites of separation, van Gennep says, there are rites of transition, and then the rites of incorporation. I cannot see so far ahead; so much of that too is in shadows. There is a time to give away the things of childhood. There is a time when the young bride must give away the things of her girlhood to her sisters. Then, after a season so long that one dreams it will never turn, there is a time to say,

Take. Take.

Often my husband is overcome by what is happening. He dreams a sister; he longs for one who must share this with him. Once more I must pretend to know what it is to be a daughter, to be a sister, I who created myself to be an only child and then, that failing, to be no one's child.

My daughters bargain with one another. They scheme, borrow, argue, make up their differences, then begin measuring again. I am amused to find that one of my sweaters or scarves or bracelets has quietly migrated to this one's closet, that one's drawer. *You only needed to ask*, I laugh. *You know I am happy to give you whatever you like.* Then one or the other of them laughs too, and sometimes even hugs me. They think that love has proofs, and that these proofs are gifts. They are almost grown; they are so young.

1980S

In a Brief Space

Peg O'Flaherty Bloom, scrivener, peer-reviewer, merchant of scribblers' dreams, bibliographer, translator, scholar, sometime poet, slept these seven selves atop the bed, her late Professor Moberg's eight-hundred-page tome, each chapter clipped into a separate folder, the whole of it parceled out into three giant-sized mailers snitched from the college printing office, underneath the box springs. From whence it sent up plumes of gentle admonition to float upon her shallow sleep, soft scurrying shapes of his shade in all the varieties of her responsibility to his memory spelling the syllables of a deathbed promise his widow imagined Peg had made. Arnie was deep in his own dreams, having done what he could for her as a confessor. Even at her third awakening, which must have been at about half-past two.

I know Perkins will insist that the thing has to be cut to half its length. For beginners. He'll want whatever's salvaged to be rewritten, too. Every paragraph, every sentence of it. So she had played the devil's advocate all day every day and through half the night, too, since the reviewer's report had arrived in the mail a week ago. Arrived amid the bills and the requests for money and the tabloids and magazines, and the postcards from vacationing friends on Monhegan Island and in Yugoslavia, and the galleys for her bibliographical guide, and still no letter from their son. *Enclosed is our reviewer's report on Professor Moberg's manuscript. If you are seriously interested in pursuing this project with our Press, could you come down to the City to discuss this? If you are free for lunch on July 1, please give my secretary a call.*

If *she* were seriously interested in pursuing, and etc. And what would there be to discuss? *This manuscript needs a lot of work. It also needs heavy editorializing,* sic. *It needs to be updated, also, in view of Regan's,* sic, *election. It needs judiscious,* sic, *pruning. It ought to be reduced, probably at least to half the length. I'd suggest a whole new structuring. Also deleting his point of view. He romanticizes.* Additional comments: *I can just picture his sitting in his study in rapture over his dreams of international peace.* And then the final gratuitous cruelty: *The tone he takes is empassioned,* sic *. Almost adolescent.*

The early book—there had been good reviews among the damning ones. But Perkins would remind her that the good reviews, numbering two in all, had been published in obscure little magazines long since defunct. Moberg is dated, his views are dated, Perkins was bound to say. He has published nothing for a quarter of a century. She would remind him, then, that it takes that long to put together a piece of scholarship of this magnitude; moreover, Moberg had been steadily losing his eyesight. Toward the end he had worked a killing ten hours a day, his wife had told her, his books and papers spread out over the counterpane on the bed in the room that doubled as his study in their retirement hotel apartment. Wearing an eyeshade, and alternating between three pairs of glasses. And listening to the tapes his wife had made of his notes while resting his eyes during the quarter of every hour his affliction covered his seeing eye with frost. Perkins would remark that effort is not enough. Although, of course, he would admire the old man for his grace under pressure. A voice-reader herself, Peg had discerned from the first telephone conversation with him that Perkins would be about thirty. In as many years again he might know the full weight of those three words.

She would ask Perkins what he recommended that she do. Knowing full well what his answer would be. She would ask him if he had informed the reviewer that Moberg was dead, that Moberg's wife was in a nursing home, that Moberg's daughters had no interest in their father's academic life, that long before retirement, even, his colleagues had forgotten him, forgotten him to his face, that to turn this tome away was to consign thirty years of unremitting labor to oblivion. *This is a business, not a charity,* Perkins might say. Ah, then, she might reply, If it's a business, why did you send this work, this classic, yes classic, to a reviewer who in these spare, hard words betrayed indifference, if not hostility, to Moberg's point of view? A reviewer who objects to Moberg's style, yet is unable to spell simple English words, among them the name of the President, whose policies, by the way, Moberg could scarcely have discussed since he died some months before the 1980 elections? A reviewer who took an entire year to write this sorry excuse for an evaluation.

Look out, Arnie had warned her. *She's probably one of Perkins's friends.*

For twenty-seven years of married life, Arnie had been reminding her it is better to leave a little in the inkwell.

It wasn't an inkwell, it was a black sea, Moberg had worked with two editors before Perkins, worked for over twenty-three years with them, up to the retirement of the first and the untimely death of the second, he had gone on revising, rewriting, *restructuring*, in accordance with the suggestions of one, then the other. He assumed, he assumed. *He assumed wrong,* Perkins would say.

The lunch was meant to be a ritual. To absolve the Press of any bad faith of which this excessively loyal protégée of Moberg's might accuse them. And if she did not play the game? Well, they had their ways, they could fix her wagon for her.

What about throwing herself at Perkins's mercy, simply telling him these revisions were impossible, they would take at least two years of full-time work on her part at the end of which he could give her no assurances of publication. (And where was it written that she had two years for this, indeed for anything?) But Perkins could say that in its present form it would be twenty years before she might find someone willing to publish it, and she'd have to pay for it at that. He would blink, he would speak calmly, reasonably. As if she were being obstinate. As if the Press had any intention of publishing the manuscript in any form ever.

It's no use, she had said to Arnie during the second awakening. But Arnie had always known that nothing's of any use; still, you do what you have to do.

Time had passed Moberg by. There had been civility, at least, in his day. So she told Arnie, who had his doubts, who said we always think the past was better. "Than now?" she'd asked. "That, too," he'd replied. "But I meant than it really was."

She asked Arnie, as if *he* had misplaced it, where intellectual modesty had gone, and common decency, how had *that* become so uncommon? She asked him how people could treat someone else's life work like this? She asked him to explain indifference to her, or was it the love of power she needed him to inform her about. "Why do you insist on making grand opera out of this?" Arnie had asked her. "Just this semester, old Wilkerson sent one of his graduate students back to the drawing-board with his dissertation. For the fourth time around. And the guy's living on four hundred a month, and his wife just had their second baby."

During the third awakening, she told him that the worst of it was that Moberg died believing.

"*Shluff.* You have a big day tomorrow."

Of the day after tomorrow, when the results of her tests would be in, neither of them spoke.

"It's impossible to shluff. Think of what's waiting for me."

He chose to think she meant tomorrow, not the day after. "Think of the poor devil of a political prisoner lying in a cell somewhere tonight, waiting for somebody to come and get him for an interrogation. Some Big Man somewhere will send for him at any minute, to ask him some questions. *That's* something to lie awake about."

Shamed by this, she slept at last.

* * *

The wind was howling with the voices of souls dead or well on their way to it. It was raining the Bejaysus, hard enough to shatter the windowpanes. Thanks to her Irish luck, then, maybe she wouldn't be going in to the City tomorrow after all. All the roads might be flooded, the bridges down.

At midnight, she had still been worrying aloud. *Shluff,* Arnie had said. And fell *on shluff* himself.

It must be well into three in the morning.

Ah, Moberg would be the gallant one. He'd take her by the arm, he'd introduce her to all his new colleagues, he'd say, *Of all my students, she was the finest, the keenest, the most promising. And I found her in the Midwestern cornfields! Now she calls herself a poet. But surely you saw what she wrote on Bergson in the* "Annals" *four years ago? Still remembers something of what I taught her, eh, Pegeen?*

The Thin Man the students called him in the Illinois of the Fifties, and not unkindly. This was in appreciation of his unfailing courtesy, even toward the occasional Yahoo who turned up in the heavily enrolled Survey of World Philosophy the dean had thrust upon the department in those days of expansion, as much as of the tall, spare frame he carried so stiffly. As though he wore a back brace. As though walking caused him pain. *Prince Shadow* Peg called him, to herself alone, until graduate school, when it was time to put away the things of the child. The Prince for his shapely thoughts, his musical voice, the silver of his grey eyes, his realms. The *Shadow* for the hunger in his long, lean face.

He will not have changed. The last year of the Sixties now, and this constancy. What did he make of the werewolves in his classes? And how would he survive this burlesque they mocked the gods by calling Armageddon?

The wind keened; she lay next to Arnie shaking with silent laughter at Moberg, at herself, at the two of them. He had delivered her from the forces of ignorance and superstition and tyranny— into this purgatory. For what was she to say of the three thick chapters he had sent her, these trellises of dreams, now that she had lost her innocence? It was just her loss that exposed his so cruelly. *I am especially eager to hear what you have to say about these fragments of my life's work, my dear girl.* Well, she had lived long enough to have learned the art of dissembling.

Twelve years before, Moberg had taken her and Arnie out to dinner, to celebrate their visit to the East. *Come out from behind that degree,* he'd written in reply to her note that they would be in the City for the holidays, *and have dinner with me.* Afterwards, he'd driven them out to his gingerbread house in Teaneck to meet his wife, who had only just returned from a visit to her family in Minnesota. He had met Arnie for the first time then, yet the two of them behaved as though *they* were the principals of the reunion, reminiscing about life on the post-war campus where their paths, strangely enough, had never crossed. And she had been set down in the armchair next to Karen Moberg's. And what was she to say to this regal presence, this famed cellist, this living proof of Moberg's ardent feminism? Legend had it that he did everything—the marketing, the raising of their twin daughters, the cooking, even. That had *she* been the wife and mother of the family, Moberg might easily have become one of the luminaries of the twentieth century. But as she dared not entertain such thoughts, Peg began to speak vaguely of how she missed the autumn and the winter now they were living in New Orleans, of how she had almost forgotten the look of snow. *Ah, yes? I think I should miss this most of all too, Margaret. The change of the seasons.* And so, while the men amused one another, the women chatted amiably about nothing. And Karen Moberg was so gracious that Peg was certain she had made up her mind what it all meant, the white marquisette evening dress with the silver sequins, the extravagant late Fifties coiffure, the revelation that Peg was meeting Arnie's family for the first time although they had been married for five years. When Arnie called a cab to take them back to the hotel in Manhattan, Moberg took one of her hands in both of his and murmured, *I didn't approve of your marrying, Pegeen. But now that I have met Arnold, I am completely reassured.* She had repeated all this to Arnie, furious, swearing she would never see Moberg again. And Arnie had prophesied she would learn to forgive her old master. So it had come to pass: her first thought when Arnie took the job at State was that she would be seeing Moberg again.

It would show, this sleeplessness.

The Broadwalk, the elms, the *nyssa sylvatica* burning in the blue October dusk. Then spring, and the dogwood blossoming, and then the forsythia, and then the lilacs. And Moberg meeting her on the bicycle path near the library. *I'd like to see you for a few moments after class,* he had said that first time. And the second time, and every time thereafter: *Don't let anyone tempt you into marriage. Into throwing away your gift.*

Her father had drawn back his bow, sent the arrow of herself into that white cloister, that dazzling dream of the virginal Pegeen at prayer flashing in the blue Catherine-wheels of his gaze. She could not look, she could not look away.

On the day Moberg asked her, *Where do you come from, you wonderful child?* she told him of her apostasy. *This confidence does me great honor, my dear girl.* And then: *I am gratified that you came to Philosophy after you swept away all the rubbish.* Then in that clear, grey sea under glass she read her new fate that was the old fate, had she had the wit to recognize it then.

Out of politeness, but only once, he asked if he might see her poetry. It was plain that he did not take this seriously. By the first year of graduate school, she lived in dread of disappointing him. So much so that, at the end of that year when he left the campus for New York—to ascend The Chair during the last days before the palace revolution neither of them saw coming—she felt soaring-free. All over again, she left her father's house for good.

Enough. She would get up, have a look at the children, a belt of brandy. Yes, it would show. And she had wanted her color to be high. She had wanted him to see that she regretted nothing.

* * *

An hour before the alarm was set to ring, she was going through the notes she had prepared to plead The Case For Andrew Moberg. Well knowing that Perkins's jury of one would be deaf and his mind in that "elsewhere place" he would suggest that she take the tome. Politely, of course. For it was understood that the distinguished university press "would be delighted" to publish the works of its illustrious alumni. *Never mind,* his ghost said to her this morning. He did not mean it.The very stones of the place were sacred to him. Dead, and he was still a believer. She closed her eyes. *Go away, please leave me be. I have sorrows enough of my own.* But he was as deaf as Perkins was sure to be.

Arnie found her in the kitchen, asleep in the chair she had drawn up to the table, and the air thick with cigarette smoke. And she had vowed never again. He would not speak to her. He would not even look at her. Humbly she shook cereal into two bowls, poured two glasses of juice, put English muffins in the toaster. He stared past her all through breakfast.

On the way to the bus station, she touched his arm. But he did not relent.

"Listen, I know I've asked too much of you. I can understand why you're out of patience with me. But those hours of talking . . . even if it all comes to nothing, I want you to know I couldn't have come this far without them."

"Okay. Okay. So I'll pick you up here at five unless you call?"

She was relieved that he was not going to wait with her. She turned around to wave at him, and he honked lightly, twice. Try as he might, he could not carry a grudge. But she was pushing her luck with the cigarettes.

The bus was crowded, thanks to the strike that had been going on since April. She worked her way to the back and took the first empty aisle seat she saw.

"Peg! Peg Bloom!"

Just in back of her, in the row across the aisle, Rita Stein was leaning forward from her seat next to the window. Her seat mate offered to change places with Peg.

"Going into the City too?" Peg settled in, embarrassed as always by Rita's effusive kissing and embracing.

"Not this time. I'm getting out at Paramus. A job interview. Number One Hundred and Thirty-Five. And you?"

"Got to see a man about a book."

"Peg! You've got a book of poems coming out!"

"No such miracle. This is my old professor's. He appointed me executor of his papers just before he died in Florida."

"That's quite an honor." She sighed. "It's quite a lot of other things too." They laughed together. Rita asked about the book of poems, and Peg told her it had been at a press for eleven months now.

"I suppose it's useless to ask if you ought to get an agent."

"Yes, it's useless."

"In the case of this professor's book, too."
"Yes. Good Christ, yes."
"How can you stand it?"
"I can't."

They laughed again. Rita asked, knowing the answer, if Peg was still teaching a class in Introduction to Philosophy at the community college; and to appease her, Peg said she expected to become America's first Adjunct Emeritus. As fair exchange, Rita told her of her adventures in job-hunting, and that she didn't have much hope for this one.

"It appears that historians are growing like fungi. And I haven't been able to impress anyone with my book and my thirteen articles."

"Never mind. Socrates didn't have much of a vita, and *he* found students."

This they celebrated until tears came to their eyes.

They talked now about the threat (as Peg saw it), the imminence (as Rita did) of nuclear war. Rita wanted to know what Peg thought about the Supreme Court ruling on draft registration that was handed down just days before. They both had daughters who felt that either way it was no good. They both had sons who were lostlings. The last she'd heard, Rita's was in Mexico. The Canada of the Eighties? She dared not ask: questions beget questions. In their own son's Canada it was hard to find a mailbox.

"If there's a draft, all hell will break loose on the campuses," Rita said with conviction.

"A young man in my class last semester made quite a speech in favor of a draft. Not that he imagined his own name might be in the drum."

"Naturally not."

"It's all coming around again, Rita. The crewcut brains, the Ku Klux Klan eyes, the goose-stepping. That young man's words left me feeling so ill I had to leave the classroom for a few minutes. In twenty-two years of teaching I've never done that. There was a full-blown flesh-and-blood blackshirt sitting in front of me. Nineteen years old, and his heart was as dead as the moon. Nietzsche's eternal return, and I didn't know until that moment that it would be on *this* side of life. It came to me that's the one justification I could accept for committing suicide."

"Or committing Life," Rita said quietly.

Peg took her hand, lifted it to her lips. "There's a lot to you, old girl."

"Just what I hope to impress upon my interviewer." Rita kissed her on one cheek, then the other. Gathering up her book bag, she reminded Peg of what Camus had said at the end of *The Plague*.

"They will always be there, Peg. Every generation has to come to terms with it all over again. That's what we forgot in the Sixties."

"*Bonne chance*, Rita." "Thanks, and the same with that mountain on your lap."

* * *

The storm hadn't been so violent after all. The sun was radiant, the air nippy and fresh. Watching the children run down the road to meet the school bus, Peg could find no sign of that Souls in Purgatory howling wind, except for a single branch that had been torn loose from the dying ash tree and flung on their kitchen doorstep like a premonition.

Arnie drove her to the bus station, putting up with her story until they got to the parking lot. She could be mugged, she said. *That's* why she hadn't been able to sleep. It had nothing to do with seeing Moberg again. But when they were walking away from the car, he let her have it. "Listen. All the criminals had a conclave last night. The whole underworld was there. They sent out a bulletin with a complete description, right down to that fluffy thing you're wearing under your throat. They'll be laying for Peg O'Flaherty Bloom."

He bought her ticket for her, reminded her how to get out to the campus, warned her he'd come after the two of them if they decided to run off.

The bus was almost empty. She took a seat near the front. He waved at her until they turned the corner, his smile quizzical.

A quarter of an hour later they were in Apple Valley, and as usual there was a long line waiting. She closed her eyes, napping while they boarded, not troubling herself to see who was settling in beside her. When she opened them again, she saw they were already winding through the Shawangunks. An autumn firelight played across the rime of the mountains; the beeches were a blur of gold, the meadows incandescent. The solitude she had sacrificed in that first rite of passage returned to her, the memory of the flesh: her viscera yielded to the dark green moss tufting the crevices in the rock walls; her lips thrummed with the scarlet of the sumac. *How can you know the beauty of this world unless you paint it?* Only seven years old, and her daughter was busy at the work of consecration with her brushes. *Mama, Mama, don't say anything, I want to feel all this forever!* The child through whom her own childhood would be restored. So had she kept her covenant with the race, the race with her. The excellent old ways. And now the old griefs lay ahead, and they would have to be brave. The trolls were waiting under the bridge. Upon the clear pool where she might behold the true reflection of her grave and tender face, the quicklime floated. And her mother could do no more than keep watch. "We are not given power,/Only the chance to be brave." Peg, who knew this when the nurses first brought her newborn son to her, and two years later her newborn daughter, had written the truth of it in a poem only months before her reunion with Moberg.

Her seat partner was working a crossword puzzle. Fulfilling Hesse's prophecy. He put down his paper from time to time to look around her out the window. His cap was on his knee; his jacket had the incense of the woods in it, and of pipe tobacco. His going-on-sixty face, his heavy glasses, his hair the color of dry sand . . . so her father was making his appearance again. Since his death, he had turned up in subway cars, in hotel lobbies and in cathedrals. Once she saw him in a Memorial Day parade in Indiana, and once on television—walking past the bier of the assassinated Kennedy. Only in *shul* could she escape his haunting.

She gathered up her overstuffed shoulder-strap bag and, rocking with the bus, steadying herself by grasping the backs of the seats all the way back, she made her way to the comfort station. *What, already?* Arnie would have asked, amazed. Even without morning coffee, she always had to do a few drops. The phantom ones were the most urgent of all.

When she came back, she found her seat partner dozing. She closed her eyes too. The resentful face of Rosenbloom bobbed up on a balloon string, the shock of his Afro exploding straight up from his white forehead as though he'd been plugged in at the other end. He was on something. Whatever it was, Arnie said, it wasn't a woman.

Like, I don't care for the way you teach. Like, we don't have to take notes, to spit this stuff back at you on exams. We know so much more than your generation ever knew. We've been places you never heard of. Kant said this? Well, Kant was stupid.

They, the New and the Now, had invented war and human suffering and the fear of a nuclear holocaust. Their virus infected her; she ran their high, apocalyptic fever; it burned away the perspective that had been the work of twenty years—dare she confess this to Moberg? Knowing better, ah, knowing better, she had grasped both sides of the lectern and declaimed against The War, pollution, the population explosion, racism, poverty, the lot. She had abandoned her post in the barny lecture hall and prowled about the room, weaving, wickedly weaving The Doomsday Spell. She was not alone; then so much the worse for them all. The students' appetite was voracious, insane. And she had capitulated. Knowing, ah, *knowing* that most of them, whatever their color, their creed, did not care, did not truly care about any vision other than that of their young selves wasting among the ruins. Arnie had said that compassion is a mutation. And, like most mutations, lethal.

The Jews read *Soul On Ice*, cooked soul food, cheered on the Al Fatah. The Catholics sneered at Vatican Two and their parents' provincialisms. The blacks, when they came to class, watched her, watched her carefully.

We're just waiting, Laura Evans told her, *for you older people to die.* Yes, and her own son and daughter at the ages of nine and seven would be waiting in their good time for Laura Evans to move out of the way. They would have a good wait, too; it was not for nothing that the sociologists were pointing in awe at the Postwar Baby Boom. But what had Lucretius written? "In a brief space the generations pass,/And like to runners hand the lamp of life/One unto other."

The lamp to Rosenbloom, his brains rearranged by LSD. The lamp to Ramón, who had shouted down the corridor, *We begin by burning down the library!* The lamp to Laura Evans, to light her way to Candyland.

The bus sped into Lincoln Tunnel. In the sudden darkness she had a prevision of the classroom in the Eighties. After the chanting and burning of incense, after playing Frisbee with prayer wheels, after Communion feasts of peyote, the return of the silent ones. And what will they be breeding in their silence? *These violent delights have violent ends.*

Such thoughts were heresy for Moberg's student. *My dear girl*, he would reproach her, *do you remember nothing of the Enlightenment?*

* * *

She found the Ladies Room in Port Authority after some searching—they were renovating; it had been more than a year since her last trip to the City—and queued up for one of the stalls. Afterwards, she repaired her make-up, brushed her hair, rearranged the contents of her handbag and her folder of notes. Perkins had said noon. It was only a little after eleven, and the cab would take no more than half an hour. She stopped at the concession stand, bought some mints and the *Times*. But the minute she walked outside into the steaming city, she took one of the cabs drawn up at the stand.

The driver, whose name and photograph were taped on the shield between the front and back seats, had just arrived in the city himself. From the West Indies. They arrived at an understanding about where she wanted to be taken through some vigorous sign language and a working map she drew under the letterhead of Perkins's most recent communication.

Moberg's ghost was at her side now. No time to study the street scenes, and it was just as well. She assured the ghost that Perkins's voice was the voice of an angel, maybe an archangel even. She conjured up for him a tall, angular, bespectacled benevolence, a

1981 edition of himself. And pitied him his eager acceptance of this fraud. Right after Perkins's call, she had told Arnie he had a bushy beard and small, cold eyes, and was about thirty years old. His voice had indeed been that of an archangel. But never had she known a voice to match its human lodging-place.

The driver's knuckles were wrapping against the shield. They were half a block away from the Press, in the midst of a traffic jam. She gathered up her things, paid him, tipped him twice the going rate for good luck for Moberg, and let herself out. *Go directly inside*, Arnie had instructed. *Do not pass GO, do not collect $200.*

In the small reception room she gave her name to the young woman at the desk, who sang it softly over the intercom. *Doctor Margaret Bloom to see Doctor Perkins*. Margaret, indeed. Doctor, indeed. She studied the photographs of the old campus buildings that marched in a straight row across the wall. There were footsteps on the carpeted stairs; a tall, severe-looking woman in a crisp cotton shirtwaist invited Peg to follow her up to Perkins's office, explaining on the way that he would be in conference until noon. Peg followed her meekly across the landing and down a narrow corridor to a room that was no more than a partition into which a desk and typing table had been crammed. The woman directed Peg to another room just beyond it—a smaller edition of this one, but graced with a window under which there was a chair which Peg was invited to take.

So in such cells as these are the fates of the labors of splendid isolation decided, where the blind threshers make the separation that foreordains their harvest. Ah, my esteemed Professor, and it was you who first placed Marcus Aurelius in my hands: "All of us are creatures of a day; the rememberer and the remembered."

The moist midsummer air drifting through the open window licked at the edges of the papers stacked on Perkins's desk. Moberg's file was probably at the top of one of these. If she cared to, Peg knew, she could manage to read enough of it upside-down to learn the fate she knew was sealed. She took off her light cotton jacket. She could hardly breathe in this stuffy cubbyhole, yet she longed for a cigarette. An infallible intuition warned her that Perkins did not tolerate smoking. She amused herself by reading the spines of the books jammed into the shelves along the walls, and noticed after a census she had not even been conscious she was taking that Moberg's early opus was not among them. So Perkins had not even troubled himself to pay tribute to the master. It would have taken no time at all to fetch a copy from among the hundreds—thousands?—in the warehouse. He might have put it in a prominent place just for this day. Or was its absence a silent message? But Arnie had told her that megalomania was the root of paranoia. Yet Freud had said the paranoid is never completely wrong.

Perkins's letter had been phrased with consummate care: anyone who read it who knew nothing about The Case would conclude that the Press was requesting no more than a few minor revisions before the manuscript would be dispatched to the printer. For the hundredth time she wondered if Perkins had consulted the Press's lawyer, if he thought she might accuse them of breach of promise. Arnie had been amazed when she suggested this possibility to him. He had reminded her there was no contract; he had also reminded her that contracts are broken every day, that all of Life is a broken contract. But the writing and the revising had gone on and on, she said, through the coming and the going of two editors; and Moberg had complied with their instructions, working with a terrible patience, for the second editor had disagreed with most of the recommendations of the first. Then Arnie had shouted, "*What difference does that make? There was no firm commitment, and even if there had been, there are ways of working out of it!*" She had been appalled at his vehemence. Ah, Arnie was sick of it, sick of it.

She heard a man's decisive footfall on the bare wooden floors of the corridor, and put the jacket of her dress back on, hurriedly, as if she'd been sitting there naked.

"Mrs. Bloom? I'm Dr. Perkins."

Even before she looked up to see the possessor of that melodic voice, she knew: although he wore a moustache, not a beard—for even her own clairvoyance was not infallible—his eyes were small and cold. And he was thirty years old at most. The hand he offered her for a cursory shake was limp, dismissive. He was wearing a slate blue shirt open at the neck. His sleeves were rolled back to the elbows, and the cloth under his armpits was soaked with sweat. She thought of the deep carpets and the spacious air-conditioned rooms of the trade publishers. Not for the likes of them, still less for the likes of Moberg's manuscript. Even so, this man was her adversary.

The telephone in the room adjoining his rang sharply. A minute later, his secretary appeared at the door. The call was from Germany. Peg listened to the conversation against her will; she had recognized the scholar's name immediately. She knew his work, and she respected it—for what it was. There was elegance in such fastidiousness, such precision. But she believed there was *hubris* in it also. Yet it was Moberg, whole-souled and far-embracing, who was accused of *hubris*. Moberg, who had instructed her well in the perils of missing the mark. Hearing the humility in Perkins's tone—no, the obeisance, the servility—she felt the old madness wind itself around her, the aliveness of her terrible lucidity in that moist and heated cloth enwrapping her. This work was a masterpiece, and it had been entrusted to her for safe passage, and she would fail. Her daughterhood put to the test a second time, and she would fail again. *Mea culpa, mea culpa, mea maxima culpa.* Too late she had become her first father's nun, too late become disciple to her foster-father. The Church was in ruins. And dwarfs sat in judgment of princes. Useless to trouble deaf heaven with Einstein's bootless cry, "Great spirits have always encountered violent opposition from mediocre minds," for Moberg would remind her that this too was *hubris*. Useless to confront Karen Moberg with the truth that Peg, a mere mortal, had not the power to grant absolution for the sin that must be committed by one or the other partner of every marriage of two great talents. "The gods told Oedipus his *moira*," Prince Shadow had said. "And thus did Oedipus become like the gods—he knew the future. Yet this knowledge was utterly useless. If Oedipus averts his *moira*, he brings chaos into the world." Useless to ask herself why *this* responsibility. "Men bind themselves to their fate by their own actions," Prince Shadow had reminded them. "This is the supreme irony of tragedy." And: "There can be tragedy only in *hamartia*. The period before the *kairos* is a term of suffering." This intense remembering calmed her, released her from the winding-sheet. When Perkins came to the door to motion her to go with him, she was ready.

On their way to the Faculty Club, Perkins pointed to the buildings, the design of each in turn earning his ever more eloquently scornful deprecations. Then, once they were in the dining room and had helped themselves from the tureens and platters and bowls set out on the long tables at the front of the vast hall, he showed her who sat where when the Washington crowd came to town and visited the campus at lunchtime.

He began after he had finished his soup and she her fruit cup. "Well, let's get to Moberg's work. What did you think of our reviewer's comments?"

She decided to play with him a while. "Just to satisfy my curiosity—your reviewer is a man, not a woman?"

"Wrong! A woman. And a good friend of mine. I thought a long time before I decided where to send it. What made you think it's a man?"

Ah, this was much too easy. The whole transaction was made by telephone, she was sure of it. After all, Perkins had so phrased his letter to her that it appeared as if the Press had every intention of publishing the work.

"Why, it was supremely objective. If I, as a woman, may say so myself, unusually objective for a woman."

He studied her face keenly. She widened her eyes, waited, entertained for a moment the vengeful joy she would feel at rising and tilting the table toward him, emptying his plate of roasted chicken and broccoli stalks in his lap. Then she began the bargaining. He moved in swiftly each time she began to advance concessions. He was telling her to save her breath; he was saying, as she had known he must, *Dated; This is a business not a charity; He assumed wrong*. He glanced at his watch several times. When it was almost over she reminded him that Moberg was dead, reminded him that Moberg had been given to believe he had an understanding with the Press. He shrugged lightly, once. She told him she did not have two years to dismantle her late professor's work and re-assemble it according to a concession with which he would never have agreed were he still living. Again that light shrug of the shoulders. But he allowed her the dignity of saying it was getting late. She longed to say, "You have no idea what you were holding in your hands, of what was almost yours." But she said nothing more.

* * *

Moberg, Room 412, between Marinelli and Moscowitz. She chose the stairway over the elevator—a last chance to primp. Her mirror nearly slipped through her gloved fingers and she put it back in her handbag without having a look, after all. Pulling open the heavy door off the fourth landing, she came into a deeply carpeted lobby. A receptionist pointed down the hallway to where he would be waiting for her.

He was sitting behind his cleared desk, his hands folded, his expression bemused. Exactly as he had appeared to her in the room off one corridor of her dreams. He smiled as he had smiled seventeen years before, grasping both sides of the lectern with his huge and shapely hands, a STEVENSON button bright-blooming on his lapel.

"Peg. My dear girl. Pegeen."

"Professor, ah, Professor Moberg."

They shook hands across his desk, and she took the chair opposite his, and they both began talking of how strange it was that she and Arnie had come to New York to live. He told her she was looking well in a way that made it clear he did not think so. Had it really been ten years since that evening at his gingerbread house?

"More than ten. And now I am on the farthest side of thirty. Going down the slope."

He frowned. "What a ridiculous thing to think about. Age."

"Perhaps it's a woman's preoccupation."

"Nonsense. You should not waste that fine instrument inside your skull with such nonsense."

She must have looked stricken, for he burst out laughing then and called her Miss O'Flaherty. And then she too was laughing. He inquired about Arnie, about the children. Then he announced they ought to be having their lunch.

"In *this* neighborhood, the possibilities are all but infinite. What's your pleasure, my dear girl? Chinese food? Seafood? A steak? German fare?"

"German fare."

So he would not be taking her around to meet his colleagues after all.

"Only once before in all the years we've known one another did you tell me I was talking nonsense. That was when I quoted Nietzsche to you after class one day: '*Do not gaze too deeply into the abyss, lest it gaze into thee.*' You said this was utter nonsense, that abysses don't gaze."

"That would have been 1950, October, after I returned your papers. You had inscribed an 'AJPM' at the top of yours. You needn't have. You were telling me, you know, what I divined anyway from the Margaret O'Flaherty and from the point of view you took in your essay on the young Rousseau. You often wore a bright green suit. You sat between the laconic Gerber and Miss Barker, She Of the Drooping Eyes."

"Memory gives people such power over one another."

"Until I read your first paper, I was not at all certain you were truly listening. Your smile, after all, could have been mocking. Or foolish. I did not discover until the semester was over that Miss Barker's heavy-lidded eyes were a symptom of the myasthenia gravis that afflicted her mother, and not, as I had at first supposed, the sure sign that she was brooding over some terrible truth."

"AJPM. *Ad Jesum Per Mariam*. Even then I knew better than to ask the gods directly to smile upon my endeavors."

"And tell me, which gods are those?"

In studying anthropology she'd learned that Tylor had traced the evolution of religion from polytheism to monotheism, she reminded him. But Tylor had not noticed, having been born too soon, that the process was reversed once you lost your faith.

"Now, Peg, let us suppose that these gods of yours do exist. Do you think they would take your mockery lightly?"

"Some time that first semester, I asked you if you believed in gods. And you lectured me. You said organized religion is a pestilence. You said you had been stricken with it too. You said that we would both survive it, being strong of soul, and that in *my* case you thought renouncing it was long overdue."

"Surely you are making most of this up. *No* one has a memory for conversations."

Ah, but the words were engraved on one of the countless tablets inside her skull. She returned them to him now: "You can't have both worlds, Margaret. God doesn't exist, and you know this perfectly well. Not in the singular, not in the plural, not as a benevolent despot nor as a horned toad. If you must pass through a stage of devolution, you will progress to paganism. And then you will come to the clearing and you will see there is nothing at all. And you will be free."

"You ought to write fairy-tales, not poetry. And what did you reply to this?"

"I said the spirits were everywhere, that you had only to close your eyes—which Protestants stubbornly refuse to do—to see them. We quarrelled."

"I'm sure we would have. I'm sure I would not have been amused." "The dear, dead days beyond recall. I propose a toast. To you." "Not to me, my dear girl. Better to the elms. Yes, the elms."

They drank to the world that would not come again. He said he had a fond remembrance even of the Parade Ground Units that mushroomed on the outer precincts of Fraternity Row. "That was before your time, Peg. One night in late spring, the engineering students wired the entire football field. A fireworks display that was controlled by timing devices went on into the dawn of the new day. After chasing their own shadows for a good long while, the campus police joined the students watching the show. And a great show it was."

"One of the last communal pranks of the innocents. Today they smash windows, slash couches and draperies and oil portraits of the emeriti. Today they overturn the book stacks and set them on fire."

"Then you have not read my work."

"But I *have* read your work, your magnificent work! I can't *tell* you how much I discovered!"

"Discovered?" He gave her a puzzled look; he had almost whispered the word.

"Books I never knew existed. But more than that—the connections."

"Which books?"

"Jane Addams's *The Long Road of Woman's Memory*. Mary Heaton Vorse's *A Footnote to Folly*. And Virginia Woolf's *Three Guineas*—I'd heard of it, but that's all. I had no idea what it was about."

"And the connections?"

"Addams's idea of the eternal opposition between Militarism and Feminism. Vera Brittain's belief that the noblest and most profound emotions that men experience can come to them only through women.

Woolf's prescriptions for ways the anonymous, secret Society of Outsiders would help prevent war and ensure freedom."

"'That the daughters of educated men then should give their brothers neither the white feather of cowardice nor the red feather of courage, but no feather at all . . . that is the duty to which outsiders will train themselves in peace before the threat of death inevitably makes reason powerless.'" He quoted the passage in a kind of chant, his eyes holding hers which filled with tears as he was speaking. He seemed not to notice this—or was this what he was after? to make her weep?—but went on to the passage from *Testament of Youth* that he had made an epigraph to his first chapter: "'I do not believe that a League of Nations, or a Kellogg Pact, or any Disarmament Conference, will ever rescue our poor remnant of civilisation from the threatening forces of destruction, until we can somehow impart to the rational processes of constructive thought and experiment that element of sanctified loveliness which, like superb sunshine breaking through thunder-clouds, from time to time glorifies war.'"

He reached across the table, covering both her hands with one of his. "You must tell me what you think. You have the foundation there, in what I sent you."

With a wildness in her heart—why had it not been enough for him, her reverence? was it not more than most disciples freely gave?—she quoted back to him. From Vorse, to show him she had read closely, to show him the absolute limits of the responsibility she was willing to assume. "'Everyone there knew that peace is a militant thing, that any peace movement must have behind it a higher passion than the desire for war. No one can be a pacifist without being ready to fight for peace and die for peace.'"

His grasp tightened. "Not what Vorse thought, I already know that. What *you* think. I can only ask a woman this. And of all women, I have chosen to ask you."

She began to weep. "I think it is this or nothing," she said. "And I think I am in the presence of someone who is building a cathedral. But I also think it may be too late."

The People's Mural, a Great Dove of Peace, flowered on the stone face of the building across the street from the restaurant. She had to run to keep abreast of him. He told her his daughters had made a grandfather of him three times over. "All girls, too; it seems to be my fate." He told her his wife's arthritis was growing worse, that soon she would no longer be able to play. Peg said she was very, very sorry. "I know; I too am sorry, and afraid for her. Music is all the world she knows or has."

They stopped at the old library, wondering if there would be time to go in, deciding against it. He steered her around cars, announcing with some heat that cars ought to be banned from all Manhattan. They stopped again, this time to read the titles in the window display of a small bookshop. The First Manifesto of feminism was enthroned on a dais in the middle row.

"Of course you've read it? The wonder is that *you* weren't the founder. You were a precursor, you know." "Yes, I *do* know. But that was before children were born to me. And changed me."

"My dear girl, that is only one of many changes. Wait. Soon they will be grown and gone. And you'll be someone else again."

He had promised he would walk with her as far as Macy's. And here they were. He was asking to be remembered to Arnie; he was saying they all ought to meet again one day. He took her hand, and then let it go, and the crowds swept over him and bore him away.

I'll never see him again, she thought. Two students, one with the face of a Christ, the other with the face of a Judas Iscariot, whipped through the revolving doors with her. Leather jackets, torn jeans. Tomorrow, they may wear togas. And her own son among them?

* * *

Wilted, carrying the three mailers stuffed with his manuscript that weighed inside the heavy covers—*I'd suggest that you not pack them like that*, Perkins had said. *It increases your mailing costs. And readers always take them out anyway*—a good fifteen pounds, she hurried through the doors of Port Authority and down the corridor, and then down the steps to the loading stations, although her bus was not due to depart for almost an hour. She had had too much coffee; she went into the Ladies Room and found it deserted except for a young woman who was just then drawing back her arm to deliver a sound smack to the bottom of her wriggling and fussing toddler. The woman glanced up at her and then went back to her business. There was a smack, a shriek, another smack, and then loud screaming and a steady pounding accompanied with promises: *This is just the start, you just wait until we get home, you'll see what's coming to you, I'll take care of you good*. She turned around to flee when the woman yanked the child by the arm and dragged her, pushing past Peg and out the door, her threats made in that tight, enraged and righteous voice that reclaimed the Primal Scene of Childhood.

Pietà, Peg whispered to herself, opening the door of a stall, then, seeing the puddle on the floor, slamming it to and checking out another before going inside. A dry floor she must have; she had to set down her burden to take care of her own business. Anyone else, she supposed, would have quite sensibly left it on the wide counter under the mirror, for what thief would want Moberg's tome on war and peace? *You and he should both be so lucky that someone would steal it and publish it under their own name*, the redoubtable Rita would have said. Peg muttered *Pietà* again to the ghost on the other side of the slate-gray door. *This is where it begins, esteemed Professor. In the shadows just beyond your Cause and Cure*. Seventy-four years he lived, and he would not confront it. Was it blind faith, was it cussedness, is there a difference?

Carefully drying the sink next to hers with paper towels, she stacked the three huge envelopes in a wobbly pillar, washed her hands, looked up into the mirror, felt his gaze, was ashamed. Then the shame passed, and she gathered up her burden without bothering to dry her hands. The middle envelope slipped, and she punched it back into place. When he was her age, and even younger than that probably, he knew, ah, he knew. But he would not let it go.

A queue had formed for her bus, even though it would be another forty minutes until departure time. She counted the passengers and took her place at the end. Number forty-one; unless people were holding places for others, there'd just be room for one more. She set the envelopes on the floor. Her arms ached, and under her ribs there was the ache where it had bitten her again and again. *At some time or another,* Arnie had said, *each of us has to carry some fox under our cloak.*

Arnie would be waiting, and the test results would be waiting, and still no letter from their son. She would have to get on with it. The peaks of brown envelopes would be waiting for her. As though she could give them safe passage too. She whose own scribblings were jammed into file boxes that filled their son's long-abandoned room. And how could she leave all this to Arnie? It was a question she might have to answer very soon. Ah, she would burn the lot of it before she would burden Arnie so. *Esteemed Professor, I'm a better man than you.* She laughed aloud. The woman just ahead of her turned around to look, then faced forward again. Yesterday, this morning even, she would have been mortified. Now she had to stop herself from tapping the woman on the shoulder of her seersucker suit and telling her never to mind, Port Authority was full of crazies, she, Peg O'Flaherty Bloom, was harmless.

The doors were flung open. They would be loading a little early, then. She shoved the envelopes ahead with her foot.

"Can I help you?" The young man in back of her bent down and picked them up. "Wow, these *are* heavy. Want me to carry them aboard for you?"

"No, thanks, I can take care of them. Here, let me have them, please, thanks just the same."

They can't spell anymore, even, she told his ghost. The man took her ticket book, ripped out the return coupon, handed it back. She climbed aboard, worked her way to the empty aisle seat she saw at the back of the bus. *They won't read it, you know, wherever I next send it. They'll let it lie around for another year, and then leaf through it and scribble a few comments and send it back.*

The young man in back of her was still offering to help. Could he put her packages up on the overhead rack for her?

"No, thanks. But you're very, very kind. I'll just hold them on my lap."

Ah, don't you see, it could circulate forever and ever. She sat back and closed her eyes. Lord, how heavy was Moberg's dream.

This isn't an age for faith of any kind, don't you see? Won't you give it up? Won't you let me go now?

At last, Moberg answered her. *"Margaret, you said long, long ago that you were choosing Life; here, take it then."*

Arnie would be laughing, jubilant, the tests would be negative, she had not been released, she would have to get on with it. It was the wrong time for her, the wrong time in her life, the wrong time in the life of the country, and she would have to get on with it. His last spoken words to her—the ones that mattered—were in that restaurant, where he would not let her hands go, but fished with his free hand for his napkin and reached across the table and began blotting her tears, saying with that terrible elation in his voice, *"It's not for anyone to say more than that the hour is late."*

When Arnie had carried in that enormous carton and watched her unwrap it and lift out the thick chapters one by one, covering her hair, her dress, the kitchen table with excelsior curls, he had said, *It's time for you to stop this mothering, Peg. You can't go on mothering all your life.* But it wasn't that, it wasn't mothering at all. She had tried to explain it to him, that all this was much older than the responsibilities that were born with their son, their daughter. It had been the only time in all their life together that Arnie had not understood her because she was a woman.

Evanescence

She stood in the dusk at the edge of the scene and she watched her shade walk from their house at the top of the hill that was the corner of Fifth and Elm and cross the road onto the campus, knowing they had returned for good. She went on up the path to the main building and looked up and saw the spire of the chapel pierce the brilliant blue October sky. She met the dean and the dean took his pipe from his mouth and the dean shook hands with her. And the dean was saying, "A new ballgame today, Laura. Your Jerry was a corker back there in the Sixties, haw." And Jerry was walking at her side now, and they were returning to their house. And Robb Payne was trudging up the hill toward them, and he was saying, "Welcome back on board, you two." And down at the foot of the hill the Paynes's house was crouching, crouching, the Paynes's gray cottage, the sadness of the place. And the bush of barberry in the Paynes's front yard was in autumn bloom. The red-orange flare The defiance

Arms lifted her over the stile and she awakened. Knowing she had dreamed It again.

The shower was running. She lifted her head from the pillow, narrowing her eyes, squinting, trying to read Frank's clock-radio without having to put on her glasses.

Twenty to six.

For the love of God, couldn't he be a bit quieter while he was at his ablutions.

Rising earlier every day now that there was nowhere he had to be. She closed her eyes. The digits of cyanic blue on either side of the flashing colon sank into the russet heath. Drowsing, she listened to the faint thrum and twitter of the air conditioner.

The second night in a row they'd slept with it on. Frank had insisted. "You need your sleep, Laura, especially during the work week. My doctor didn't say *never*, and the heat's been *stifling* this week."

Sealing themselves off from daybreak. And from the matins of the birds. Someone in the natural history society had remarked only last week they were singing this Orwellian year of 1984 as though for the last time.

Frank's solicitude. His most strategic weapon yet.

Not that the earlier ones were any less effective.

"Laura, dear, look." His small, shapely numerals marching in columns down the ledger page, marching in lockstep to the trenches of incontestable sums. "If you add all your work-related expenses and subtract them from your salary, what is left simply doesn't justify this sacrifice of your time."

What was her weak defense? That it was the principle of the thing. That a woman wants to have her own money to spend.

His reproach, gentle and kind, richly deserved. "When in our eight years together have we made a distinction between your money and mine? Can you recall even one occasion when I gave you to feel obliged to seek my approval before spending money?" Selling the house, divesting themselves of the things of their separate pasts, moving to this apartment, furnishing the place, hadn't they shared equally in deciding about these matters? Gifts, vacations, visits to and from the children, hadn't they decided about these things together, and always amicably?

They had, they had, she was sorry, the truth of it was she wasn't ready for retirement just yet, she needed more time to make up her mind about it.

"But that's just *it*, Laura, time is just what's in short *supply* now. How many more good years can one hope for, after all?" What of the travelling they ought to do while their health was reasonably good, still. What of the classes they could take together. Think of the luxury of honoring season tickets to the theatre and the symphony orchestra. "And you could get back to your painting and drawing at long last, Laura. You could get back to your creativity after too many years."

Give me a little more time, Frank, I need to think about it a little more. As if there were anything more to be thought about it. First the honeymoon: the trips, the concerts, the Tai Chi Chu'uan class, the new sketchbook. Then, on the pages in about the middle of that sketchbook, palm trees, the stretch of beach. On the easel in the bedroom of the small, air-conditioned condominium the fierce yellow of the sun in a sky so pale blue it was almost white. The condominium in the retirement village playpen filling up with older women lostlings abducted by their aging husbands.

And then the final abandonment.

She heard the little thump the pipes made when he closed the faucet. Then the brushing of the wicker clothes hamper across the floor tiles as he pulled it up to the tub, he was groping for the bath towel he draped over the side handle. Now the swish of the shower curtain as he swept it aside, now the clopping as he peeled the bath mat from the porcelain.

Silence. He was toweling himself, putting on his robe. Now the faucets were running again, he was rinsing the tub for her. His fastidiousness. Gone the way of all virtue, gone to vice.

How very long life is.

It was the dream that had poisoned her mood, the eternal return to Erskine, to Cranford College. The dean with his infernal pipe. And bearded Robb Payne, Gauguin's Yellow Christ in the sallow flesh himself. And that tumbledown shack where Janice Payne had made a cuckold of him. And that blasted shrub, how it had bloomed their last fall at Cranford when the two of them, Jerry and Janice, fell in with one another.

Her last sketchbook, *Cranford Critters*, pages of Janices. Gawks, flamingos uncoiling their serpents' necks, their mealy-skinned rumps in plain sight under tattered plumage, waddling into the margins. Janice always asked to go upstairs to have a look at the children, one would think Janice was a fancier of children, Janice who proclaimed to the entire Erskine community that the four little Payneses were lucky to have been blessed with an Underprotective Mother. Those were the days when it was a mortal sin to sacrifice your children for the sake of navel-gazing, what a precursor Janice had been, now they canonized you for it in some circles. Of little Joey and Annie Kendrigan, Janice would whisper reverently, "They're something else." Peering into the darkness from the doorway, her breath a warm scarf of white wine and tobacco. Janice's rose-scented soap, her Judas-kisses, her gall. *They're something else*, indeed.

But she had heard that Janice had come to grief too.

Where was her forgiveness, it was all so long ago.

Frank's footsteps padding up the carpeted hallway to the kitchen.

The click of the cabinet door opening, the squeak of the drawer sliding out on its runners, the rustling in the pantry. He was taking down his cereal now.

She sketched him inside her head with sure, quick strokes: the bloodhound's large, wistful eyes. The long, deeply-lined face. Crosshatches for the ruddiness of his complexion. Tufts for his sideburns. And now a tufted circlet, his tonsure.

He would be sitting stiffly upright over his bowl of granola. Presiding over his granola. As he had presided for so many years over the board meetings of the corporation.

He would wince. Arthritis of the spine. Like all somatic signatures of temperament made plain in God's good time.

His perfectionism, his reserve. His chivalry.

If the dream were a gothic horror, now. If it would give her a good heart attack and be done with it once for all. The thuds of that tell-tale heart driving against the ribs, the surf of fear pounding over the shores of awakening, if only it were one of those. Off to the afterlife she would go. And gladly, too.

But it wasn't a nightmare, it was a vampire-dream. So she had said to the priest she'd visited on that trip to Boston years ago. She would see a priest, she had told herself on a whim she would see a priest. She had been a desperate character back then. "Bless me, Father, for I have sinned, it has been twenty years since my last Confession, may God forgive me. Father, this dream is draining my vitality. And I have two young children to raise alone, now." And what had been his reply but that a recurrent dream is the Devil's distraction from the sacred obligation she owed Joey and Annie.

She heard the soft scrape of the chair as Frank got up from his breakfast. She heard the water running, he was rinsing his dishes.

He was going to a three-day conference on toxic waste trouble-spots, that was it, that was why he was up so early, how could she have forgotten. "I'll miss your company, Laura," he would say, waking her just before he had to leave. Before he went to town meetings, to workshops, to seminars, to conferences she felt too tired to attend with him, "I'll miss your company, Laura." A widower for three years when they first met, a survivor of a long, childless marriage to a fellow chemist, Frank was a man in as heated a pursuit of responsibility as Jerry Kendrigan had been in flight from it, Frank had fathered Joe and Annie in their teens so devotedly that her relief over seeing how well they'd got on turned into jealousy. A private club they'd made, an exclusive secret society of three members only. He had taken her place as the Parent-in-Chief that Jerry had forced her to claim.

Feast or famine, that was the way of it then, that was the way of it now.

How could she have known when she married Frank that there soon would come a time when she would outgrow the need for human company? Since his retirement he could not have enough of hers. Wherever she took herself he stalked her. If she was pottering in the kitchen, he had to see what she was up to. When she went out to do the gardening, soon the dark billowing around the shadow cast by her sunhat would announce his presence. At the desk in the den, absorbed in writing a letter, soon would come that tapping on the door she had pointedly closed, he was going for a stroll, was there anything he could pick up for her at the store. The thrust of a spear deep into her back, that was what the sound of a voice had become when she was in the bliss of solitude. "The twelve years between us do make a difference, Laura. The children and I will get along fine, but what about you and me? You're still very youthful, how can this old duffer hope to keep up with you?" Forty-five years old at the time, she had permitted herself to be distracted by this descant of gallantry from the plainsong of doubt that was its theme. A *grass widower* he often called himself when she . . . withdrew.

He was the loneliest man she had ever known.

His footsteps were padding softly down the hallway. He was coming back here now. The flick of the light switch in the bathroom, he had stopped to make a last inspection. The rustle of paper. He was unwrapping a fresh bar of soap for her bath. The flick of the switch again.

She closed her eyes.

He came into the room and went to the dresser to take out a clean undershirt and shorts. When he crossed in front of their twin beds and went into the walk-in closet, she stirred. He came around to her bed and bent down and kissed her forehead.

"Go back to sleep, dear. I'll call you just before I leave." He was whispering.

"Frank. You smell delicious." She wrapped her arm around his legs, tugging. He made a little sound of surprise and pleasure. She tugged at his legs again. He knelt and took her face in his hands. "No," she murmured, her eyes still closed. "*Here*." She pulled at his shoulders until he raised himself up and sat down beside her. Then she pushed his robe aside and nuzzled the soft down on his thigh.

"Laura." He cradled her head. Still whispering, he asked, "Laura?"

"There's time," she laughed, drawing him down to her. "There's time."

* * *

For the third time, Mrs. Krause pushed herself forward in her wheelchair and stood up, calling "Emily, will you please?"

"Sit down, dear." Without looking up from the crossword puzzle, Laura lay her arm along the arm of her patient's wheelchair. "Sit down, dear," she repeated. A bluebottle fly was walking down the stairwell she had just filled in with her intricate lettering, O B E R O N for "medieval fairy king." Just the landing stage for the creature, this trembling iridescence. She steadied the wheelchair as Mrs. Krause sat down obediently once more. A moist breeze light as a catspaw ruffled the newspaper; the fly vanished.

She put the puzzle down on the bench and looked at her watch. A quarter past two. Mrs. Krause was not due for therapy for another fifteen minutes. She would wheel her around the grounds again after a moment, let them stay here a minute longer in the gazebo, in the shade and the peace of this place. They were alone here, she and this woman who thought her nurse's aide was her daughter Emily, this woman who wanted to take her Emily on her lap. *Poor soul,* the others would sigh, *Poor thing,* but they shunned this wrecked colossus grieving for her lost daughter as though Mrs. Krause were one of the Erinnyes.

And who could blame them for averting their eyes?

Pity. Pity is quicksand.

Across the wide lawn the voices of Mr. Ames's visitors drifted toward her, a spume of sound riding the wavering brightness of the air. Five figures in folding chairs encircled the old man who was celebrating his ninety-third birthday today. Cousins, one of the nurses said, the sole survivors of the family. He had outlived even his two grandchildren. No one else was out in the heat of this August afternoon but Mr. Dakin, who was promenading back and forth in front of the building complex reciting poetry aloud to himself with that smile of beatitude some blind people wear.

Mrs. Krause pushed herself forward in the wheelchair again.

"No, dear. Stay." Laura took a packet of tissues from her pocket and daubed at the spittle gathering at the corner of her patient's mouth.

"Emily, would you please?"

"I'm fine right here, dear. We'll be going for a stroll now." The wisps came fluttering back, the feelings with their floating images.

Before she had met Frank even, for it was that long ago, she had consulted a therapist, a Dr. Corday, a small woman, even shorter and more slender than herself, as dark as she was fair. Her Other, she had imagined at the time. Dr. Corday had advised her to refuse the dream.

"Throw it back into the cauldron, Laura. If you talk back to it often and strongly enough in your conscious mind, you will be able to confront it when you are dreaming it. And then you can reject it outright. Even in your sleep." Dr. Corday proposed that she take the point of view that a true dream comes to you once and once only. That recurrent dreams are not dreams at all, but visitations of The

Evil One. "You have to get tough with a recurrent dream, Laura." Dr. Corday had taught her thrilling curses and epithets to hurl at The Thing.

And so she had played the reel over and over inside her head, saying "No" to her shade, "No, I *will* not follow you across the road and up the path, I *will* not go back there with you," shaking her fist at the spire, offering to push the dean's pipe down his wattled throat, roller-skating down that hill with a blazing torch in her hand, burning that shanty to the ground once for all, tearing the barberry from the soil with her bare hands and flinging it on the pyre.

But The Thing rose from its ashes, came back, came back. Exasperated with her, Dr. Corday said she must confront it as an artist would. That she must personify every symbol and sketch or paint each one. And then destroy this black art.

And so one evening she took out the sketchbook she had not opened for years, and on a blank page a woman took form, a mermaid who was braiding her hair with the blossoms of the witch hazel. Leeks sprouted in her eye sockets, her nipples were snails, her tail was a fretwork of moons.

And she tore out the page and burned it in her last good faith. And that night she stood in the dusk at the edge of the scene and saw her shade leaving the house on Fifth and Elm, crossing the road to the campus, knowing they'd come back to Cranford for good. And the spire of the chapel was piercing the sky and the dean was taking his pipe from his mouth. And the dean shook hands with her, he was saying it was a new ballgame today and Jerry had been a corker back there in the Sixties, haw. And then Jerry was at her side, and Robb Payne was trudging up the hill toward them, welcoming them back on board, you two. And the gray cottage crouched, crouched. And the barberry bloomed red-orange.

The wheelchair shook as Mrs. Krause lifted herself up, calling, "Emily, will you please?"

"Sit back down, dear, we're going for a spin now."

She patted the heavy arm absently and got up from the bench. Looking back over her shoulder to see if the sweat had soaked through to her skirt, she was caught off guard by her patient, who grasped her firmly about the waist and backed into the wheelchair pulling her down onto her lap.

"Emily," Mrs. Krause exulted. "Emily, Emily, Emily, I've got you now."

Mrs. Krause was tightening her hold now, and Laura was squirming and wriggling in that powerful embrace. "Oh, this is—" she sputtered, and waved for help at the circle of Mr. Ames's visitors. But no one seemed to be looking her way. "Halloo!" she yelled, "Do you see?" She waved frantically. After a few moments, two of the group looked over their way.

They had misread her signal, they were waving at her.

And now they were re-arranging their chairs with their backs to her. So they would not seem to be intrusive.

"Please, dear," the tight voice in her throat was saying, "Oh, God, this is awful." She strained against the arms encircling her. They clasped her even more firmly. She felt her hips rolling upon the great thighs of the old woman as Mrs. Krause began a slow, rocking movement.

And now Mrs. Krause was singing, her voice like the pipes of an organ badly out of tune, sliding from falsetto to alto and up the scale again: "When it's springtime in the Rockies,/I'll be coming back to you"

"Please, let me go," Laura implored.

Mr. Dakin was approaching the gazebo, his arms folded like the wings of a giant bird that had alighted on the palm tree printed on his shirt, his smiling lips moving in silent recitation of his prayer-poem to his long-dead wife.

"Once again I'll say I love you/While the birds sing all the day" The blind man stopped in front of the gazebo, listening intently. Then he nodded in their direction, and wished them a good afternoon, and continued on by.

Worse things have happened to you, Laura reminded herself. She would wait for the verse to be finished.

"In the Rockies far away."

"Mother," Laura said.

"Emily."

"Mother, thank you. We have an appointment now. We mustn't be late, dear."

Slowly, so as not to alarm her, Laura began unlacing Mrs. Krause's strong fingers, fingers that had been clamped like a cestus over the middle of her body.

* * *

On their drive back to Laurel Hills, Kem recounted his professor's lecture. "It was a good word that he used, the word *elusive*, in speaking about the life of a people's culture. He told us it is cunning and swift. And *elusive*. A people's soul runs on the path ahead of them. The way they pursue it, this is how one can take the measure of the quality of a people's life in community, he said. The point of anyone's life is your part in that chase. You find a path, and then another, and that vision is always a little ahead of you. You can never catch it, he said. People build temples, halls of justice, universities. To catch it in. But it will seep through the stones and float away. Always a little ahead of you. Always beyond your reach."

She turned the wheel and their car joined the halting procession across the bridge. The waters of the Hudson were green, dark green as the skin of cucumbers. *To every thing there is a season.* The light in August was incandescent, pouring in a dazzle of silver-gold through the delicate blue veils of summer sky. Soon, September. Frank would want to take a week-end trip to Vermont in another six weeks or so. "To see the leaves." The red would be as burning, the yellow as deep, the orange as brilliant here in the valley of the Shawangunks. But it was the journey he wanted, with her at his side. *I'll miss your company, Laura.*

"Like Tantalus," Kem said. "Do you know the story of Tantalus?"

"Yes." She looked over at him and smiled.

He returned her smile, his white teeth dazzling in a dark face round as a johnny cake. He had the deer's poetic, velvety eyes. Large, glistening acorns they were.

His appalling personal history. He had confided it to her not long after he took the summer job at the Home. "My people's names are difficult for Westerners to pronounce. Call me Kem." He had fled his country just in time, just before a massacre of the people in his village. He hid in the fields by day, he ran at night. His mother's and sisters' bodies were in a mass grave. "How they died was merciful, when I think what happened to my father and my brother before they too died." There was another brother who had escaped. Kem did not know if he had survived, or where he might have found asylum. "If he lives, I know that one day I will find him."

She had insisted he ride to and from work with her. After all, he lived in Laurel Hills, and there was plenty of room for a passenger in her car. She had tried for years to organize a car pool, but finally she had given up. "Everyone for himself in this society," she had told him. "I'll be glad to have your company." He had insisted on paying fare for his passage. "You must respect my pride," he had said, and she had cried out, "You must respect *mine*! That's *unthinkable*!" So they had struck the bargain that as he rode beside her he would share with her what he was learning in his College courses.

Just now they shared a companionable silence as the long line of cars crossed the bridge. When they rounded the curve in the road on the other side, she picked up speed, and felt the quickening in her thoughts. "Look, Kem." She waved at the marshy fields beyond his window, the lush green purpling with loosestrife. "That is an infallible sign that summer is ending in southeastern New York country."

"Will you take vacation?" he asked politely.

"Not until mid-October." They would go to Washington first to see Annie, and then to Chicago to visit Joe and his wife. In between there was the conference on nuclear arms control. Or was it on world peace, she could not remember.

"When does the fall semester begin?"

"Right after your Labor Day."

"Will you take a full schedule of classes?"

"Yes. Full time. I am going to take a job in the food service in the fall."

"You will go from serving the old to serving the young. Those close to your own age."

He shook his head. "We are side by side in the classroom, in the library. But we are not in the same universe. They are good kids, most of them, but we do not have a common language."

"In the Sixties it was different, Kem. And it's not that long ago."

"In 1960 I was born. An eternity ago."

"An eternity ago," she echoed. Family, a homeland, good causes. Losses he had reaped when he still was in his youth, Kem had outgrown millenarianism in his teens. Before then, even.

He would endure, yes, he would go on to bear witness. Inscribing his portion on the tombstones of fear and desire.

Somewhere there must be an abbey where all the records are kept.

And roosting in the tree that shades the clerestory, a small bird of ancient sorrows.

"Excuse me, please, for saying that. I must not ask you to carry what it is my burden to carry. I am in your debt for the understanding you show me. And I am proud. And I do not know how to repay you."

"Kem." She heard the shading of tears in her own voice and cleared her throat. "Before I met you, I did not know what life was made of."

"You are a gracious lady to say that. But it is not right, this. My people believe you show thanks for every gift by giving a gift in return. I want very much to give you something more than my professors' lectures."

They were passing the sign welcoming travelers to Laurel Hills. To their right was the new shopping mall. The parking lot that filled the horseshoe of stores was jammed with cars. Thursday night. There would be shopping until nine o'clock. Frank wouldn't be home tonight, she would have herself to herself.

"Very well, then, I have just thought of something. But wait, please." She drove through town and up onto the campus in silence, and parked in back of the tennis courts. "Kem?"

His expression was respectful, attentive.

She told him about the dream.

He listened, staring straight ahead, and when she finished the story, he said as if to himself, "It is always the same. And you have been dreaming it for a very long time."

"Always the same, yes. And I have been dreaming it since the last year of the Sixties. We left for New York in June. In August, I moved with my children to Laurel Hills. The dream began, then, after the separation from my first husband, but a long time before the divorce was final."

"How do you treat dreams in this country?"

"Those who take them seriously try to read them. To decode them. A long time ago, I consulted a priest about it. But as you see, the dream was not dispelled by my having gone to confession. Some years after that, I consulted a psychotherapist. She could not help me, either."

"The modern way to confess." He smiled.

"That is very well said," she laughed. "As a matter of fact, both of them thought it is the Devil's work."

"Perhaps it is something else. Something much simpler than that. Let me think how to say this."

She had parked so they were facing the college pond. Wisps of haze drifted across the slate blue mountains. Above the twin peaks, in the calm sea of sky, a shimmering cascade of light augured the sunset.

"It is so beautiful a planet," Kem whispered.

"Yes."

"The dream is reminding you that you left something in that place.

Whatever you left, it is calling you back. That is why it returns."

"An actual *thing*? An *object*?"

"An object, yes, I think so. Perhaps you can recover it. Or you can make something that is the same, what is your word?"

"A replica?"

"A replica, yes. You were meant to keep that object. Its spirit pursues you because you abandoned it. If you bring it back into your life, I believe it will be appeased. Then your dream will not come to you again."

* * *

The dean's costume party that last spring, how could she have forgotten. Jerry, of course, thought it all up in a flash. He would go as The Ugly American, she would go as a leprechaun. He brought her scraps of pink calico and purple and red-striped seersucker to sew in patches on his old shirt. The YANQUI SÍ placard he wore on his back. His sunglasses, his visor cap, his sandals, his cigar. The pockets of his jeans stuffed with Monopoly money. "You'll need Kelly green leotards and a shirt long enough to work as a tunic. And ballet slippers, and my old corncob pipe, and a pouch-bag full of that sparkle-dust stuff, you can get it at Woolworth's. I'll take care of your hat myself. It'll be a masterpiece, Babe."

The pair of them in their costumes, they had been a sight to behold, what was it he called out to that startled student they'd run into on their way to the party. "I lost a bet."

That morning they moved from Erskine, he'd come back from a last inspection tour of the moving van, wearing her leprechaun hat. "Got to make some offering to the household gods, kiddo." He'd left the hat in the basement, on top of the washing machine they'd sold to the new tenants. It wasn't even a superstition, his leaving an oblation for the *lares* and *penates*, but a flash of fancy such as came and went with the variable winds of his moods. She might have run back to fetch it. He would not have cared, he would not even have noticed. He could not remember from one moment to the next what he thought, what he wanted.

She had bought enough cardboard to make *two* of the things. Never mind. She shaped a cone eighteen inches high, leaving an air space at the top. She wound the stiff material around and around and fastened it at the peak with the heavy-duty stapler. Now the wide circle of cardboard for the brim. "Keep the sombrero in mind. But the part for the turned-up edge has to be made separately, watch."

She could hear his very voice.

One by one, she tacked the green felt strips onto the cardboard. "Small, close stitches, kiddo, or the thing will fall apart in your hands." He had made her drop everything to come and admire his handiwork, must he breathe over her shoulder now? She covered the underside first, then the top; then she joined the brim to the cone with short strips of tape, and sewed the two parts of the hat together.

Now the edge for the brim out of another cardboard circle. It had turned up about three inches, she remembered. She joined this to the circular frame. And now she was ready to cover the cone with the green felt. She remembered to cut enough material to overlap the place where the crown was joined to the brim. First she sewed the big silver buckle onto the fabric. Then she twisted the soft stuff around the cone, sewing it down at the bottom and then making a strong seam up the side.

Last, the covering for the pointed peak.

And now she poked two holes in the brim, one on each side, and pulled through the elastic for the chin strap. And the knots to hold it in place.

And the hat was done.

Banshee! he had roared, and the children hiding under the table, sobbing, and there was no saving it, though they agreed to give it one last try up East. So they had gone off to that party like any loving couple.

The costumes. The dean in the kilt his wife had brought back from her yearly sojourn to Scotland, so much for the dean's imagination. Janice in a black body stocking, giggling all evening about who might put a run in it. Robb Payne the Great Pumpkin, his head stuffed inside a plastic Jack-o-lantern, tripping over the hem of Janice's orange caftan, couldn't she have taken up the hem a few inches for the occasion. Morrison, the leader of their inner circle of campus radicals, in the yellow winding-sheet, his freckled face covered with pancake make-up, his red hair stuffed into a yellow bathing-cap, announcing he would immolate himself at dawn. And the dean, who had fired the lot of them, Jerry too that year, pounding his pipe bowl on the table. "Haw, you're a bunch of corkers, haw!"

First prize went to the dean in the kilt his wife brought back from Scotland, that was the way of it at Cranford. Second prize to Morrison, that was all the more the Cranford Way. And third prize to Janice, to serve notice that Robb, too, had fallen from grace. "The Ugly American came close to winning," the Bursar commented at the end of the award-giving rites. "But he disqualified himself by trying to bribe the jurors with his Monopoly money. And the leprechaun is guilty by association."

"Politics! It's all politics!" Jerry had fumed, he had all but foamed at the mouth in his wrath. "You were a natural for first prize in that hat. *My* hat!" He had kicked the porch steps, what a boy he was still then, had he learned by now the wages of originality, good God he would turn fifty-five this coming November, wherever he was.

She pushed her chair back from the table, picked up the hat, and carried it down the hallway to the bathroom. Flicking on the light switch, she stood in front of the cabinet mirror over the sink, turning her imitation of his invention over and over in her hands. Not bad for a copy of the Real Thing, even *Jerry* might have to concede her memory had served her well.

Fifteen years ago.

It had taken her too long to discover that one artist is all even the best of marriages could be expected to abide, and they had made sad work of their own ill-advised union.

It was the bitter truth that he had abandoned her and the children. "They'll grow up anyway," he said. And they had.

She put on the hat.

A gnome gazed solemnly into dust-gray eyes magnified by the lenses set in tortoise-shell frames. Now the gaze shifted to the lower half of the face. The deep scores made by the Graver that were forming parentheses around the wide, humorous mouth. The jaw line becoming a man's. Her father's.

In the greengloom dusk cast by the wide brim of the hat, the taper that was the face of this creature flickered and smoked. And in these waverings the calipers of memory pointed to lettering flashing across the screen-

God is Dead Project Camelot MINISTER DIES OF WOUNDS RECEIVED AT SELMA Watts Biafrakwashiork or the Establishment the Apocalypse KEEP OFF THE GRASS Burn baby Burn Keep the faith We Shall Overcome MCCARTHY FOR PRESIDENT Hell no I won't go

Now the letters crumbled into grains of black powder, swirling into shapes and shades drifting up from the pages of all the sketchbooks she had filled before the day she had closed them for good and stored them away. An image of the kiosk across the path from the chapel at Cranford floated past, the manifestos festooning it fluttered with her breathing. And now she was inside the polyethylene maze Jerry had created for his last Happening at Cranford, she knew she had lost her way, she knew she was about to be suffocated. He had wrapped himself up in cellophane. A glistening mummy.

She was afraid of him, afraid of his critical judgment. She had allowed it to work as a curse on her creativity. No work of art she made could pass muster with him. *Can't you ever get it right, kiddo?* She had given him the license to kill, and he had used it.

Fifteen years ago. And in another fifteen, the end of the century. And all the somedays spent.

The gnome in the leprechaun hat beckoned.

Time to put away the crossword puzzles. Hand to the plough again. Had she learned nothing from Mrs. Krause who had made a vocation of mourning her loss, had she learned nothing from Mr. Ames who had made a vocation of mere surviving? The hour was late and she was long past her prime, yet when was the prime of the young man who had shown her the way, the young man who had been born an eternity ago and yet still could feel reverence for the beauty of this planet? The hour was late and she was tired, yet had she no memory. What of her fatigue when she had lived at the edge of that force field, had she forgotten that ravening energy pouring, pouring from the source the artist knows is inexhaustible?

It was the bitter truth that he had abandoned her.

And it was the bitter truth she was in his debt for having done so.

What a marvel his gift was, what a torment it must have been for him too.

The telephone was ringing.

It must be Frank.

I miss your company, Laura.

He had been holding the gate open for her so patiently, he had been waiting for so long for her to set herself free.

She went to answer, still wearing the hat.

The Cameo

Carolyn's piano music was painting the western skyline of the village on the canvas of the ceiling. It was dusk. An autumnal dusk. Miriam saw an aureole of coral light around the watch tower in the divide between the two peaks of the Shawangunks. She saw that above it an incandescent band of blue-white was holding back the mulberry fields of coming night. Bright pink quills floated away from the wing bow of the vanishing light, moving back and forth, back and forth. And now they were dissolving. Pink shafts were thinning into pink needles darting over and under the darkening fleece, pink barbs were melting like dreams in a scattering of cameo pink petals down the grave of deeper sleep. Stars were winking on. Miriam could feel the moonrise. She heard Mr. Becker's sibilant baritone: *"One reads the moon as one reads a Hebrew text, Mrs. Ferris. Can you guess why?"* That afternoon she had been reading Powys's *Wolf Solent* to him; the passage made some reference to the moon. Miriam could not remember what it was, but she remembered how the kindly pudding of his face trembled as though the tiny flames of myriad candles were flickering under his skin. That was his soul, she had thought; his whole soul was coming up into his face. It's the kindling of the last lights in the branched lamp of bone inside our bodies that gives the dying this look of beatitude. *"Come, take a guess,"* Mr. Becker had urged her. She remembered the terrible eagerness in his smile as he lifted his sightless moss-eyes toward the region of her voice. A silver wine-cup where the twenty-two letters of the Hebrew alphabet are stored during silences, she had asked, did he mean that? No, no, he had simply meant that one reads it from right to left to tell what phase of the cycle it's in. *"The way you complicate, Mrs. Ferris! Your mind spins webs like orb weavers!"* He had joked that, like most poets, she had been a spider in one of her former lives.

The beaded curtain of grey crystals on the ceiling was dissolving in a shimmer of light rain.

And now it was clearing.

And now there was nothing.

She had been lying with her head back in the armchair across the room from Carolyn and Hugh. She brought herself upright. "Thank you, darling. That was . . . enthralling."

Carolyn made a slight movement as though tossing back the ghosts of wings of long hair that used to fall across her cheeks as she played the piano. Above the mandarin collar of her red silk blouse her black hair was combed into a sleek duck's tail. "Oh, Mom, you always overpraise." She turned halfway on the piano bench to face Hugh, pinpoint fires flashing in her crystal earrings. "Like that, Dad?"

Hugh made an appreciative murmur. He had been staring straight ahead, his fingers playing the imaginary keyboard spread across his knees. When he looked over at his daughter, Miriam saw two mandrake roots of light sprout in the lenses of his glasses. "What about an encore?"

"Not now. That was enough." Caro began putting her rings back on.

"Not even a little Bach?" Hugh persisted. "I thought you might give us a bit of Bach in honor of his 300th."

"Maybe tomorrow. Or Sunday. Bach's 300th was two weeks ago yesterday, anyway, so another day won't make any difference. What did you see *this* time, Mom?"

"Sky," Miriam said after a moment.

"Sky," Caro echoed.

"Our sky over the mountain. At sunset. In another season."

"Hmmm." Caro glanced down and scratched at a pleat in her navy blue skirt.

A familiar claw was tightening its clasp on Miriam's right shoulder. She reached up to massage it just as Caro lifted her head. Under the blue search of her daughter's gaze, she began patting the folds of the cowl neck of her dress. "Have either of you ever noticed the light in November at dusk? It has a bitter beauty, I think; the bitterness is what gives it that beauty. And the blackness of the trees against the horizon just after sunset—that's what gives Novemberlight its drama.'

"November light," Caro repeated. "Novemberlight."

Caro was looking at Hugh now. Miriam saw that Caro and Hugh were forgetting her presence, that she was free to contemplate the tableau that presented itself to her. She saw the dark fringe of eyelash, the ski-slope nose, the lovely curve of Caro's mouth, the stalk of her neck, the soft rounds of her shoulder and breast under the cherry-red blouse, as a carving in high relief against the ivory shell of blank wall above the piano. She saw the afternoon sunlight graze the shards of stained glass inlaid in the casing of the pendulum clock impending above the heads of the two seated figures. She saw how Hugh's face shone with a waxlike luster. As onyx shines.

Hugh bent his head, rubbed his ear, pulled inquiringly at the knot in his tie. "Let me hear *your* version of the Caravaggio show. Your mother came home in a trance over one of the paintings."

"And I know which one, too. It was *Still Life With Birds*, right? The museum was *jammed*, Dad, did she tell you? I couldn't get near enough to see more than three or four of his. I remember *The Magdalen in Ecstasy* best. Gil said he liked his energy. Too much blood and thunder for my taste. I liked some of the works of his contemporaries more—what I could get to *see* of them, that is! There was a Rubens I loved, *Equestrian Portrait of Something-or-other*. Mom, do you remember that magnificent horse? MOM?"

"Your mother's still coming back with the tide," Hugh laughed.

"Your mother is back." Miriam smiled at her daughter. "Yes, I *do* remember that magnificent horse. I can empathize with what you say about the blood and thunder, by the way."

Judith With Holofernes. The crowd in front of that painting! But, then, she probably could not have borne a closer look. The avenger's eyes had stared straight into her own; the fierceness of that gaze drew the blood up into her throat. Suddenly Gil had materialized at her side. "Pretty brutal, eh, Miriam? She was a Jewess, wasn't she?" Caro and Gil had proposed they walk all the way to MOMA. She remembered the cold spatter of the first raindrops, the bluster of the March wind, the table they took at the deli. *"A quarter to one, poor Mom, you must be starved,"* Caro had said. *"Gil and I had an enormous brunch just before we left to meet you."* Caro had ordered a soda, just to keep her company. Gil had ordered a "snack" of a BLT and fries; *"gladly,"* he'd said, accepting her offer that he share her omelet. She hadn't touched her toast; he ate that too. Caro had dampened her napkin in her water glass, lifted his chin with her forefinger, patted at the corners of his mouth. *"There, Greedybaby, will that hold you for a while?"* They had become so absorbed in their little ritual they had forgotten her; she was free to contemplate her daughter's husband across the table. Caro's Greedybaby dwelled in the rangy casing of a Daddy-long-legs. Friends who thought he bore a facial resemblance to Raymond Burr called him "Perry," a nickname Miriam thought ill-chosen. Gil Parker had done nothing to earn the lineaments of probity and large-heartedness she read in the portraiture of the actor's character. At MOMA they had gone first to the exhibit of Rousseau's paintings. His green jungle-wilds had revived her, his crafty-eyed beasties, his exuberant orange moons. "Rousseau 'inhabits his paintings as we inhabit our dreams,'" she had quoted to Mr. Becker. "But my daughter complained she felt as though she were back in nursery school. *She is stuffier and more disdainful of playfulness every passing year. I miss the Carolyn of Eld. It probably has to do with her profession. A biostatistician in an enchanted garden is a displaced person, I suppose."* Mr. Becker had suggested it was Caro's age that accounted for her formality. He had asked Miriam if she'd noticed how elderly one becomes in one's early thirties. *"Wait until she has children, then she'll be a happy child herself again. So will you, Mrs. Ferris. For you, it will be the third time around, eh? People say that grandparenthood is as much of Paradise as we can know on this side."*

"What do *you* think, Mom? MOM!"

"Your mother's been wandering again. She hasn't heard a word we've been saying."

"Not at all, you two, I've heard *every* word! That was the high point for Gil, wasn't it, Atget's vacant rooms—"

"*Vacant!* Mom, you are not being fair."

"Uninhabited, then. Unless you count those shadow-shapes of tables and chairs as living presences."

"That's just the *point!* They *are* living presences." Caro stretched and started to get up from the piano bench, but then changed her mind. "Grey on grey, Dad, I could just hear Mom thinking that. She was bored by Matisse's drawings too."

"Your mother craves excitement. Living color."

"And drama." Caro pointed at him. "And that's where *you* come in."

"What time is Gil coming tomorrow, did you say?" Hugh asked.

"One, two o'clock. He'll call us tonight. Dad, neither of us can *wait* to see Hugh Ferris's James Tyrone. We read the whole play aloud to one another last week-end, did I tell you? You're right, Eugene O'Neill was brilliant. And Mom gave us rave reviews of your performance."

"Your mother is biased. Her reviews are based on only one rehearsal, and it wasn't even the *dress* rehearsal we're having tonight. 'This play of old sorrow, written in blood and tears,'" he mused. He reached up and tapped the crown of his head. "And I have to carry it off without a tonsure. I wanted a tonsure, but your mother objected."

"Your mother has no voice in such matters!" Miriam protested. "The tonsure was the director's idea, darling, and it's your *father* who wouldn't hear of it." She caught herself massaging her shoulder and was about to take her hand away when she realized neither of them had noticed. Hugh was saying that in all the Big Apple, Gil must be the only one grinding away in his office on Good Friday afternoon. *Not to mention the afternoon before Erev Pesach,* Miriam thought. *Most of the buildings in Manhattan must be deserted by now.* This was a monster case, Caro replied. Mind, Hugh went on, he wasn't *criticizing* Gil. Quite the contrary, one of the reasons the country is going down is that so few people believe anymore in the ethic of hard work. "Wait until I tell you the latest developments in this case," Caro began.

Van Gogh's *Starry Night*. She had taken the whole of the painting inside herself, to bring back to Mr. Becker, and to the children in her Sunday School classes, and to her poem. It all had dissolved on their cold, windy way back to the Met, when a panhandler with a cane had reached out of the crowd towards her. He had thrust his cane at her, called out something—what? what? She had caught only a glimpse of him before Gil grasped her elbow and marched her past the man, but she would see him henceforth and forever. His face rose up in her thoughts as a face floats up through the nebulae of a dream: his moist, reddened eyes, the pink heart of his mouth, his blond Vandyke beard. He could not have been much more than thirty—a stocky figure in jeans and a tan jacket that looked as though it were made of deerskin. *"I'd never beg,"* Gil had muttered in fury, *"I'd do anything, carry boxes,* anything, *before I'd beg."* Pulling up the black dandelions in the budding grasses of the soul. Casting out devils who come back, come back. That night she had told Hugh about the encounter, and asked him, *"Isn't that what I do every time I send out my poems? I, who think of myself as a proud person, don't I beg?"* Hugh had replied he thought she saw it as a kind of game, like the lottery, and that if she felt it was begging, she ought to stop. *"One flop by the Palatine Players, Miriam, one disaster on that stage, and I'm out. They need me more than I need them. I'm with Gil. I'll not give charity, and I'll not seek it or accept it."* People's cocksureness in the time of plenty. They were young souls, Gil and Hugh, both of them young souls. *And Caro? And Caro?* By the time they'd got to the Met that afternoon, she'd felt walked out. Caro and Gil wanted to go the last mile, the exhibit of The Treasury of San Marcos. She had told them to go on without her, that she was "all out at the eyes." After they left, she had gone looking for Rembrandt, and finally found him, and gazed and gazed at him until Rembrandt took pity on her and returned her gaze. Afterward, she'd gone downstairs to wait for them on one of the benches outside the cafeteria, and a sighted Mr. Becker had materialized, a sweet elderly gentleman she had rescued as he was about to go into the Ladies Room. Even the voice was the same; had she dreamed *him* too? Even now she could hear his profuse thanks after she showed him the right door, and the rapture in the Mr. Becker Voice when he exclaimed on his way in, *"Caravaggio is a* sensation! *This is the greatest painting I've ever seen!"* She had closed her eyes, the better to see the procession of

Italian-looking Christs and Italian-looking St. Francises pass by. St Francis's perpetual smile, his incorrigible happiness. His faithful companions, his skulls. They say he sang as he lay dying, that the monk who attended his deathbed was greatly annoyed by his singing as he lay dying, they say he sang Psalm 142 as he lay dying. "Maschil of David, when he was in his cave; a Prayer." . . . She heard Gil ask, *"Pretty brutal, eh, Miriam? She was a Jewess, wasn't she?"*

"TEN TO FOUR!" Hugh was getting up from the couch. "Anyone for a constitutional before the usual banquet?"

"I could *use* a walk! Mom, do you mind? You and I have the whole evening to visit—"

She waved them away, reminding them they would have to sit down at the table by 5:30, if Hugh was to be on time for the dress rehearsal.

Out in the kitchen, she heard their voices fading away as they crossed the lawn, Caro asking how work was coming along on the beams in the basement of the Andries Wibau House, could he give her a quick tour of inspection, and Hugh replying there probably was someone around the historical society office, it was better to wait until Sunday morning. He could give the three of them a private look-see while all the Christians in Palatine were in church celebrating Easter.

Easter Sunday. Hugh had not gone to Mass on Easter since his mother died. Wasn't the failure to go to church on Easter a mortal sin? she had asked him when he told her opening night was to be on the Saturday before Easter and they began talking about the coincidence of Good Friday and Passover this year, hadn't he told her it was a mortal sin for a Catholic not to attend Mass on Easter? Sounds more like something his *mother* might have told her, Hugh had replied testily. He had said he went to Mass on Easter all those years only to please his mother, and now that his mother was gone he was free to please himself. But his mother lived in *Beloit, Wisconsin,* she had protested. So how on earth could his mother know whether or not he was going to Mass on Easter? It wasn't a matter of what she *knew,* Hugh had rejoined, it was simply that so long as his mother was alive, he hadn't felt he could be his own man. *"I just don't hear the same music that religious people hear, Miriam, and*

I told you that before we married, remember. It was out of respect for my mother that I kept my promise to go through the motions. Case closed, now that she's gone." Wasn't that what Poppa had said to Mama when Bubby Pinsky died, weren't those his very words? *"Case closed, now that she's gone, Gemini."* Except that Bubby was *Mama's* mother, not his, and Poppa was making up Mama's mind *for* her. Of her own return to Judaism Hugh would say no more than that she was free to go her own way, now that Caro was grown and they both had kept their agreement to raise her as a free-thinker.*"Well, you and Dad each have been going your own way on* many *fronts, Mom, so to me, this is just one more added to the rest."* That had been the thrust of *Caro's* commentary on the matter.

She began chopping onions for the Chicken Kiev. Gil *could* have driven upstate with Caro today. A pity he hadn't. Gone were the days she wanted Caro all to herself, gone forever. Now that Caro had told her the decision was Final, what more of substance was there to be said between them? Their mother-daughter talks belonged to another era. The new era had begun, the closing era, the era of observing the proprieties between parent and grown child who, in the fullness of time, ineluctably become beloved strangers to one another. Perhaps she and Caro ought to go to the dress rehearsal tonight after all. Why suffer and put Caro through the suffering of an evening of parrying at the edge of the abyss that had opened between them?

The phone rang just as they were finishing their soup. "That *can't* be Gil, it's too *early!*" Caro protested. Hugh folded his napkin and got up. "Someone wants James Tyrone, probably. I'll get it."

She pointed to Caro's empty soup bowl to ask if she would like a second serving; Caro shook her head. "Hey, how *are* you?" Hugh called out in a startled tone. "What's *up?* Oh. Oh." She set down the bowl Caro had just handed her to stack with her own, and went out to the kitchen to stand beside him. "Yes, she's right here, just a minute. Miriam, here, sit down. It's Eric, it's your brother Eric." She shook her head to say she didn't want the chair, and took the receiver from him.

"Eric?" she asked. Hugh was patting her shoulder. Caro had come into the kitchen. "I'm sorry that I don't have good news, Mims." She waited. "She's gone, Mims." Hugh was hugging her. "When?" she asked. Caro started to cry. "Just now. The Home just called me. They all just sat down to the seder and she . . . slumped over. Just like that." She was trembling violently, tears were standing in her eyes. "Ah, Eric." Her brother's calm voice asked, "Think you can come?" "Of *course* I can come," she sobbed, "right away." "Listen, Miriam, all the flights probably are full. It's Passover, Easter, all the college kids are on spring break this week-end. To get three flights—" She cleared her throat. "Hugh won't be coming," she said. Hugh reached for the receiver, and she made a sign telling him to wait. "Hugh's starring in a play, Eric, *Long Day's Journey,* he can't come with me. Don't listen to him if he argues. Caro is here, Gil will be here tomorrow. . . . Let me come by myself. *Please?*" She looked straight into Hugh's eyes. Then she gave him the receiver, and Caro held out her arms to her, and she went into them, and Caro rocked her and kissed her hair.

The chicken roulades had dried up, the needles of rosemary and flecks of crushed sage leaves had gone stale, the matzo meal in the paste had crumbled into sand, the potatoes in the kugel had lost their crispness, the mash of carrot and honey and ginger had grown cold; the wine was wormwood in her throat. Caro helped clear the table, helped her with dishes, then followed her into the bedroom and helped her pack. Gil called and Caro answered and told him the sad news. Eric called back and Caro answered and told him that Hugh would be going to the travel agency in Kingston first thing in the morning. She put her hand over the receiver. "Uncle Eric says you don't need to come until Sunday. The funeral home is arranging for a service on Monday morning." "Tell him I'm coming tomorrow," she said. Caro repeated this, and promised to call him back in the morning to let him know what time Miriam's flight would arrive in Miami. After she hung up, she asked, "Want to borrow the navy blue coat I wore home for this week-end? It's perfect, so lightweight." "But it's brand *new,*" Miriam said. "What difference does *that* make? Mom, *please* take it. You don't *have* a cloth coat for spring. It would mean so much to me if you'd wear it—" Caro began to cry. Miriam embraced her. "Don't," she said. "It isn't your fault. It isn't anyone's fault. I'll be glad to take your coat."

They were about to go into the living room when she remembered the congregational second seder. She called the Millers. Don answered, and she told him she couldn't be there tomorrow night, that there had been a death in the family. "Miriam, I'm terribly sorry. Is there anything we can do?" There was nothing, thanks, she told him, but she was the one who was bringing the haroses. "Oh, don't think about the haroses at a time like this! Gerry can find someone else to make haroses. She can make it her*self!*" "No. I said I would bring the haroses, and I intend to supply the haroses. I'll arrange for it before I leave." The tightness in her voice. Taffy eyes stared out of the stark white face in the mirror, the face of a bird, the white-tailed kite, was staring out at her from the glass. "Well, sure, Miriam." She heard the amazement and the hurt in his voice. Caro was hovering in the doorway. After she hung up, she explained about the haroses, and Caro said they could take care of it in the morning.

Hugh would be back around eleven o'clock. And then there would be the long night to be got through. Caro sat at the other end of the couch, leafing through her mother's stack of literary magazines, respectful of this silence her mother had ordained and that her mother alone had the right to break. The lamplight buttered an errant lovelock at Caro's temple.

Orphan. With Mama gone, she was fully an orphan now. *"It's quite a feeling,"* Hugh had said. *"You're out there on your own. You're free. For the first time in your life, you're really free."* Mother Ferris had been a widow for sixteen years before her Tom came to guide her across to the other shore. Mama had been widowed for thirty-six; Poppa died in '49. Mama was fifty-four then. Only one more month, and Mama would have turned ninety this year of 1985. *"Gemini,"* that was Poppa's love-name for Mama. And that was when she knew the last of Mama had faded away, when she showed Mama the photograph album, when she pointed to the laughing-eyed sylph that was Mama in her jubilee year. *"Gemini in her prime,"* Poppa had said, Mama had been so proud Poppa had said that. 1945 . . . the whole world had seemed in its prime that year. The Germans had surrendered in Italy, then all of Berlin had surrendered to the Russian troops, then all of Germany had surrendered to the Allies, the fighting in Europe was over, and Eric would be coming home. Gemini was fifty, and the lights were going on again all over the world. *"'Gemini in her prime,' Mama, remember?"* she had asked. And the white-wreathed head was nodding Yes, shaking No. *"I'm Miriam, Mama, don't you remember me?"* The bashful fall of Mama's eyelids over her hazel eyes, fear flickering like firelight across her high cheekbones . . . Mama looked like an ancient Indian priestess. Again the white-wreathed head was nodding Yes, shaking No. *"I'm Miriam, Mama, I'm your* daughter!" The biscuit-brown face raised to hers, afraid, afraid to offend this stranger with the familiar face, this pestering visitor who would not leave her in peace. *"I'm Miriam, Mama, I'm your* daughter!" The dry, cross-hatched pale lips forming the hopeful response, *"That's nice."*

The faint twit of the pendulum of the clock above their two heads. The light breath of warming earth and early grasses plucking at the hems of the closed drapes, Hugh had put in the screens only last week.

"Chametz!" Mama had shrilled, Mama said she had to sweep away the last crumb of *chametz*, Dorrie came home from work that afternoon and there Mama was, running around the house with the dustpan and whisk broom, sobbing that she wouldn't be able to get all the *chametz* out before dark. A panic attack, Dorrie said. They finally had to give Mama a hypo. Dorrie had to refresh Eric's memory, Eric had forgotten what *chametz* is.

Eric had been twelve at the last family seder in '36, Bubby died later that year and Poppa announced, *"Case closed, now that she's gone, Gemini."* "I was only five-going-on-six," she'd told Dorrie, "and *I* remember you weren't supposed to eat bread or cake or cookies or cereal during Passover. *I* remember that *chametz* is leaven, why can't Eric remember?" A six-year-old is impressionable, Dorrie had replied. And besides, Eric was already well on his way to being a scientist at the age of twelve. Eric had been calling religion "Retrogression" as far back as Dorrie could remember. *"Farther back than* that!" she'd said. *"Eric is his Poppa in his bones."* Then Dorrie had confessed she'd have to admit there's good sense behind some of the old taboos. Miriam had thought Dorrie meant the ancestors' discovery that one can get trichinosis from eating pork, but Dorrie had told her, *"That's only the most obvious one, Mims. Ever thought of the side benefit to cutting out yeast for a week? There's a regular epidemic of candida yeast infection, they call it 'candidiasis,' half the country's got it. Ask your observant friends from the Palatine congregation if they noticed they feel better during Passover. Americans are bread junkies, know that?"*

Dorrie is brilliant, she had told Eric when he got back on the line during that telephone call, she herself would never have thought of making a connection like that. *"Okay, she's brilliant,"* Eric had laughed. *"But you're* bright *too, though in a different way. She's a pragmatist, you're a dreamer. Like Mama."*

Like Mama. From Nowhere, Mama went into a panic over clearing out the *chametz*, and they put her out of her misery with a hypo, and Mama never returned. One afternoon, when Eric and Dorrie were at work, Mama turned into Bubby. And then Mama vanished.

Bubby. Small and pert, Bubby hopped about like a little wren. *"Ess, ess, zei gezunt!"* The taste of ginger—

She had made a little sound deep in her throat. She looked up and into the blue compassion-flowers of Caro's eyes.

"Mom? You okay?"

"I was thinking that my Bubby, your Great Grandma Pinsky, used to make a sweet at this time of year."

"A sweet?"

"It must have been the taste of ginger that reminded me of it. You cook carrots and then you mash them and put them into a saucepan with sugar. Sugar and ground almonds and the ginger. After it's thick, you sprinkle more sugar and ginger on a board, and you turn it out on that. *Carrot Ingberlach* I think Mama called it, Mama made that dish every Passover. You wait until they cook a little and cut them out before they harden. Into diamond shapes. Or squares." She smiled. "Passover Brownies."

"Passover Brownies," Caro echoed softly.

"Bubby was the great love of your Grandma's life."

"Poor Grandma. To have to live so many years like that . . . . Did Uncle Eric say he was calling Sidney? I forgot to ask."

"So did I. I'm sure he's called Sidney. But he wouldn't expect him to fly all the way from London."

"No, I guess not. You saw Sid when you were there last May, at Aunt Dorrie's—?"

"At Aunt Dorrie's Unveiling. Yes. Remember, in '83, Aunt Dorrie died right after I came back to Palatine from my visit, and Uncle Eric didn't let me know until after the funeral was over. He didn't want me to turn right around and go back to Florida. Which is what I'd have done."

"Vic came with Sidney both times, didn't he? In '83 and '84?"

"Yes, both times."

"Sidney and Vic have been together for a long time now. Four years?"

"Oh, more than that. Your Aunt Dorrie and Uncle Eric told me back in '81 that they both felt good about it. *More* than good, *grateful*. Way back then, they said they thought Vic was very, very good for Sidney. I remember it was '81, because it came up when we were talking about the assassination attempt. Everyone was very shaken up by it, don't you remember? Vic's a Catholic, and so the talk naturally came around to religion, family . . . ."

"Assassination attempt? In '81? Oh, you mean on the President's life. What did that have to do with religion?"

"No, no, not the President, that was in March. This was in *May*. Someone tried to kill the *Pope* in May, just before my visit. Don't you remember?"

"I guess so," Caro said doubtfully. "Poor Uncle Eric. First his wife, now his mother. And Sidney lives so far away."

Sidney and Vic had taken her to the airport after the Unveiling. They had planned to visit Mama at the Home on their way back to Eric's. *"Dad's tough, Aunt Miriam, he's a survivor. He's got his work; he doesn't believe in looking back."*

"That's Dad's car I hear, isn't it?"

She got up. Her neck and shoulder were throbbing with pain. "I'm going to take a hot bath, dear. If I go right on to bed, say Goodnight to Dad for me, will you?"

Their low murmuring was lapping on the shores. She breathed in, breathed out, with the rise and fall of the humming in the living room. *Gil.* Caro was talking to Hugh about Gil . . . .
"She was a Jewess, wasn't she?"
Holofernes was a general, Mr. Becker said, a Babylonian general. His troops were attacking the city of Bethulia, and they destroyed all the wells and springs. The commander finally decided if people's prayers for rain weren't answered in five days' time he would have to surrender to Holofernes's troops. Judith was a widow, very wealthy and very pious; she fasted except for the Sabbath and the Feast of the New Moon and the Holy Days. She had a secret plan to deceive Holofernes into believing she had left her people and wanted to turn Bethulia over to him. She brought food with her—wine and cheese, bread, figs, oil. On the fourth night that she was in his camp, Holofernes made a banquet for her. *"First eat some of my food, then I'll take some of yours, that was the bargain she struck, Mrs. Ferris. She got him drunk on the wine, and he fell asleep, and that's when she killed him. She cut off his head with his own sword. So she saved her people, she saved her city. End of story."* Why isn't the story in the Bible? she asked Mr. Becker and he replied that he thought the story had been written too late to get into the Bible. He thought it happened during the time of the Maccabees, and that's why the story is remembered at Hanukkah time. She wondered aloud how a *woman* artist might have painted *Judith With Holofernes.* Mr. Becker told her then about the works of Artemisia Gentileschi. She wrote the name down in her pocket notebook. *"So much to learn, Mr. Becker. And we have only one lifetime."* Mr. Becker laughed. *"Maybe yes, maybe no. I'll soon find out. Meanwhile, is there time for another chapter of* Wolf Solent? *In case it's Maybe yes."*

Hugh called from the travel agency while she and Caro were finishing breakfast. He could book a flight at half-past two or a flight at four. She decided on the earlier one. What about coming back? he asked, what about 12:30 Monday, was that too early? She said it sounded all right, and when she hung up she asked Caro to call Eric to make sure. While Caro was talking to Eric, she began chopping the walnuts and the fruit for the haroses. "Can I help?" Caro asked after she made the call. She divided the labor, Caro chopping the dried apricots and apples while she finished chopping the prunes and dates. "We don't want to make a paste," she told Caro, "just to chop it enough so it has the consistency of mortar." "Mortar," Caro repeated. "They made bricks out of it for the Pharaoh," she explained. "Bricks for palaces, for pyramids. When they were slaves to the Egyptians." Caro nodded. After they finished chopping the fruit, she gave Caro the wine and the brandy to mix. Then she added the honey and spices, the cinnamon and nutmeg and cloves, and poured it into the bowl of fruit and nuts. "Now mix in the matzo meal," she told Caro. "Go ahead, don't be afraid, you'll know when it's the right amount." When Caro finished mixing she put in a splash of lime juice. "Gerry Miller gave me this recipe," she said. "Poor Don last night. They must have been in the middle of their seder when I called. Gerry jokes that this is Reconstructionist Global haroses; the Ashkenazic recipe is a simple mix of apples and nuts and honey and wine and cinnamon. I'm going to call her to ask if she'll pick it up at our house. You and Gil will stay in until after she comes, okay?" "Can't we bring it to her on the way to La Guardia?" Caro asked. "The Millers live on the other side of the mountain," she explained, "so there won't be time." "You wouldn't let me go with you to Florida," Caro said quietly. "And now you're telling me you won't even let me go with you to the airport." "But you have to be here to meet *Gil*," she reminded Caro. "I called Gil before you got up," Caro said; she was almost whispering. "And he's to meet us at the airport and come back here with Dad and me. He's waiting for me to call him and tell him what time to meet us."

Caro folded her arms. Her face was a white wall of stone, of granite, her eyes were tiny points of chicory blue, her mouth was a purple stain on the hard white mask of her Furies face, purple as the flower of the poisonous monkshood. Something thrummed deep inside Miriam's body; she wondered if she were going to pitch forward, and put both hands on the back of the chair nearest her. She hung her head and closed her eyes, and tried to remember how it had happened, that she and Caro had become antagonists. "I don't know what all this is about," she said after a moment. "Neither do I," Caro whispered. "Call Gil and tell him to meet us at the airport then. Tell him we're going to try to be there by a quarter to two. And then I'll call Gerry and ask her to pick up the haroses on their way to the seder. You three should be back before then; it begins at sundown."

She looked up and saw tears standing in Caro's eyes. Hugh was just pulling up in the driveway.

They took Caro's car. Hugh sat up in the front, in the passenger's seat. He had insisted that Miriam have the whole back seat to herself so she could stretch out. Last night, awakening for the half-dozenth time, she at last had felt him lying beside her; and when she stirred his arm went around her in the old way. *Sleep,* it said. *Sleep.* And so she had slept until morning. She had felt too shy to tell him she'd have liked for him to sit back here with her. She stretched out as he'd suggested she do.

Caro did not like much conversation when she was driving. And Hugh was saving his voice for tonight's performance.

She closed her eyes and entered the body of one of the three figures in the lawn chairs on the grounds of the Home. Sun-canaries fluttered across her face, she smiled as she listened to their small talk, Eric's and Dorrie's, smiled and said nothing. May after May after May, the years, the years. It's mostly a Haitian neighborhood now, one or the other was saying; then they talked about another drug war, and then about the hurricane winds in September. And now they were talking and laughing in Cuban Yiddish. And now they were talking about Mama's roommate Essie.

"Miriam," Essie introduced her to the man behind the counter, "Miriam Ferris." The man was chewing gum, heavy glasses in tortoise shell frames rode on the pocked schooner of his nose, his fir-green shirt sprouted purple palm trees, *"she comes to see her Mama every spring, so she's taking me shopping, she's taking me on an outing. Bras I need, a couple of good bras, size 38, but the cup's never right in the ones they bring me, an A is too small and a B is too big, here, I'll show you—"* Essie opening her blouse, reaching into her slip, lifting out her breast and holding it out to him, a small white partridge with a peach-colored eye quivering in her hand, holding it out to the man in the fir-green shirt sprouting purple palm trees.

Fir-green. The colored squares of the afghan folded at the foot of Mama's bed, a row of fir-green, cream yellow, earth brown, apple green, a row of cerise, buttercup yellow, cameo pink, burgundy, a row of lilac, yellow-green, peacock blue, another cameo pink, then the fold. She would curl up at the foot of Mama's bed and draw the afghan around her shoulders like a shawl . . . ."*Please, God, let me die,*" the old woman in the wheelchair in the corridor was sing-songing, "*Please, God, let me die.*" . . . ."*A death-watch,*" Eric was saying, "*For years and years, a death-watch.*"

"Slowing to a crawl!" Caro muttered. "Wake-up call, Dad. We're on the Triborough."

Hugh straightened his shoulders. "Great time. You made great time."

"Wonder if Mom's awake."

She closed her eyes just as Hugh was turning to look. "Still asleep," he reported.

"I hope she'll be okay, Dad."

"Your mother will be fine. Eric's meeting her plane, and after that they'll be together the whole time."

"Grandma almost made it to ninety."

Hugh cleared his throat. "It's better this way. All around."

"Uncle Eric said Grandma died a long time ago."

"So she did. Funny thing, your Grandma Ferris died on All Souls' Day, and now your Grandma Goldman passed away on Good Friday."

"Passover too."

"What? Oh, yes, Passover too."

When she and Caro came out of the Ladies Room, Gil was standing in the lounge talking with Hugh. He looked up and waved and hurried towards them. "Hey, Babe." He kissed Caro's cheek, and held out his hand to Miriam. She felt that he wanted to embrace her. When she gave him her hand, he clasped it in both of his. "I'm sorry. I'm really sorry, Miriam." She thanked him, she said she knew that he was. Was there anything they could get her? Coffee? A soda? A sandwich? The paper? Nothing; she'd brought things to read, and she was sure they'd give her a snack on the plane. Again she thanked Caro for the coat, again they reminded her to be sure to stop at Caro's building on Monday afternoon if there'd be time before her five o'clock bus back to Palatine, again she wished Hugh good luck for tonight. Boarding time was announced. Hugh hugged her, Caro hugged her, Gil hugged her. then they went into a little huddle all together, and the three of them said, *"Give Eric my best,"* and then the refrain, *"Take care. Take care."* When she turned around for a last wave good-bye, Caro blew her a kiss. The three of them, they were complete, they were a family, Caro at the center, her father's hand on one of her shoulders, her husband's on the other, they had no more need of her, they had outgrown their need of her, the quickening, deep inside the sere womb, down, down, wild freefall, a blaze of silver, rumbles, screaming, off the coast of North Carolina, one of the estuaries there swallowing the plane whole . . . she smiled and waved and turned around and went on into the passageway to the cabin.

She'd been assigned the aisle seat. Her seat partner, a young woman, had settled in. After she buckled her seat belt, she fished for her book and opened it to the page where she had last closed it over the bookmark with the print of the unicorn and the cameo pink fringes. An afterimage of the trio in the lounge floated up from the print, waving at her as they drifted by. Three. Three is a mystic number. For Christians more than for Jews? *"She was a Jewess, wasn't she?"* Miriam closed her eyes. Four cups of wine. The Four Questions. The story of the four sons. The four cardinal points, the four seasons, the four elements. Four is an earthly number. Jewish.

* * *

The stocky figure in the pale yellow safari jacket and beige slacks coming towards her—*Eric! Eric!* He held out his arms and she ran to him, and he hugged her, hugged her *hard.* "Hey, Mims. Hey. Hey." Patting her back, patting and patting her back, then he took her by the shoulders and held her away from himself to have a look at her. "Another year gone by." "Almost." "You don't change, Mims." "Neither do you," she lied. *The boy with the laughing face, short and slender, Tuesday's child full of grace, swallowed up by the teen-aged pudge with glasses, overspread by the roly-poly Navyman whom the post-war years kneaded into this portly professor . . . . Time working with its terrible patience, saddening his face in making Poppa's face come out and stand.* He took her small suitcase. "How's the arthritis, any better?" "*Some* better," she lied again. They walked down to the luggage claim area with their arms around one another's waist. "What are we doing down here?" she asked. "I only brought that one suitcase you're carrying." "I thought so. But we'll be closest to where I parked if we go this way." He held the door open for her, and she walked out into the smoky fruitflower wavering gauze of Miami air. They would go home, he said, and she would unpack and he would get her a tall, frosty drink of something. And when she felt ready, they'd go out to dinner. They'd go to the Home tomorrow to sign papers and collect Mother's things, they had the whole day for that.

They were halfway home when she saw it in the unending sapphire sea of the eastern skies—the ghostly arch bridge of clouds, and swimming across it a giant, puffy dolphin, bright pink. A colossus dolphin crossing the dissolving bridge, a dolphin between the dissolving piers.

"I turned the Big Six-Oh," he reminded her after the pretty young waitress had served them their entrée and he had winked at her and flirted with her and Miriam had scolded him for it. "I'm getting to be a Dirty Old Man eh? Four years to go. I *could* stay on, but I've been putting off writing that book for too many years. It's now or never. Besides, I'll still have my place at the lab, I can keep my office, I'll have my library pass. Academe is top-heavy, you know. I don't want to be one of those duffers who won't get off the pot. You miss it?"

She thought for a moment and then told him truthfully that she missed it *some*times. "Pittance that it was, Hugh and I could use that extra income. But adjuncts are expendable. Last hired, first fired. Not that it makes any economic sense; if it weren't for our cheap labor, colleges across the country might as well shut down. So far as missing the work . . . you don't miss teaching Freshman Comp like you'd miss teaching a Lit course."

"Manage to keep a hand in?"

"Things come up. Workshops, conferences, a book review assignment here and there."

"How's the poetry writing?"

"Languorous slow, as ever."

"Think you'll be getting another book out?"

"I'm pedaling as fast as I can. Now that I've been retired I have more time. Well, you have four years to go. Four years is a long time."

"The last two were the longest I've ever lived."

"I can imagine," she said softly.

"Dorrie hadn't felt well for about a week before our trip."

"That's what you told me last year. But she wouldn't cancel—"

"I blame that cardiologist of hers. Left it up to her, did I tell you? Said he didn't have a crystal ball. I never had any use for that guy, but Dorrie swore by him. Eager. Eager to get to . . . ." He was staring so fixedly at some Presence on the wall behind her, she turned around for a moment. Nothing there. "Leningrad, Mims. Who would have believed Dorrie would die in Leningrad?"

She leaned across the table and covered his hand with both of hers.

"What a hassle getting back. Sid and Vic, I couldn't have got through the nightmare of it without them. They flew out the day after I called. I had *two* sons at her funeral, Mims. I've had two sons ever since."

After the waitress filled their coffee cups, he asked about Caro. Caro would be going into the Ph.D. program this fall, she said. "How long? Four, five years?" "I suppose." "Caro's how old now, let's see, thirty-two, that won't leave much time for a little Parker to get in under the biological deadline." "There isn't going to be another little Parker," she said quietly. *"Another?"* Eric repeated, puzzled. "Gil was married before," she reminded him. "Gil already *has* a son. He lives in Texas with his mother and his stepfather." "Well, sure, I remember that, Mims. How's that going?" "Now that the boy's getting closer to adolescence, the visits are becoming . . . strained," she told him. "In any case, Gil says he's done his duty by the human race." "What does *Caro* say?" Eric asked, "What does *Hugh* say?" "Caro says, and Hugh says he agrees, that the world doesn't need another unwanted child." "Maybe Caro will change her mind, Mims." She shook her head. "Caro told me a few weeks ago that the decision is Final." Eric looked at her keenly over the rim of his coffee cup. "The line stops here, eh, Mims? With you and me."

On the drive back, she told him about her work at the hospice and about Mr. Becker. And about teaching Sunday School at the shul. "Shul keeps you busy, eh?" "It's Pesach, Eric. It's Passover. The second night. Our shul is having a congregational second seder tonight at a place we rented for the holiday, and I was supposed to bring the haroses. Caro helped me make it this morning." There was a long silence, and then Eric said, "If it makes you happy, Mims. To me, it's a step backward." She told him there is a world of difference between Reconstructionist Judaism and the Orthodoxy they'd thought was synonymous with Judaism when they were children. He replied that he had sent telegrams to twenty Senators before the vote on the MX. "And I'm on the state environmental commission, and on so many committees on campus that I can't get a leg up on my own research. Where would I find time for all this if I went running to shul? Poppa was right, Mims, you don't have to be a Marxist to see it. Borrow a leaf from Dorrie's notebook. She learned early on that I'm my Poppa's son."

And you're Mama's daughter, was that what he was thinking? Now Mama and Poppa were *both* gone, must they still play the old game of dividing their parents up between themselves? And hadn't Eric won them both in the end? It was Eric Mama went to live with, wasn't it, soon after her daughter Miriam became Mrs. Hugh Ferris?

"We settled it when Mama went into the Home, remember, that she'd be buried here. Nobody's left on her side, and that's *Poppa's* family there in Brooklyn, and they never let Mama into The Club. Anyway, the Funeral Home's arranging for some kind of service at the graveside. Mr. Greenspan's taking care of everything. He's the one who handled everything at Dorrie's. A Burying Sam's part of the package. It just occurred to me you might want to have some say about who and what, now that you've got Religion."

"No. Whatever's arranged will be all right." *Getting Religion has to do with Life, not funerary rites,* she wanted to tell him. But Dorrie would have advised her not to give him the satisfaction of knowing his tease had hit the mark.... Dorrie knew her customer, all right.

There were two Erics in the double armchair across from the sofa where she sat hunched against the pain that was wringing her neck, two Japanese Erics in their kimonos and sandals, two chubby hands caressing the stems of their brandy glasses, the glasses on their two faces spangled with lamplight . . . and in the darkened Florida Room at her left hand, rustling things sat in the windows like watch keeper cats looking out at the yard sloping down to the bay. The two Erics wanted The Lowdown on The Men in her family. "Hugh first," they were saying, "Hugh's the Big Star of the Palatine Players, eh?, and now he's on the Board of the historical society. One of the big *machers* in Palatine, eh?" "Joseph in Egypt had nothing on Hugh Ferris in Palatine," she heard her drowsydrunk voice telling the two Ericos, "Hugh is out every night keeping the wheels of the town turning." And the two Ericos chuckled as in the Days of Yore. "And Gil is Yuppie of the Year, eh, wowing them all on Wall Street, eh?" "Gil's wowing them all on Wall Street," she heard herself saying, her tongue was coated with molasses, and she asked the two Ericos, "You know what his secret is?" "I can't wait to hear," the two Ericos nickered, and she pulled herself upright on the sofa and blinked her brights on into the fog where the two Ericos were hiding, and she puffed out her cheeks and she said, "I'm a meat-and-potatoes man," and she patted her middle and said, "Gotta bulk up, Caro, Greedybaby's hungry." She lifted her hands and made a monocle and brought it close to her left eye and pushed the two Ericos into one. Erico lifted his glass. "Long as Carolyn's happy. Here's to my lovely niece Carolyn." "She was a Jewess, wasn't she?" she asked. "Who?" Erico asked back, "Caro, you mean?" "No, I mean Judith. Doncha know, the lady in all the paintings who beheaded Whatshisname." Erico shook his ruffly head. "That wasn't Judith, Mims, that was Salomé. The gent's name was John the Baptist, I believe." She made a face at Mr. Smartness and told him that *was* Judith, and that the gent's name was Holofernes. "Doncha know Judith and Holofernes?" "Haven't had the pleasure, Mims." "If we'd brought her up one way or the other, Erico. We gave her a week without a Sabbath. We could've given her *both* and asked her to *choose*. This way, she ended up with nothing." "*So did Sidney!*" Erico yelled, "And Dorrie gave him the whole *routine!*" "You're hollering at me, and

I'm pickled," she moaned. She put her glass down on the coffee table and bent down to look for her shoes. "Pickled and potted and pie-eyed, Erico. Shellacked and gilded." She started to cry. "None of that," Erico said, he wasn't mad anymore. "Here, let Erico help you toddle off to bed." He picked up her shoes and put them on the coffee table and put his arm around her. *"That* way, remember?" He pointed to the hallway. She put her arm around his waist, and he steered her in the direction of Sidney's old room. "Ladies to the left, Gents to the right." They bumbled to Sidney's room, and Erico started singing about old Mimsie, the all-time Mimsie, *"All mimsie were the borogroves/and the nome graths outgrabe,"* and he parked her at the doorway and toddled off, and she waved at his Japanese Erico back, *"g'night, Erico, g'night, g'night."*

The nurse at the station called one of the aides to accompany her to Mama's room. "They're all having lunch," the young woman said. "You'll have privacy." She asked about Bessie. The young woman did not recognize the name. "I just started working here last month. They moved Sarah in the day before I started, so I guess your mother's roommate passed away." *Sarah.* The name of the matriarch, the first name of a woman old enough to be this young woman's grandmother, spoken with such . . . familiarity. *"I can't stand it that they call Mama by her first name!"* she had cried to Dorrie, *"It robs you of your last semblance of human dignity!"* And Dorrie had replied grimly that's what old age does, *"old age is a thief, you want to be spared, pray you'll die before you meet up with him."* Was that why Dorrie had been so eager? Did she know that she was keeping an appointment? If only she'd been able to see Dorrie and Eric on her trip here in '83. But they had left just before she'd made her yearly sojourn.

Mama's bed was neatly made up, the dresser top was bare. They'd packed all her things into a carton and sent it down to the Office where Eric had gone to sign the papers. The young woman pulled back the sliding door of Mama's side of the closet. The rack was neatly hung with Mama's colorful collections of robes and gowns, blouses and skirts, dresses for special days. "Always wanted a daughter to dress up," Dorrie used to say; half Mama's wardrobe was from Dorrie, the other half from herself. The nurse's aide asked her if she'd like to sort through Mama's clothes. "That won't be necessary," she replied. The young woman said this was a generous donation she was making to the Home's Thrift Shop and that they appreciate it. She reached under the clothes and pulled out a plastic bag. "That's what she was wearing when . . . . You can stop at the desk on your way out to pick up the personals, Mrs. Ferris." Yes, there would be Mama's wedding band. And her watch. Odd, that was the one thing Mama insisted on wearing at all times, her watch. People at the Home told her Mama would bring the dial right up to her eyes and squint hard so she could read the time. And Time had become Mama's foreign language.

When she was left alone, she opened the bag. Mama's beige and white dress, neatly folded. The matching beige jacket. A white nylon slip, white cotton bra, panties, footlets, Mama's shoes. As she packed the things back into the bag she noticed a soft little bulge in the pocket of the dress. She reached in and pulled out a wad of Kleenex. Mama had used it and folded it. Folded it like the ray flowers of a daisy over its disk. Mama had used this tissue between the time they dressed her up for the seder and the time she died at the seder table, it was still damp. She stuffed it into her purse, and lifted the dress to her face and sniffed at the armpits, sniffed deeply. Nothing. She put her face into the bodice and breathed in. A thin scent, timid . . . like . . . like dusty, stale cookies and faded flowers, faded sweet peas.

"Mama," she whispered. "Mama."

The nurse handed her a small yellow envelope. Mama's wedding band was inside. "The watch?" she asked. "Watch?" the nurse repeated. "Yes, my mother must have been wearing her watch when . . . ." The nurse looked through her papers. This envelope was the only one she had, she said. She hadn't been on duty Friday. "Would you like me to have this checked?" "No," Miriam said. "No, never mind."

"Let me direct you to the Office." The nurse came around the counter and took her by the arm. When they went around the corner to take the staff elevator, Miriam recognized the old woman in the wheelchair at the other end of the corridor. The figure was too far away for her voice to carry, but Miriam knew the words she was sing-songing, knew them by heart.

They had spread it all out on the dining room table, and now they were storing the last of it away into the four cartons on the chairs Eric had lined up in a row against the wall, two for him two for her. The biggest items were on the bottom, Poppa's gas mask from the Great War was at the bottom of one of Eric's. The welter of photographs, they had given up trying to sort them after an hour of crying out to one another, "Look! You've *got* to see *this* one!" "C'mere now, you won't believe this!" "Where was that, that *had* to've been on Eastern Parkway!" "This was the first time we took Sid and Caro to Flamingo Park, remember?" "Enough, we'll be here all night."

Eric had brought out the big brown envelope they used at the university for Campus Mail. He helped her pack the photographs in them; she had agreed to take them and sort through them and send him his portion. And Mama and Poppa's wedding picture, he would have a copy made for her. The packets of letters—he would keep the ones he sent from overseas, those would go to Sidney; she could take the rest. Except for Poppa's letter from King George commending him for his service in the Great War. That and Poppa's pin, and the box of Poppa's mementos, the belt buckle that belonged to Uncle Joe, Poppa's cufflinks and tie pins, those Eric would keep. And Mama's collection of scarves, and all Mama's jewelry, those would go to her.

"Halfies-akeys on the knick-knacks Mama saved after she packed up and moved to Florida?"

"No. I've got enough to get rid of as it is. I still haven't finished going through *Dorrie's* stuff."

"Don't you want to look through them first?"

"No and double no, I'm ready to *pay* you to take them off my hands. Don't worry, nothing will happen, I'll send the whole kit and kaboodle First Class Insured with special handling. You *can't* shlep anything on the plane."

"The cameo," she reminded him.

He snapped his fingers and hurried back to the master bedroom. She heard him opening dresser drawers. She would take the cameo with her back to Palatine. And Mama's wedding band. She had put it on next to her own, back at the Home.

"Here we are."

She had not heard him come back into the room. He handed her the tiny white box. "MIRIAM" Dorrie had written across the top in her big, flowing characters.

She opened it.

The cameo was wrapped in pink tissue paper. "Want to see it?" she asked him, unwrapping it. She lay the brooch in the palm of her hand and held it out to him. Eric leaned down, squinting. "Onyx?" "Her head is onyx, it's carved on sardonyx, I think they're both in the chalcedony family. Lovely, isn't she?" She traced the raised head and neck and shoulders of the young woman with her thumb. The abundance of hair, the swirls of rich hair. The soft folds of her gown. Her profile, so tender, so young. "Why'd you leave it with Dorrie?" he asked, and took it from her and began wrapping it up again in the tissue paper. "Didn't Dorrie ever tell you?" He shook his head. He was about to put it back into the box. "I don't need the box." She took it from him. "You know that it was Bubby's? From her mother?" He rubbed at a temple. "I guess I remember that." "That it's to be passed down through the first granddaughter born in each new generation?" "Okay, I know," Eric said, impatiently, "and that's why I asked you why you left it here with Dorrie." "After Mama . . . after Mama got sick, that first time I came here after Mama went into the Home, Dorrie told me to take it back with me. But I said to wait." "Wait? Wait for *what?*" Eric's lips were trembling; there was hurt in his eyes, and accusation. "Forgive me, I didn't mean—" She lay her head on his chest. "I told Dorrie I had this feeling I shouldn't take it until . . . until I earned it." She was sobbing now, sobbing and choking, and Eric put his arm around her and patted her back, patted and patted her back while she wept and wept.

"Listen, Mims, Mama *had* to have family around her. After Poppa died, she couldn't stand the loneliness. She had no other life, you know. If you and Hugh'd had Carolyn before we had Sid, maybe she'd have been with *you* all these years, she had that thing about the first-born grandchild, lots of women do."

She shook her head. She couldn't speak.

"Being a grandmother gave her a whole new life again, Mims. Mama lost her center when Sid grew up."

She nodded to say she knew that.

"Mama did love you, Mims, she didn't mean to abandon you, she did love you."

She hugged him and pulled away. "It's all right, Eric, thanks. Let me go wash my face, and then I'll get us some supper."

"Still sure it won't be too much of a hassle?"

"I'm sure. I *want* to cook; cooking's therapy for me. Go read your newspaper, and make that call you told me to remind you about. I'll make supper."

"Here, don't forget this." He held out the box Dorrie had kept the cameo in.

"No. I'll keep it in my wallet. In the coin purse."

Eric watched her put it away, and laughed. "Still the same old Hugh. He still fills up your coin purse with quarters, I see. Hugh and his quarters!"

"Hugh and his quarters!" she echoed, laughing. "It's an obsession with him."

"Hey, while we're on the subject, let me give you some cash for the return trip. How much—" He pulled her wallet out of her hands and counted the bills, frowning. "Twenty-five. Might not be enough."

"It's *more* than enough!" She pulled the wallet away, her face flaming.

"But Mims, you have to get from the airport back into Manhattan, that'll be twenty right *there*. And you'll need a bus ticket back to Palatine."

"I already *have* my bus ticket!" She put her wallet back into her handbag and slung it over her shoulder on her way to the bathroom. "Hugh gave me a whole *book* of round-trip tickets to the City!"

She turned on the faucet full force and began splashing her face with the icy cold water. In the beginning was Erico, when she came into the world he was already there, two albums stuffed with pictures of Erico the Great all by himself; and even in the photograph of Mama leaving the hospital with her newborn daughter, there was Erico the Great standing next to her. *"No, no, dolink,"* Bubby used to say. *"Jealousy kills, jealousy kills."*

While they were stacking the dishwasher he told her about Irene. He'd known her for years; she worked in the campus library. Divorced a long time ago, she'd raised two sons, one lives in Washington, the other gave her a lot of grief, he was out of her life now, and good riddance. Companionship. They both needed it. "We'll have to see where it goes. You don't seem too surprised." She replied that she *thought* she'd noticed traces of a woman's touch around the place. "That was the cleaning lady's, Mims. We don't get together over here much. That was Irene I called before, by the way." She pretended surprise. "I just didn't think this was the right time for you to meet her. Maybe if things develop you'll meet on your next trip here." She asked if Sidney knew. "Sid knows. He and Vic are happy for me." She said she was too. "Funny thing, when I first went out with her I felt guilty. Like I was cheating on Dorrie." Dorrie would understand, she said. "You're right, Dorrie *would*. She was that way . . . . Say, that was a *dandy* Gazpacho. And your omelet was great. Sorry you wouldn't have any of the rye bread, it's the bakery's finest." She reminded him it still was Pesach. "No *chametz* for eight days, remember?" "Even if it's *Jewish* rye?" "*Chametz is chametz*," she said, and laughed. And then the words she had just spoken played themselves back inside her head, and a clamor rose up in her chest. Eric had his back to her. His hand froze for an instant; then he pushed the dial for START, and a loud, merciful whirring filled the kitchen. He cleared his throat. At the door he asked her, without turning around, if she wanted to *shmoo-ess* for a while. She told him she thought she had better finish her packing first, that if they had to be out at the cemetery by nine-thirty they'd better make it an early night.

"Yitgadal v'yitkadash sh'mei raba," the rabbi prayed, the heavy rain beat down on the green canopy where the four of them stood, the Rumpelstilskin rabbi, and the kindly-faced Mr. Greenspan, and Eric, his face crumpling, "b'alma di v'ra khir'utei, v'yamlikh malkhutei," the three men in black, and this statue of stone in Caro's new navy blue spring coat, "b'hayeikhon u'vyomeikhon," the rain drumming down, and the black crepe ribbon pinned to Eric's lapel, she had unbuttoned Caro's coat lest the rabbi put the pin through the cloth of Caro's new coat, she had bunched the material under the collar so he would pin hers on her blouse, but there was no ribbon for her, only for Eric, did the rabbi think she was Eric's wife, had they forgotten to tell him that Mama had *two* children, or was it that she was only a female, only a daughter, that only the son wears the badge of mourning, only the son tears his clothes when the mother dies, "u-v'yayei d'khol beit yisrael," the coffin looked so small, all that there was of Mama was inside this little box of pine, had they been gentle with her when they bathed her, had they remembered this was the casing of one of God's creatures when they wrapped her in her shroud, mortal remains of Bubby's jewel, Bubby's Queen Esther, of Poppa's regal, laughing Gemini, of Fairy Godmother Mama with hair black as the raven's wing, skin white as driven snow, Mama's red, red lips, "ba-agala u-vi-z'man kariv, v'imru amen," plain, plain, unadorned, a plain wooden box, Mother Ferris's had been heaped high with flowers, the hooves of that November rain pounding on the roof of the canopy over Mother Ferris's grave, the huge cross of carnations, white and pink, on the flower-heaped coffin, the Ferris clan huddled under the canopy, bound on all sides by the zigzagging fence of the downrushing earthbrown rain, seventeen grandchildren mourning Mother Ferris's passing, Hugh, her Crown Prince, the apple-of-her-eye, her first-born, flanked by his three brothers and two sisters, Grandma Ferris's six children, one a nun, one brother widowed, a brother and a sister divorced, the other two Mrs. Ferrises, herself and Daniel's Geraldine there, and in the outer circle the grandchildren, some had come with their mates, their own children, seventeen children the five married Ferris children had produced, *"every faith under heaven including one freethinker in the younger generation,"* Hugh's brother Jack had remarked at the wake, *"You really got that ball rolling, Huey,"* Carolyn among her cousins, her head bowed, *"In the name of the Father,"* the priest began the closing prayer, and as some of them began making The Sign of the Cross, Caro raised her eyes to Miriam's, the blue haze of her look asking, asking, and the foreverness of the rain, of the drumbeat rain, falling in the Catholic cemetery there, falling in the Jewish cemetery here, "y'hei sh'mei raba m'varakh l'alam u-l'almei' almaya," seventeen grandchildren gathered at their Bubby

Ferris's graveside, and here there are none, there the whole Ferris clan assembled, and here not even as many mourners as there are fingers on one hand, *"The line stops here, eh, Mims? With you and me,"* the branch withered, barren, barren, the punishment of the barren womb, the radiant Carolyn born to them, then one after another the three miscarriages, the radiant Carolyn was to be their One and their All, "Yitbarakh v'yishtabakh v'yitpa'ar v'yitromam v'yitnasei," the small cry, was it Eric's, was it her own, "v'yit hadar v'yit'alah v-yit-halal sh'mei d'kudsha, brikh hu," the piercing of the flesh deep inside her, the first incision of the graver, the cutting, cutting across the core of her hidden under her navel, etching deep, deep, the sharp coldburning point riving, riveting, sundering, infixing, tearing, engraving—

"Miriam." There was a light *click!* and Mr. Greenspan's black umbrella opened, and he lifted the great black flower over their heads, and Eric cupped her elbow in his hand, and she stepped off the green tarpaulin onto the sodden grass . . . . *Hugh handed her the umbrella, she fumbled with the clasp, pushed hard, a broken wing half-spread and fluttered and crumpled, "Damn!" Hugh muttered, "did you have to force it?" Daniel opened her car door, then he leaned over and fetched the umbrella from the back seat and handed it to her, Geraldine came out of the other side and took shelter under the black umbrella Hugh had borrowed from the funeral home, Hugh slammed the car door shut, he took Geraldine by the one arm and Daniel, coming around the car, took Geraldine by the other, and the three of them made a dash for it through the driving rain, they had forgotten her, she pushed the clasp and it sailed up the pole, and a bright pink half-wing spread, then the ribs collapsed and it fell, rain was running in streamers from the brim of her hat . . . . The cold absinthe of November air, Hugh's look when the three of them stopped and turned around at the church door and saw her plight, his look of displeasure, the impatience of his stride back to where she was standing, the glisten of the rescuing shade drawing nearer, glossy black as a raven's wing*

Tock-tock, the windshield wipers were saying to themselves, Eric took his hand from the wheel and patted her arm, she murmured her thanks, *tock-tock, tock-tock,* the grey-blue skies of Miami were shedding tears, rainstripes were running down the glass, "We made good time, Mims, they'll be boarding less than half an hour after we get there," *tock-tock, tock-tock,* mother-of-pearl fingerings were running down the glass, "Getting back into the old routine, and the sooner the better for both of us," *tock-tock, tock-tock,* "Almost Goodbye Time again," the relief in his voice, *tock-tock, tock-tock,* "Try that candy I gave you? Here, in my right pocket, that's it, take a handful, closest thing to an orange you'll ever taste in the Candy Department," *tock-tock, tock-tock,* "Tell Hugh that Mohammed's coming to the mountain one of these years, that's a promise to Caro too, give her a hug from her old Unc, will you?" *tock-tock, tock-tock,* "Mims, I *wish* you'd take some extra cash, just in case. You and your pride, what's a brother *for*? Better not run into any panhandlers that won't take a couple of Hugh's quarters, then," *tock-tock, tock-tock,* "Don't grieve too much, Mims, we lost her a long time ago, you know. One thing we have to learn if we want to move on, we have to bury our dead, eh?" *tock-tock, tock-tock,* "We have to bury our dead."

She imagined her seat partner was taking note of how hungrily she was devouring the lunch he passed up in favor of a second Bloody Mary. Once, when there had been a slight vibration in the cabin, their sleeves of grey crepe and grey gabardine had grazed one another. They'd both pretended it hadn't happened; a murmured "Sorry" risked invading spheres of privacy they had drawn around their persons with the signings that strangers in close contact make. Ravenous, that was how she must appear to him to be. Starved. How was it that grief, that had taken away her appetite for the seven days of mourning after Poppa died, now left her so famished her hands were trembling as she served herself this midday feast of consommé, chicken cutlet, a potato pancake, green beans, Waldorf salad, carrot cake? Who was this child inside whom she was nourishing, for what was she shoring up but for yet another hurried moment with Caro, followed by yet another parting? *"A time to plant, and a time to pluck up that which is planted."*

The stewardess stopped to take her tray with all but the cake devoured. "Finished?" She nodded. Her seat mate took it from her and handed it up; then he settled back into the cloak of his ruminations. She turned her face to the window where white plumes floated and dissolved across a sunlit field of hyacinths in a dance, a pavane of whites and blues.

"I would have liked it," Hugh had said after a long silence. "I would have liked having a grandchild. But we can't live Caro's life. Only Caro can live Caro's life." "'The world doesn't need another unwanted child,'" she had echoed bitterly. "You know very well whose words those are that Caro was parroting. Why did you parrot them too?" Hugh had sighed. "What would you have me do, then? I also *know very well there will come a day when she will regret she never had children, and I pity her on that day, pity her with all my heart. But it isn't the kind of knowledge I can give her, it's the sort we have to discover for ourselves. When it's too late for a remedy.*" He had reminded her of the words in *Ecclesiastes*, "*For in much wisdom is much grief;/And he that increaseth knowledge increaseth sorrow.*" He had repeated, "*Only* Caro *can live Caro's life.*" "Caro's life?" she had echoed even more bitterly. "Gil Parker, who says he's done his duty by the human race, this is Gil Parker's *plan for Caro's life, you mean. To be the mother of his Greedybaby.*" "There's the difference between us, Miriam, maybe it's a religious difference, after all. Or maybe it's the difference between our vocations." "Vocations?" she'd asked. "Or is it avocations? *Not a bad choice, mine, acting. Parroting. That's what most people want, isn't it? They find a parrot to be a most pleasing companion.*"

"You wouldn't want us to have a child just to please our parents, would you?" Caro had asked her. "Or even to please humanity? There are many ways to make a contribution to humanity besides having a child. In fact, having a child is a modest gift compared to many others I can think of."

"*You were ours*," she had thought, but did not say. "*Gift and return gift, both. Seed and harvest.*"

Harvest. Caro had been born on the harvest feast-day, on Succoth. On the fifteenth of Tishri in the year 5713. But Caro did not know what Succoth was, Caro did not know that the month of October had another name, or that the fourth of October in 1952 was the fifteenth of Tishri in 5713 by that other calendar.

"*If not to please ourselves, or our parents, or Humanity, then to please whom?*" Caro had asked her. *Then to please whom?*

The soul, longing to be made flesh . . . she could almost feel the warmth and weight of the infant in her arms. Small ghost in that limbo where souls wait to be made incarnate by that primal desire. Caro did not have that desire? She could not believe it. Hugh had given it up. She could not give it up.

Words were shaping themselves in the hedges bordering the path her thoughts followed. The covenant between the generations: the promise of continuance upheld by honoring the sacred trust. Replenishment. Returning gift for gift. Requiting Love, requiting Life. The cherished in turn cherishing. The lessons of the mind and spirit and heart fully received only by passing them on. *"The Talmud teaches there are four classes governed by the laws of inheritance: those who inherit and bequeath; those who inherit and do not bequeath; those who bequeath and do not inherit; and those who neither inherit nor bequeath."*

"Your Great Uncle Eric," she would say to the child, drawing the covers over the small form, *"has the same deepfroggie voice and the same wobble-cheeks as your Great Zayda, yes. Great Zayda used to take off his glasses and huff and puff on them like this, with his underlip, the same way, and then polish them with a bit of his shirt-tail. When he took them off, you could see the little pods under his eyes. And even if he was laughing and slapping the table just like Great Uncle Eric does when he is happy, you knew that was where he carried his tears. I only saw them once, that was the night before Great Uncle Eric went into the army, and your Great Zayda put down his knife and fork and lifted both hands up to his face and covered it like this, and his shoulders were quivering, and he kept making a strangled little sound, like the one you make when something you eat gets caught in your pipe part-way down, and your Great Bubby Goldman jumped up and ran over to him and put her arms around his head. And you know that little tuft right on top of your Great Uncle Eric's head that stands straight up in surprise? Your Great Bubby Goldman patted it and patted it 'Jolliper,' she said. 'I promise you he will come back, Jolliper.' Jolliper was her love name for your Great Zayda, he called her Gemini. They had many love names, but those were their favorites. And when he took his hands away, his face was all pink and wet with tears. He couldn't see through his glasses, he took them off and* got up to go wash them, and the little pods were all flattened out." "My Great Zayda popped them?" the child would ask her gravely.

The FASTEN SAFETY BELTS sign flashed on, the shushing sound was whistling through the cabin, the microphone was clucking, a male voice muzzled in metal announced they were landing, a piston of pain slid up and down the burning rod inside her right ear, far, far down the tunnel she could hear the little melody Bubby Pinsky hummed when she made a turban of towels over Mimsele's head and lifted Mimsele up on the chair over the stove to hold her aching ear over the boiling magic get-well brew, a little tune without words, she was humming it now to the child looking up at her with great round eyes bright blue as the blue of delphiniums in the shadowing dusk of her longing, under the roaring thunder and the muffled keening of the bagpipes she could hear Bubby humming her melody, she could see Bubby's eyebrows climbing her forehead, eyebrows pointy as lancet arches, she could see the little scallops Bubby's index finger was drawing on the air, marking the tempo of her tune, as the silver mock-eagle who bore her on its wings screamed down the airways to the landing field.

She had taken off Caro's coat and folded it. She lay it atop her suitcase on the back seat of the cab. She would have almost half an hour to visit Caro in her office before she would have to leave to catch the five o'clock bus. Caro would want to walk with her to Port Authority, but she would not let her. She would be firm this time, Caro would have to learn that her mother was refusing the fate of the woman buried that morning, that she refused to become the daughter of her grown daughter. It would have to be enough for Caro's own lifetime, mothering her own two children, her Greedybaby and the ghost-child waiting patiently, patiently to be welcomed into the world.

She closed her eyes. *"You see,"* she would say to the child riding at her side, *"for your Great Bubby Goldman, Family was All, first the family you grew up in, and then the family you made when you married and had children of your own, you grew under the one roof and then you grew your children under the other, and it was love that connected the roofs and that made them into one roof over your head, like the roofs of the succahs the Israelites built when they wandered for forty years in the desert, if you looked down from high above you would see the whole encampment in the desert, how one roof was joined to the next, fragile booths they were, with roofs of foliage laid atop the wooden slats, spread loosely so that when you looked up you could see the stars through the green boughs, and you would remember the Presence of the Guardian guiding you on your way to freedom. Passover,"* she would say to the child, *"marks the miracle that set us free from bondage, and Succoth, your mother's birthday, marks our journey after we were set free."*

She opened her eyes. They were only a few blocks from Caro's building. Spring flowers were set out in front of the shop at the corner up ahead. As the cab rumbled to a stop, she rolled down her window and leaned out to look at the feast of color the flowers made, the white and rose and bright purple of the cyclamens, the pinks and reds of the geraniums, the pinks and deep reds of the begonias, showy oleanders red and white, and the pink hibiscus, and the sweet williams white and pink and purple and rose, and the blue delphiniums, blue as the eyes of the grandchild she was never to have, never to have, and the tulips butter yellow and red, the *red* red of Mama's lips. She drank the wine of the April air, the blend of the perfume of flowers with exhaust fumes, and motes of grit were dancing in the dazzle of the tear-speckled sunlight where her eyes gathered a bouquet to bring to her mother, to lay in her mother's arms.

"I'll walk from here," she said. The driver glanced sharply into the rear-view mirror and then he nodded. She opened her bag and pulled out her wallet, trying to steady her hands, but she could not. She passed the bills for her fare and the tip up to him, and gathered her belongings and Caro's coat, and scrambled out, hurrying between the cars up to the sidewalk.

Spring, it was spring, spring had come and her mother was gone, and she was coming into her own harvest-time, and there would be no one after her to remember them all, to remember the ancestors. Gone, they all were gone into herself, and they would die a second and final death with her own death, and there would be no one to mourn them.

"Everybody in the whole world is family," Mr. Becker had said gently, after that long silence, "one big, quarreling family, I don't deny it, but we're all related, all the children are our grandchildren, look at it that way."

The words had come and gone, her mouth waa a desert dry and barren of words. She stood at the edge of the curb looking up at Caro's building, in front of her and in back of her the traffic was hurrying by, hurrying by.
"Guard our coming/and our going, now toward waking, now toward sleep."
Caro's building of stone. Solid walls of stone, a solid roof, impervious and apart: a stronghold, a fortress. "We dwell in fragile, temporary shelters." Spring, it was spring of the year of 1985 of the Common Era, it was the 54th year of her earth-wanderings, she was in the autumn of her life. It was Passover in the year 5745, at the seder they had commemorated the Exodus, the miracles blazing the trail of their departure from the land where they had been enslaved, commemorated the moment of their taking leave, the moment of liberation. Autumn, it was Succoth in her own years, the time for the gathering of the harvest, at the Feast of Ingathering they would commemorate the years of wandering in the desert. Succoth, and their prayers for rain had been answered, the rains had come. And in the rains she had buried the last of her dead, and now she was orphaned. There in Miami, under a green canopy, her mother had left her orphaned. And here in Manhattan, shut up in her fortress of stone, Caro had left her without issue. And orphaned and without issue she must recommence her wanderings, she must retrace her steps, reading her life from right to left, as Mr. Becker his moon, reading by the light of the stars shining through the green boughs, by the Novemberlight, by the afterglow of love faded from the eyes of the beloved, by the bitter beauty of that afterglow at the hour of dusk.

She would not go up to see Caro. It was too late. She could return Caro's coat another time.

She looked at her watch. Ten after four, and it was a good twenty-minute walk to Port Authority from here. Better to wear Caro's coat than to lug it on her arm all that way. She set her suitcase down on the sidewalk and pulled the coat on over her right shoulder, then, as Caro had so often cautioned her to do, pulled it over the left, keeping the shoulder strap of her handbag on the inside, out of sight, out of temptation. She picked up her suitcase and began walking, quickening her steps to keep pace with the early rush hour crowd heading the same way.

Twenty-five to five. She had made excellent time. She passed the candy and newspaper stand and headed for the stairs, taking off Caro's coat as she walked. She stopped to fold the coat over her arm.
"Got a dollar, lady?"
The voice was throaty; the face of its owner loomed out of nowhere so close to her own that the lips speaking the question might have brushed hers. Acorn eyes passed over her eyes, traced a circle around them, came to rest on the bridge of her nose.
Pink cross-hatches in the whites of the eyes, a pockmark near the tip of the nose, the mouth half-open, red-brown hair pulled up into a topknot, staring acorn eyes looking out from a mask of waste and want at the space between her own: a child of no more than fifteen. A waif.
"Got a dollar? I'm hungry."
"Yes, yes, of course," she mumbled. She reached inside the coat sleeve, opened her bag, took out her wallet. "Here, I don't have any bills, but you're welcome to my change, there must be seven, eight quarters in here." She shielded the pink tissue-wrapped packet with her thumb and extended the open coin purse, meaning for the girl to take the coins. The whey-colored hand moved, stopped still, turned over, the palm making a cup.
She flipped the change purse over to pour Hugh's quarters into the outstretched palm. Her thumb slipped from its hold; she heard the singing notes of the coins and the little thud of the packet striking the floor.
In an instant she and the girl were crouching, heads close together, picking up the spillage. The child's fingers closed quickly over the scattered coins.
"Here." Miriam handed over the two quarters she had retrieved.

The girl was straightening herself.

"Wait!" A hoof was pressing down, down, down on her chest; she caught her heel in the hem of Caro's coat and heard the ripping of the lining as she scrambled to her feet and reached out her arm, closing her hand over the child's wrist. "Wait, *please,*" she implored. The anguish was choking her. *"Please."* The words were trapped under a bar of bone. "Tissue—" she squeaked, "tissue ... paper ...."

The girl shook off her hand. Glistening brown eyes stared into hers, seeking her, seeking her out.

In that eternity, the child opened her hand. And Miriam, tears running down her face, took back her cameo.

1990S

After Many Days, a story of coming-of-age

You were already on your way here when the travel advisory was issued on the seven o'clock news. The weather bureau people repeated what we've been hearing all day, that the biggest snowstorm of the season is heading toward the East coast tonight. So you were following its path. "Take care," I would have said to you if the circumstances were ordinary. It's just as well they aren't, so that I didn't say this. Half a lifetime in academe has taught me that when the young turn to you for guidance, they're quick to translate any counsel of prudence into rejection. Youth has that keenness. And that pride.

I recognized you immediately, yes. The voice can brave the passage of the years. The years, those "great black oxen" treading the world—do you remember the last lines in Yeats's *The Countess Cathleen*? But I knew you also by the first words you spoke to me. *I've got to have some answers*, you said. *I'm in a dark place*. Forgive me for my corrective to your words. It was experience, that imperialist, that prompted me to reply, "You mean you're at a critical point in your life. A *turning* point." I have to admit that your swift rejoinder was right on the mark—*They're the same thing, remember*? Yes, I remember.

War nerves, you comment, and I hear the old self-mockery in your words. *War hysteria*. It's contagious, I tell you. At least half the country is drunk on the world news. To give you an example very close to home, my husband's favorite nurse was just leaving his room when I came in this morning. She called out to me, "*Four more days*, the doctor says! We'll be letting you take him home on Tuesday!" "Hear that?" I asked him. For an answer, he pointed to the date on the newspaper I'd just handed him. "It's *also* four more days to the deadline," he said. "Four more days before all hell is unleashed."

January 11, 1991. Four more days for Saddam Hussein to comply with the terms of U.N. Resolution 678, or—Yes, it's the second paragraph that authorizes the use of "all necessary means" to evict the Iraqi invaders from Kuwait. What do I think of the Congressional debates? It seems to me it's been half a century since those chambers resounded with such eloquence.

Almost midnight. Just twelve hours ago in Vilnius, Lithuania, Soviet army troops used tanks and live ammunition to storm the Lithuanian press center and a building occupied by the civilian militia. Seven people were injured. One was a civilian guard. He was shot in the face by an army colonel who sprayed the press building with machine-gun fire in his rage at having been doused by a fire hose. *It's written that there's nothing new under the sun*, you remind me. Youth instructing Age in lessons learned by head, lessons the heart resists still, even at this hour of our reunion.

I've got to have some answers, you tell me. But you know that I've reached the age that accepts there are no answers. *Even so, there are guidelines*, you argue. *There are signs*. You're right. You've put me in mind of something I read in the *Foxfire* books. The Old Ones in the Appalachian Mountains of North Georgia say that folks living there used to plant by the signs of the moon, and that some still swear by it. Shall we go outside and see what we can read in the midnight sky? *That's* another *people's set of guidelines*, you protest. *I want to talk about ours.*

I am coming to that. Have you noticed the year 1991 is a palindromic number, that it reads the same backward or forward? The last one was 1881, the next will be 2002, and after that not until 2112. But we're talking about the *civil* calendar here. According to *our* calendar—and by the way, it's lunar as well as solar, and we read the moon too, from right to left—our next palindromic-numbered year will be 5775. If I'm still walking above ground then, I'll be 85, older than Moses when he had that conversation with Pharaoh—

You're wandering, you say. And we both laugh, because in this, at least, I'd be following our old way. But I'm not wandering, as you'll soon see. By the way again, I don't want you thinking that wandering's a story exclusively ours. Wandering is very much a part of the rite of passage for Pit River Indian males when they're at the critical point known as coming-of-age. In his INDIAN TALES, Jaime de Angulo tells us that it was Robert Spring, a Pit River Indian, who first made him understand about the *dinihowi*. The Old Ones say that a young man will never amount to anything unless he goes out and catches a *dinihowi*. There comes a time, he told de Angulo, "when a young fellow starts to feel uneasy, kind of sad, kind of worried, that's just about the time he's getting to be a man grown up." And that's the time he starts wandering. People say to one another, "Leave him alone, he's wandering." That's when he goes to the hills. He doesn't come home at night. "You get scared," Robert Spring said, "you cry; two, three days you go hungry. Sometime your people get worried, come after you, but you throw rocks at them." You tell them to go away and leave you alone. You get hungry, dizzy, you're afraid of grizzly bears. Then it can happen that you fall asleep and a wolf comes, or a blue jay, or maybe a fly gets into your ear. That's your *dinihowi*, your animal protector from whom you get Power.

What's the point of the story for us? For now, let's say that when you're on a vision quest, you're actively waiting for a sign. That's an oxymoron, I know. While I sat at my desk this evening waiting for you, I happened to pick up my Book of Days of the Literary Year. I read that on January 11, 1842, William James was born in New York City. And that on January 11, 1928, Thomas Hardy died at his home near Dorchester, at the Biblical age of eighty-seven. Did you know that the heart of Thomas Hardy was buried in the grave of his first wife in Dorset? And that his ashes were inhumed next to the ashes of Charles Dickens in Westminster Abbey? You ask what our guidelines say about cremation, dismemberment. My husband and I had occasion to look into these questions before he went to the hospital; we'd been told his chances weren't good. We took it as a Sign that just about then a band of fellow Jews who live in this community asked us to join them in having a portion of the town cemetery set aside as Jewish burial ground. We've lived here so many years, where else? he asked. His parents are buried in Florida, and mine—as you well know—in Chicago, the one in a Jewish and the other in a Catholic cemetery. So we made arrangements, as they say. Where were we?

Wandering again, you answer. *Looking for a sign.* You ask if I think there's going to be another Vietnam, you ask what I think will happen. I don't know, I'm not a prophet, but God forbid we'll have another Vietnam. By my age, one ought to have learned that all wars are alike in too many tragic ways and that every war is different, *also* in too many tragic ways. You know better than I it's the Korean War, not the Vietnam War, that's been haunting me since the second of August last summer. The *forgotten war*, they call it, you remind me. You needn't; I know all too well that you were drafted forty years ago this coming summer. Our guidelines say forty is a significant number for an anniversary, keep that in mind.

I fell into a kind of drowse while I was waiting for you. One of those half-sleeps that tempt the soul to go wandering. The biblical "dream that was not a dream." That's when Harriet made her reappearance. Tall, big-boned, with the redhead's freckled pallor, remember? Crisp auburn curls in a "poodle cut." Mild blue eyes bracketed by those flesh-colored glasses frames. A wide-winged nose. A shapely mouth, a bit on the small side; it was always lipsticked poppy red. I saw Harriet plain only once before since I left the Midwest; and that was on the April morning I received a letter with the news of the accident that took her life. The letter said she'd been killed instantly. Elaine, who had been driving, lived another several days. "Mercifully, she didn't regain consciousness," my correspondent wrote. "She'd never have forgiven herself."

Harriet. Harriet. *Beware, Maureen. Maturity is almost upon you.*

The name on our mailbox? I changed my given name to Miriam forty years ago this coming summer. And my maiden name, Gold, to my husband's, when I married. In 1953. Meet Miriam Feldman, alias Maureen Gold. Alias—

Matchoor-it-tee, Harriet pronounced it that night. Like Miss Reardon in Paul Zindel's play, our Harriet drank a little. And smoked like the proverbial chimney times ten, as you say. *Matchoor-it-tee*. And a ray of ruby-red floated on an eddy of the cigarette smoke that was her emblem.

Maturity. Rites of passage. Coming-of-age. Be patient. Remembering is harder work, and often more painful, than Youth imagines.

In that "dream that was not a dream," Harriet was wearing the grey pinstripe suit she had on the September day in 1950 we first met her, the day she interviewed us for the part-time job in the secretarial pool of the university's Institute of Social Research. Some months later, when Harriet and I were a little pie-eyed, we argued about which of the two of us was more skittish during that interview. "*You* were, by *far*," I insisted. "And I figured my name was what perturbed you. Maureen Gold. It baffles a lot of people. A name with a Joycean lilt to it, don't you think?" Then understanding dawned in her eyes, and she gave me a look of reproach. That's when she took off her own mask. By quoting Shakespeare's "There's no art/To find the mind's construction in the face." "Your name," she said, "didn't ring any bells. If I seemed agitated, it was because I felt a little in awe of you. Because the Student Employment Office told me you already *had* one part-time job." I went up like a match when I heard that. I accused her of having hired me out of charity, because this was a choice job and she must have had any number of applicants. "Charity had nothing to do with it," she protested. Then she said, "Proud people wear blinders, Maureen. It's true that some others applied. But I hired you only because you were the most qualified. If you *must* know what was on my mind during that interview, it was admiration. You have the courage to do what a lot of us only daydream about doing. Until it's too late."

In animal or human form, your protector *dinihowi* comes to you when you're wandering, and shows you the way. Harriet showed me the power imagination has for saving lives. I know for certain she never heard of The Many Worlds Interpretation of Quantum Mechanics. But she knew that we have alternate lives. "There are all these Harriets," she said to me. "Whenever I'm in a dark place, I give a Roland for an Oliver." She told me that she was on especially familiar terms with one of her Olivers. Harriet Two, she called her. "Now that I've told you my secret, it's *your* turn. An I for an I." That's when she made the acquaintance of Maury Golden, whose destiny to be a draftee in the Korean War was a possibility I mentioned the last night she and I were alone together.

You know very well that if there's war four days from now, it won't be the first war in history in which U.N. troops acted as police to fight an aggressor nation, that the *Korean* war was. "The Korean *Conflict*," they called it then. Or "Truman's War," remember? Have I ever talked about it with my students? Yes. What have I told them? The facts. That it lasted three years and one month. That on June 25, 1950, troops of Communist-ruled North Korea attacked South Korea, that their goal was to unify the country by force, that a truce was declared on July 27, 1953, that both sides agreed to an international conference to resolve the issues. And then I reminded them that right now there are hundreds of thousands of Korean troops on both sides of the demilitarized zone dividing the peninsula, and that among those massed south of it are more than thirty thousand from the U.S. Flashpoints wherever you look, as you say.

NO BLOOD FOR OIL! the demonstrators chant. One of our Senators said today that Kuwait's fortifications are reminiscent of those in The Great War. A member of the House spoke of the lessons of history taught us by World War II; many spoke of the Vietnam War, and many of the carnage every war is. But not one of them recalled that the Korean War was one of the bloodiest wars in history. I heard one of the members of the House say today that it's a "fig leaf" to call the U.N. coalition forces in the Persian Gulf a "multinational force." The dead numbered more than four million Koreans, military and civilians, nearly one million Chinese, and about another 50,000 of the 350,000 from the U.S.

Yes, we've been promised a bloodier war still, "the mother of all battles." You remind me of the threats: That the desert will become a killing field. That half of Israel will be burned. My husband told me that early this morning he'd been paid a visit from a kind young man wearing *peyes* and a *shtreimel*, who asked if he's Jewish. A

Feldman is a Jew, my husband laughed, and when the young man asked how he could help, he laughed again and said there's not much help for coming of age. His visitor then said something about reading the coming-of-age story of Israel tomorrow. To change the subject, my husband asked him if he thinks there will be war in the Gulf. The answer was yes. Will there be deliverance? my husband asked, and again the answer was Yes. How soon? Purim, was the answer. Saddam Hussein is Haman, the young man explained, so it would be Purim. If you've got to have some answers, maybe you should look up this fellow and ask about the story he has to tell, instead of coming to me.

As in reading any story, so in life: the first view is often oblique. In ours, that was also the *literal* truth, remember? Harriet's typewriter was on a side table against the wall, at a right angle to the front desk in the secretarial pool. When I came in, she was at work transcribing dictation. Her trademark king-size cigarette was burning in the ashtray between the Dictaphone machine and the telephone, which rang just at that moment. She motioned for me to take the chair alongside her desk, and picked up the receiver. It was a short business call. After she hung up, she said I must be the person Student Employment told her they'd be sending over. "You're Maureen...."

"Maureen Gold."

I knew nothing of this at the time, of course, but The Many Worlds Interpretation of Quantum Mechanics says that every time we make a choice, the universe splits into different branches of reality, each with a different edition of our life-story. In fact, over the years a few of my colleagues have confided to me that they have some sense of living parallel lives, and that this sense of multiple selfhood may be what attracted them to the study of anthropology in the first place. I've read interviews with people in the theatre who say much the same thing. And writers. But someone in any walk of life might apprehend this. Did you know that when Geraldine Ferraro was on the campaign trail, she said that she imagined one variant of herself as a little old Southern gentleman from Texas? "Perhaps," Proust wrote, "there are other worlds more real than the waking world." This other world comes to life in my memory just as Harriet hangs up the phone:

"You must be the person Student Employment told me they'd be sending over. You're Maury . . . ."

"Maury Golden."

Some months later, when both of us were pie-eyed, Harriet and I got into a scrimmage about which of the two of us was more wary during that Opening Scene. "I had the feeling I was the first half-breed you ever met," I accused her. She stared at me, perplexed. Then understanding dawned in her eyes. "How many people know the name Golden is Irish?" she countered. "I only learned that from you tonight." She said people with overactive imaginations aren't the best mind readers, and then she quoted Shakespeare's "There's no art/To find the mind's construction in the face." She said she'd been a little in awe of me because Student Employment told her I already was holding down one part-time job. That got my Irish up; I said she must have hired me out of charity, then. "Charity had nothing to do with it," she protested. And then: "Proud people wear blinders, Maury. If you must know what I was feeling, it was admiration. Because you have the courage to do what a lot of us only daydream about doing. Until it's too late."

She asked if Student Employment had said what my duties would be.

When I replied that they'd told me she needed someone to operate the ditto and mimeograph machines and help her do some proofreading, she said, "I notice you're an English major. Did they tell you I specifically asked for someone majoring in English?" I said they had, and I'd wondered about that.

"This is off the record, Maury, but I need you to help me do some editing, too. There are papers coming in here that I have to . . . rework somewhat, before I parcel them out for final typing. I couldn't be explicit about that in the job description." I understand, I said, and it would be my pleasure.

She showed me the back room where they kept the copying machines, and promised to have a desk moved in there for me by the first of the week. That made it sound official, but I had to be sure. I asked how soon she could let me know.

"If you're hired? You are. You'll be paid by the hour, did they tell you?"

"By the hour, right. And they said a minimum of ten hours a week."

"Right. Anything beyond that will depend on my work load. It varies during the semester. I know yours will, too. Things could get hectic for both of us around exam time, but we'll manage."

She was hovering in the doorway. I sensed she was having as much trouble with closure as I was, and I mumbled something about having a class the next hour. We danced an awkward After You, Alphonse. I lost, and she asked my back which class this was. Bird's Greek and Roman Philosophy, I told her. "The Number One course—" she began.

Just then, the phone rang and the door opened—Mary Ellen and Lois were coming back from their coffee break. There were three typists on Harriet's staff that year. Rita was on sick leave that day. She was older than the other two; she still lived with her parents. A devout Christian, she always wore a big gold cross on a chain around her neck. Lois used to say she was earning her PHT degree. That meant Putting Hubby Through, remember? Her husband was a graduate student in Engineering. Mary Ellen was seven months' pregnant when I graduated in June of '51. I heard later that she had a baby boy. Born at the right time to come of draft age during the Vietnam War.

"The Number One course at this College. I'd have signed up for it if I'd had your courage." Some weeks after I began working there, Harriet told me that's how she'd intended to finish her sentence. "That's a major symptom of malignant maturity, Maury. Regret for the road-not-taken."

I told her I'd learned in Bird's class what Heraclitus had to say about this, that Character is Fate. "If free choice is an illusion, then there's only one road. Tell you what, Harriet. Up to then I used to resent hearing older people's regrets. I thought either they were preaching a sermon or making alibis. Then I caught *myself* regretting that I hadn't learned Character is Fate in time to get back at my parents during their divorce wars."

"Maybe the most unforgiving looks are close-ups."

"Maybe. But that was my moment of truth. There I was, looking back with regret myself."

"Beware, Maury. Maturity is almost upon you."

Matchoor-it-tee. A ray of cardinal red floated on an eddy of her cigarette smoke. Hiccupping. Silence. Then: "It's a coat of mail. I once had a turtle for a pet. A captive turtlet has to grow a strong shell if it wants to survive to adulthood. Ever notice how strong an adult turtle shell is? That's what protects you from rough treatment by the young of the species."

I could set my own hours. The office closed at 4:30, and I used to put in a couple of hours of work on late Friday afternoons. Harriet got into the habit of bringing coffee to me from the take-out counter in the basement lounge before she left for the day. She'd put the carton down on the sorting table with that shy chipmunk smile of hers, and linger. Hovering in the doorway, remember? The amber glintings of the fading light in her auburn curls and in the frames of her glasses. The wistfulness in her eyes, so pale blue they were almost white.

The first epiphany happened on the last day of classes before Christmas vacation. Forty years ago, Christmas was on a Monday. On the 22nd, there was an office party in the basement lounge for everybody who worked in the building. It was the last day of classes before the holiday break, and I had a French Lit class that met at two. In those days, the penalty for an unexcused absence from the last class before or the first class after a vacation was a failing grade. So there was a queue of suitcases along the wall. Our prof handed out song sheets with the verses of Christmas folk songs, and led us in a round of some full-bodied rustic caroling. I was in a festive mood when I joined the party in the lounge.

The tables had been pushed together in the middle of the room and covered with holiday paper tablecloths. There were big platters of fancy sandwiches and Christmas cookies and fruit cake, and punch bowls with eggnog and a spiked glögg we called Kickapoo Joy Juice. Harriet was presiding over the one with the glögg. When I came in, she asked someone to take over her duties so she could squire me around and introduce me to the people whose work I'd been editing. Names corporealized. Remember Beavers? It must have been the cup of glögg I emptied. His four front teeth all looked a shade on the orange side and seemed to be curved as incisors. But you don't have to be pie-eyed to notice that some people's names happen to personify their idiosyncrasies.

Elaine had left for Kansas earlier in the day to spend the holidays with her sister, so that epiphany was postponed. After the round of presentations, I went into a huddle with Harriet and the Mary Ellen-Lois-Rita trio. A phonograph playing Christmas carols raised its muffled voice between breakers of caws and guffaws. When someone began a singalong with *Adeste Fideles* and my co-workers joined in, I wished Happy Holidays all around and went looking for my jacket. "Wait!" Harriet called. "I'm coming with you!"

There was no snow on the ground that raw, windy day. The whiteness was all in the sky, like melting tallow. The light was dark yellow as old gold.

"Where are you going, Maury?"

The rust-colored babushka she was tying under her chin with mittened fingers aged the heart-shaped eager face inside. The wind was at her back, and it came up and flung the hem of her coat toward me. I felt her loneliness reach out and ask me to grant her a favor as yet unnamed.

I looked away, at the Broadwalk. Not a soul to be seen through the bare branches of the elms. I thought with a kind of exultation that by tomorrow almost all the students would be gone, the campus would belong to us, to the foreign students, ones who didn't have a family to go home to. To the ones who were free. In my senior year, my other part-time job was in the library. I used to look forward to closing time, to clearing the stragglers out of the stacks and then turning off the lights. For those few minutes, the building and all its treasures were mine.

I said I guessed I'd be going back to my room.

"What are your vacation plans? Besides cramming for Finals, I mean."

I guessed I'd be spending some part of the vacation in Chicago, I said.

"Next week?"

"Probably."

"Why don't you come over for a while? You look sort of cold. And lost—" She laughed in that embarrassed way of hers, and reached over to button the top button of my jacket.

Her car was in the lot next to the Gym. She'd bought a small house last year in Briarwood, she told me. I'd heard of Briarwood, a new subdivision a few miles east of campus. "Eat-in kitchen, one bedroom, one bath. Small, but at least it's all mine. My mother died about a year and a half ago. She'd been a widow for a long time, and I'm an only child. So I came into a little money."

We stopped at a Piggly Wiggly to pick up some items for a special supper she said she felt inspired to cook. "Lately, Elaine and I have been taking turns having the other one over for supper once a week. She's a meat-and-potatoes type and I'm the adventurous type. But the real fun of it is sharing."

She asked me to come inside and do the honors with the shopping cart. Following her up and down the aisles, I had *déjà vu*. My worst moment came at the check-out counter. There I was, helpmate of the older woman wearing the babushka again. I'm an only child too. The tang riding on the bitterly cold air outside was sharp and medicinal. Like the creeping thyme that grows over rocks and waste places in the countryside here.

"Careful, there's a step up," she warned me at the threshold. She apologized for going in ahead of me. "Have to shed some light," she laughed. She switched on a table lamp next to a wine-red couch along the far wall, and turned and held out her arms for the groceries. "Here, let me take those. Make yourself at home, let me fix us a quick drink. I'll show you the rest of my domain later, after I do a quick spot-check. Didn't know I'd be bringing company home."

Later, she told me the couch had been her mother's. In front of it was a kidney-shaped coffee table with a miniature Christmas tree on one end and a stack of art books on the other. A book lay in the wide tray of the floor lamp next to the wing chair, M. D. Herter Norton's TRANSLATIONS FROM THE POETRY OF RAINER MARIA RILKE; it was still in its dust jacket. I was about to pick it up when Harriet reappeared in the doorway to ask what my pleasure was. She had put on fresh lipstick and fluffed up her hair. I followed her into the kitchen. She poured bourbon on the rocks for me,

Scotch on the rocks for herself. When we said Cheers, I caught a whiff of toothpaste mint mixed with smoker's breath and rose water. She asked if I wanted a Cook's tour, or should the cook get moving on the curry first. Either way would be fine, I said. She told me to feel free to do my own sight-seeing while she put on the rice.

I went back into the living room and took the hassock in front of the two rows of bookshelves under the picture window. At first, all I noticed was that she was a serious reader, because the books were arranged by subject and not by size. Then I recognized a number of the titles that had been adopted as texts for popular undergraduate courses, and I realized what it was Harriet was trying to do.

The meal was a feast. I still can taste the seasoned lamb, and the blend of chutney and peanuts and coconut. Elaine gave her the Rilke for a Christmas present, she told me during dinner. "Upon request." Later that evening, she asked me to read one of the poems aloud to her. "Which one?" I asked, and she said, "You choose." I knew very little about Rilke's poetry at the time, but I was too proud to admit this. After I leafed through the volume, I turned back to the first poem, "Das ist mein Streit." The English was on the right side, the German on the left. I read it aloud, first in my native language, then in my German Jewish parent's.

"You read beautifully."

"He *writes* beautifully."

"I recognized him as a kindred soul when I read somewhere that he believed we carry our death within ourselves."

"What about accidental death?" I challenged.

She took a long, meditative puff on her cigarette. "We carry around whatever it is that makes us vulnerable to it, so in that sense, no death is accidental. No *life* is, either, I'm beginning to think. I was married once, Maury."

I asked her what he was like, and she said he was a Scandinavian version of Tennessee Williams's Stan Kowalski. "Every Friday night, he'd have his buddies over for beer and poker. It lasted just over a year. I didn't keep his name. The year's been a little more difficult to edit out."

I asked her how it had happened, and she said it was because she hadn't known there was anything else. "I was born in a little town on the prairie. My mother was a cold woman. Puritanical, unresponsive. My father had more feeling, but he didn't know how to express it. After I graduated from high school, I took an office job. Along came my streetcar named Desire, and I thought I saw my chance to escape. An I for an I, now it's *your* turn." For an answer, I asked if her parents were of the same religion.

"My father was brought up Episcopalian. But ever since I can remember, the three of us went to the Methodist Church on Sundays. He wanted to keep the peace." She looked at me for a long moment. "It isn't the end of the world, Maury, being the child of a mixed marriage."

"Try Judaism and Catholicism."

She stubbed out her cigarette and lit another. "Which way did they decide to bring you up?"

"They never *did* decide. After the war between them broke out, they left the choice to me."

Her eyes were blue with compassion. "Will you be seeing them next week?"

I shrugged. "I'll probably spend a couple of days with one and then a couple of days with the other. They live across the city from one another now. That fits. Did you know there are only two kinds of people in the world, the ones who live on the North Side of Chicago, and the ones who live on the South Side?"

"You'll forgive them one day, Maury. By the time you reach my age, you'll realize none of us can help much what we do. What we are."

"'By the time you reach my age.' What's it like, being your age?"

She exhaled. A dove-colored feather floated toward me. "If you want to know, it's hell. You feel everything, and you feel that Everything intensely. No day is like the one before. And you can't take hold anywhere."

"That's what it's like on *this* side, too. It's the same. You forgot."

"I haven't forgotten, and it's *not* the same. One thing about youth, it has an exhilaration that carries over from mood to mood. Even despair has a curious kind of joy. Because youth glories in itself. It glories in the envy of those who've lost it."

"So that's my consolation? That older people envy me?"

"Jack be nimble, Jack be quick, there's just no substitute for a college education, is there."

"I'm sorry, Harriet."

"Don't give it another thought." She put out her cigarette and looked at her watch. "Almost one a.m.! No point in asking again if you'd like to stay over, I suppose. I thought so. Now, where did I put my shoes?" For an answer I said I could use the walk home. She gave me a sharp look over the rims of her glasses. "I'm a safer driver tanked on Scotch than most people who're stone-cold sober, if *that's* what you're worried about."

She hadn't even backed the car out of her driveway when she said, "There's no consolation for being *any* age, truth be told." When she got the Ford on the road, she told me, "You don't know what the hell you're doing when you're young. And when you're older, that's what you do know, that you don't know what the hell you're doing. But by then, you don't have youth to excuse you anymore."

Somewhere along the way back to my place, she pounded the wheel with her fist. "Try *this*, Maury! Young people say to themselves, it's the first time for this, the first time for that. *Older* people know every time could be the *last* time. *Now* do you understand the envy?"

I was beginning to, I lied. "Only one semester left to learn the lesson," she laughed.

That spring semester of 1951 flew by with the swiftness of dreams. *Remembrance of things past*: My fateful choice for an elective, the Anthropology course. The evenings at Harriet's. *Bring friends*. The smorgasbord covering her kitchen table, the cornucopia of chipped ice in the kitchen sink, the beer and wine and spirits flowing with the abundance of tap water. The cigarette ashes strewn everywhere. Meeting Elaine. *Elaine Edgerton, Ph.D.* The name corporealized at last. The denseness of the writing on the pages I edited in the back room of the office, the obduracy in the regulation passive voice of the Institute staff, made flesh. Elaine's eyes moving from Harriet's face to mine to Harriet's again. Cat's-eyes, yellow-green, chartreuse. Watchful. Dryden had a phrase for her affliction, "the jaundice of the soul."

Spring came around again, the forsythia blossomed, the dogwood flowered, and then the lilacs. "Elaine says I need to be used, and that's why I court the young," Harriet said one afternoon in early May. "But I know better. I court the young because they help me forget who I've become and they help me remember who I used to be. And that's considerable." She smiled, but not with her eyes. "Brave words as the courting season draws to a close, eh?" A few weeks before graduation, Elaine moved into her house. Things got hectic in the office for both Harriet and me as she'd predicted they would. There wasn't much time for talk.

One night during Final Exam week, we met by accident. She'd gone alone to see the film *Open City*, and so had I. Afterward, I walked with her to her car.

She said the film took her breath away. "*Weakness*. It leads to betrayal."

"It does that every time, Harriet."

"At least you're half Jewish. You don't have to carry the whole burden of Christian guilt around."

"Thanks for the consolation."

She made an odd sound, half laugh, half sob. She asked me what I would tell my children about the Holocaust, and I said I didn't even know what I would tell myself, never mind any children I might have.

We found her car and stood next to it, having the old problem of closure. Still leaving for New York after graduation? she asked. The plan hasn't changed, I said. What will become of Maury Golden? she asked, and I told her that with his Irish luck, he'd probably get drafted and sent to Korea. She said that Harriet Two took her inheritance from her mother and used it to go back to college fulltime and get that degree. "She went to some university very far from here. Where there's no Elaine. You'd have liked Harriet Two."

"I like *all* the Harriets."

"Don't throw away your gifts," she begged. "What's that line from the Bible, 'Cast thy bread upon the waters—'"

"'For thou shalt find it after many days.'" She chimed in at the last three words. And then we were laughing, laughing for no reason at all.

And so Harriet One went home to Elaine, and the Roland I gave for *that* particular Oliver became an anthropologist. And after *many* days the anthropologist learned that everyone walking above ground is on a vision quest. That all of life is a rite of passage. Remember she warned you and me at the threshold, *Take care, there's a step up.* She even apologized for going on ahead. *Have to shed some light*, she laughed. That's a *dinihowi* for you. Every time.

The second epiphany? It so happened the first Jewish burial ground in this community was consecrated on my sixtieth birthday. We had just turned to leave; I happened to glance up beyond the row of poplars where a low stone wall marks the entrance from the road. And I saw the figure of light with auburn hair leaning against the wall, and knew he'd been watching us. The entire field of my vision came ablaze with a silvergold burning with an inner fire. The light seemed to ripple as I began walking toward the figure. I felt I was wading into a river of shimmering silvergold. Then, in an instant, the light faded, the figure vanished.

Almost midnight. You ask if we should read our lives backward or forward, you ask how the country got into this bog, you ask will there be war again. I hear your anguish in the voice of every student who has come to me over the past forty years seeking counsel at a critical time for the life of this planet and its inhabitants, every student wrestling with the question of individual responsibility to the world beyond the self, every student in love with the world and its beauty, yet aware of its vastness and complexity and cruelties, and of the limits of *any* vocation to comprehend it. I recognize the species of anguish born of some torn-ness felt in the morning of life and ripening in the shuttling back and forth between two sides of some city. I hear it because one of my parents lost both parents and an older brother in the Holocaust, and the other believed that hell is a location in an afterlife. To answer your questions, I don't know, I don't know, and Yes, there will be bombing and bloodshed, death and destruction, and after a while some sort of truce will be declared, who knows how long it will hold, troops are massed on either side of the dividing line in Korea to this day, remember.

Matchoor-it-tee. Planting by the signs. In our culture, one comes of age so much later than the Pit River Indians do, and life seems to offer so many more possibilities. Our young people wander the hills of our wisdom books. You remember Aristophanes' discourse in Plato's *Symposium*; he said there originally were three sexes, all of them round, back and sides forming a circle, with two faces looking opposite ways; there were man, child of the sun, and woman, child of the earth, and the man-woman with the double nature, child of the moon. You remember how the gods punished them for committing hubris by cutting them in two, *like a sorb-apple that is halved for pickling*. Afterward, the two parts, each desiring its other half, came together in the embrace, *longing to grow into one*.

That was Harriet's Number One wisdom book; once she told me that she'd have to study Greek some day, that maybe then she'd find the word for the man-woman Aristophanes said had been lost long before his time; she had been amazed to learn he said the word *androgyne* was a term of reproach. That was Harriet's torn-ness, that was Harriet's Judaism and Christianity, that was Harriet's North Side and South Side of Chicago, her Youth and Age, her North Korea and South Korea that couldn't be unified by force, that's how Harriet Two came to be, and then all the other Harriets. If she'd lived to be *my* age, she'd have seen the figure of light and recognized who it was as I did, just as it vanished, she'd have known it for the template it is for every being of light on *all* the roads-not-taken, she'd have known that this is what the journey turns out to be when you look back at this angle and from this distance, that this is what all our explorations turn up, this multiplicity.

And to think that at the time Harriet and I met, I was the one who thought I'd probably die young.

Brief Gallantry

It was a day of strong sunlight and blustery winds. Unseasonably chilly, after weeks of suffocating summer heat. The winds harrowed the tall purples of the loosestrife in the fields. They whipped in through the car windows the two men in the front seat kept rolled halfway down, and sang in the shrouds of the silences falling between our talk. Whenever we came out into the open air, they blew their breath of cold vermouth in our faces and disheveled my daughter's hair, and mine, and rumpled our clothes.

The tide was at the full.

The scientist in our small company, my son-in-law Alan, taught us that, like ocean tides, the tidal movements of the atmosphere rise and fall. But at the surface of the earth the speed of these tides in the air, called "lunar winds," is too low for us to feel them. Their rhythmic ebb and flow can be read in the changes in diurnal temperature.

Tides in the air come twice every day, that was one of his lessons. Another was that lunar winds blow eastward in the morning and westward in the evening.

* * *

"Who has seen the wind?" Carol asked as we started out on our journey. "*Winds*," Abigail corrected. *Lunar* winds," Alan amended. After his discourse on atmospheric tides, Abby confessed she had been an animist in a former life, and knew them by name. "Aeolus,

Typhon, all the pantheon of lesser gods. You know the story of my return to the faith of the ancestors, Frank. I broke *two* bad habits that day. And all this had nothing to do with your anti-smoking crusade."

Carol and Alan demanded to hear Abby's story.

"The afternoon I set my hair on fire, the fiends shook loose all the leaves on the lower branches of our silver maple. They tore down the bird feeders and stripped our linden almost bare. Elves of October, the leaves. Broken shells the colors of earth and old-gold, tossed up and then flung about, *scattered and amassed*, and then blown down the ravine where I stopped to light a cigarette and my hair went up in flames. Their *voices*! *Taunting* me! And the reek of my burnt hair, falling about my face in a rain of ashes!"

"Mom! So *that's* how you were cured of your addiction!"

"Not cured, *redeemed*. And even more, from my *other* addiction—to paganism. I was reminded that all Creation is multiple. That only the Creator Who blew the breath of life into the winds—into *everything*—is One."

We had a moment of silence. After that moment, Alan remarked that it was his impression that paganism is still the Number One world religion. "People think they're monotheists of one kind or another, but the redeemed and the truly repentant are in a tiny minority, Abby. By the way, did you know that the alchemists *numbered* those fellas you heard taunting you? And then they brought them into line with the four cardinal points and the signs of the zodiac. They thought they could decipher all sorts of cosmic meanings from this setup. Sound familiar?"

"Zodiac," Carol echoed. "Marvelous word. Where does it come from, Frank? Greek? Or is it Latin?"

I turned around to answer, and saw they were holding hands, Abby staring out her window, Carol straight ahead. A second later, my stepdaughter's eyes met mine in the rear-view mirror.

"*Zodiacus* is Latin. It's from the Greek word *zoidiakos*, meaning of *carved figures*. Zodiac comes from *zoidion*, carved figure, sign of the zodiac. From the diminutive of *zoion*, living being. Related to *zöe*, Life."

"Sounds pagan to me!" Abby called out. "Whaddyasay, Alan?"

Alan bent his head and squinted into the rear-view mirror. "I think I've said just about all I know in that area, Abigail. All *zodiac* means in my limited vocabulary is the figure that stands for the signs of the zodiac and their symbols. The circle dividing the sky into twelve parts, with equal segments of thirty degrees each. I think the smart-heads worked this out about the third century before the Common Era. The Greeks and Chaldeans put their heads together and came up with the names of the twelve constellations. Your pagan of a daughter tells me I'm a Leo, she's an Aries, Frank's a Gemini. And you're a Libran. The scales. The only *in*animate symbol of the twelve. Did I get that right, Carol?"

"You got it right. Libra. Builder of bridges. Lover of harmony and beauty and justice, that's you, Mom."

"And no lover of wind, right, Abigail?" We had another moment of silence, waiting for an answer that never came. After a while Abby cleared her throat and recited as if by rote, "Air is the element of Libra. And wind is air in the active state."

She had spoken the last four words with finality. *Case closed.*

"When I was a little girl," Carol said brightly, "you once told me the wind—the *winds*—were your enemies, remember?

Silence.

"Because you used to get earaches . . . ." Carol's voice faded into Abby's humming, velvet-toned, insistent, of the bars of a song, or perhaps a hymn, I did not recognize.

When we turned onto the road leading to the first of the historic sites we visited that day, Abby wondered aloud what name she would give the light in the eastern sky. "That pale orange color. Like apricots."

"Apricots!" Carol echoed. "Do you remember the apricot trees, Alan? You wouldn't see them in this part of the country, Mom, Frank. They only grow in mild climates, like California. It's because they blossom so early in the year. You can't grow them anywhere that has spring frosts."

"Only in California," Alan sing-songed.

"No, not only in California, Mr. Know-It-All. They grow them in Utah, too. And also, I think, in the state of Washington."

"Washington," Abby repeated. "That's where I abandoned him, that's where I abandoned Tom Moran." And again, as she had done so often that last summer of lucidity, she conjured up the lost character in her novels, Tom Moran. He was visiting his married daughter in Washington when he suffered a massive stroke. Abby had left him in a Veterans' Hospital, "*sans* speech, *sans* sense, *sans* everything." That was in December of 1986. Although her novels move on to 1990, nowhere, "on-page or off-page," does Tom Moran live or die. "There's a Veterans' Hospital in Walla Walla, you know. 'The place of many waters.' That must be where Tom Moran is to this day, in that other Reality. Where there are *also* apricot trees."

* * *

Up there on the headland overlooking the Hudson, the winds blew over the water, rolling it this way and that. The furrows shone with the luster of pewter under the acid yellow of the sunlight. As the confusions of the heart under Abby's intense, unsmiling gaze. She had left her shawl in the car, and refused my offer to go back for it. I draped my jacket over her shoulders, expecting a protest that never came. She even took my hand as we went down the incline from the parking lot to the gift shop in the Carriage House where tour tickets are sold.

A strong gust of wind came up as I held the door open for the three of them. It blew all of us inside. The door harp was trolling; we were laughing, out of breath, as the door slammed shut behind me. A sharp scent in the indoor air stung my eyes—winter bayberry, Carol identified it for us later—as I apologized to the woman behind the counter for our noisy entrance. She waved my words away. "Same thing happened to the young couple who were in here earlier. That wind means business today, doesn't it! And in *August*! Let's see, two adults, two seniors, that's eighteen." As she handed me my change, she invited us to stop by afterward and browse. "Looks like there'll be only the six of you on the first tour today, you four and a lady in a pink dress and her husband, they must be up to the mansion house by now. You folks are in luck. Mrs. Wanamaker will be your guide this morning. And she's at her very best with a small group." She pushed the Guest Book across the counter and handed me a pen. "You do the honors," I said to Carol. Abby lay her hand over her daughter's. "Don't, please, not now. That way, we'll *have* to come back here before we leave."

* * *

We were just passing the Orangerie when the couple appeared on the path a few yards ahead of us. "The pink lady," Alan whispered, and Abby stage-whispered back, "*That's* what I call *pink*! Like strawberry ice cream! You can almost *taste* it!" Carol frowned at her mother and put her finger to her lips, stopping at the head of the trail to the formal rose gardens. Abby covered her mouth with her hand and stood in quiet contrition by my side.

The moment of silence there. Of peace. Sunlight and shadow. The pebbled trail and the brindled branches of the hemlocks at either hand. The wind—*winds*—rustling the leaves. And her scents, my wife's scents, the lemon fragrance of her hair and the musk of her skin, sandalwood and some nameless flower. "*The days turned into the Past.*" When Carol remarked that morning how swiftly time had flown away, how ardently she wished the four of us could live our few days of their visit all over again, I quoted the phrase, "*The days turned into the Past.*" She exclaimed, "That's *beautiful*, Frank!" and turned to her mother and asked, "Is it one of yours?" Abby smiled absently; I don't think she had been listening. "In a way, it's *all* of ours," I said. I told her I'd read it in *The Book of J.*

Our guide was a tall handsome woman in a royal blue gown of the b*elle époque*, with chestnut brown hair piled in a rich coil atop her head and waves and curls on her forehead and at her temples. She gave her Tour-spiel in the grand manner, in a lilting soprano, with dramatic gestures of her shoulders and hands.

It might have happened to any one of us out there under that burning sunlight, squinting, looking up, following the arc described by our tour guide's hand as it swept over the central block and symmetrical wings of the two-story Georgian mansion, dazed by the brightness of the yellow walls and white columns. When I raised my eyes to the second floor, the white columns and white wooden swags between them, and the white rails of the balcony, all seemed to begin vibrating. I counted the panes of the tall Federal windows, focusing on each dark square, to stop the pulsing of the whiteness of the trim.

Thank God she was so close beside me. I caught her as her body thudded against mine, and helped her to the nearest lawn chair. She revived in a matter of minutes and got up, declining Mrs. Wanamaker's offer to bring her a glass of water. She insisted she was fine and wanted us to go on with the tour. "Are you *sure* you're all right?" Carol asked, too many times. I understood when at last Abby glared her into silence and then shook off the hand I had been cupping under her elbow.

And so we were chaperoned up the steps and through the front door into the great hall with its Doric columns supporting the three arches that divide it into two sections. There we saw the magnificent central staircase leading up to the huge sun-filled Palladian window. Our guide said we might go into the formal parlor first. Lifting both hands palms up, she motioned for us to precede her. Alan and Carol and the young couple moved to the left; I made an *after you, Alphonse* motion to Abby. "No, it's on *this* side!" she called to the two couples, and turned and walked through the doorway to the right.

Mrs. Wanamaker clapped her hands in applause."This is a little test I give unsuspecting visitors, and I can't remember the last tourist who got it right. That the formal parlor is to the right, I mean, and no pun intended. Not that there's any rule about parlors being on one side or the other in these elegant Federal-style homes. But have you ever noticed that when people are in any large space they automatically move to the *left*?" She turned to Abby. "How did you *know*? Didn't I hear you people tell me none of you has ever been here before?"

Abby smiled. "This is my first visit."

"You must have seen the floor plan in one of our brochures, then. In any case, the mistress of this house dictated every last detail of this country estate her adoring husband built for her. And she decreed that the formal parlor should be on *this* side. There she is, by the way, above that sofa, which happens to be one of our finest Duncan Phyfe pieces. Some say the portraitist captured the young bride's strong will right along with her extraordinary beauty. Both were legendary."

I heard a sharp intake of breath; perhaps it was Carol's. Under the high brow, the hazel eyes set very far apart sought the eyes of her life-likeness in the pink dress who was standing next to my stepdaughter.

Mrs. Wanamaker cleared her throat. "You all see the resemblance, of course."

The Pink Lady stood motionless, contemplating the image framed above the shimmering pale green moreen fabric of the sofa.

"Maybe she's one of your long-lost ancestors, Glo." The Pink Lady's husband turned to our guide. "Was the family Irish, by any chance? My wife—Mrs. Pearson—is of Irish descent."

"He was English. *Born* in England, as a matter of fact. And she was French. A descendant of one of the earliest Huguenot families in the New World. The Huguenots were French, you know. They came to these shores in the 17th century. When this was still Dutch territory."

"They do know," Carol said eagerly. "My mother and my stepfather live in Palatine, which was founded by French Huguenots in 1677."

Mrs. Wanamaker clapped her hands. "Palatine! A *charming* and most historic community! I must make a return visit. I was there for the Tricentennial. Did you folks take part in that delightful pageant and play?"

"They would have if they weren't away honeymooning," Carol laughed.

"Carol." Abby put her finger to her lips and then turned to the guide. "That's what they call a bird-cage table, isn't it?" Mrs. Wanamaker replied it was indeed a bird-cage table, and went on to catalogue the furnishings of the room—the lamps, the draperies, the fire screen, the Duncan Phyfe chairs and the settee with the dolphin carvings on the front and the lion's feet, the collection of shells, the ceramic and pewter family heirlooms. When we filed out into the great hall again, she hoped aloud to hear our impressions.

Abby obliged by commenting on the stonework pattern of the wallpaper and the linoleum-like floor covering that is hand-painted to resemble marble.

In the second parlor, we were invited to notice the carving on the rosewood of the sofa along the north wall and on the square piano opposite it across the room. Abby wondered aloud when the furniture had been moved. "You quite take my breath away, you do!" our guide exclaimed. She told us there had been a slight structural problem that over the years had affected the slope of the back rooms on both floors. When the house was redecorated prior to opening it for exhibition, it had been decided to re-arrange the heavier pieces. To her recollection, no guide ever had mentioned this while conducting a tour, much less that the sofa and rosewood piano had traded places.

"And that information isn't in *any* of our brochures!"

Six pairs of eyes came to rest on Abby's face. Her eyelids fluttered; a smile played at her lips. "No," she said quietly. "There is no way I could have known that."

She withdrew into herself for the rest of the tour.

We recrossed the great hall into the dining room. As our guide pointed out the table in front of the window looking out toward the river, the settings of china and crystal and monogrammed silver sparkling in the sunlight, the Federal sideboards, the chairs carved to resemble bamboo, I read Abby's thought of how it might be for Carol and Alan to have a permanent address. A place where they could invite both sides of the family for Thanksgiving dinner. A place where Carol could grow a garden. A home of their own where they could grow a family. Carol had commented only that morning that this was to be Alan's seventh transfer in the ten years of their marriage. After next week's visit with his family, they were going to return to Denver and begin packing for their next destination. Boise. "For how long is anybody's guess."

Unwinding the scroll, everything I saw was translated into one of Abby's *if-onlies*. The china and porcelain behind the glass doors of the cupboards in the pantry that were handed down from one generation to the next. The portraits of the ancestors on either side of the staircase landing. The desk in the great library and sitting room where the autodidactic gentleman-scholar of independent means bent over his studies. Abby's expression of intense concentration told me she was replaying Alan's words inside her head. *"Sorry to have to tell you folks that it's call-up time again. Ever notice how corporate life models itself on the military these days? A member of a Rapid Deployment Force, that's what I feel like. Carol never forgave the company for that transfer out of California, and now I'm told we have to be on the move again."*

When we went outside through the kitchen door, Pearson took his camera out of the canvas bag strapped over his shoulder and asked us to stop in the formal gardens to photograph his wife and himself. *"To show the little stranger some day."* A strong gust of wind puffed at them, molding the small roundness under the Empire-high sash of the pink dress into the small cello that coming life makes of the trunk of a woman's body.

On our way back to the Carriage House, Abby began humming a melody I did not recognize. Then she broke off and told us that it was an art song she had learned in her youth, and that the heavy scent of the roses and the pink of Gloria Pearson's dress and of the geraniums and begonias in the garden had put her in mind of it. She announced, as she had so many times that summer of 1991 in taking her last stand against an invincible foe, she was about to test her memory. "It begins, 'Your hands lie open on the long, fresh grass,/The fingerpoints look through like rosy blooms,/ Your eyes smile peace.' And it ends, 'O clasp we to our hearts/ For deathless dower/This close-companion'd inarticulate hour/When twofold silence is the song,/The song of love.' I've lost the whole middle part. As they say happens in old age. But I don't feel I'm *there* yet!"

"It'll come back, Mom." Carol said tightly. "Won't it, Frank?"

"*Everything* does. What's the old saw about what goes around comes around?" I tapped my forehead. "It's all stored in there somewhere."

"*Some*where, I suppose," Abby mused. "What do you say, Alan? You're the scientist in this party."

"*Some*where, Abigail."

"Mmm. Or some*when*."

"Hey, Carol, sounds as though your Mother's been reading up on Physics! *Somewhen*. I like that! It's the same thing, by the way. Even if Frank tells us there's no such word."

"There is now," I said.

* * *

We stopped for lunch at a restaurant about half an hour's drive from our next destination. Abby and Carol took out the souvenirs they had bought at the gift shop and displayed them on the table in our booth—the scented soaps, a potpourri of winter bayberry, a pair of braided candles, the art books—one by Kate Jennings on John Singer Sargent's paintings, and the other *Monet at Giverny, A Book of Days*. Leafing through it, Abby came to the month of July. "'*Le Repos sous les Lilas*.' Look, Carol! Isn't the young woman wearing the same gown and hat as the woman in one of Monet's paintings in your book on Sargent? Here, let me find it."

"You don't need to, I know exactly where it is. Here, right at the beginning, here it is, 'A Woman in a Garden, Springtime.'"

Alan made a spyglass of his hand and peered at them through it.

"Two heads of auburn hair growing together across the table from us, Frank."

"Ignore him, Mom."

"I am. Look, here it says Sargent wasn't an Impressionist himself, but that he admired their work. Especially Monet's."

"The lilacs are almost the same pink, aren't they? Maybe we're too far from the scene to be sure."

"Maybe. In both paintings, the figures are shadowed—I mean *over*shadowed—by the lilacs. Look, they're the same shade of pink as Gloria Pearson's dress. Like tea roses, would you say? Or Rose of Sharon pink?"

Carol told her that could not be. "Rose of Sharon is St. John's wort. It has big *yellow* flowers. But there's also a Rose of Sharon tree. A little shrub of a tree with flowers shaped like bells. White ones, and purple, and also rose. But you won't find a pink that delicate except in the wild rose, or the swamp rose mallow. To me, it's a pink that belongs to early spring. Creeping phlox. Or spring beauties." Her smile as she looked up from the glossy page was meant only for Alan. "And then there are our apricot trees. The apricot blossoms form masses of this delicate pink in the spring."

"Apricot." Abby stared at some point above Alan's head and mine so intently that he turned to see if there was anything there. "That's what I wrote that Patty Dean's mouth was, an apricot. In 1958, when Tom Moran's sister goes to Florida for his wedding, and sits on the porch with his bride, Patty Dean, and her mother, Lady. And Lady says, 'We'll see if we can make a Southerner out of Tom. We'll see if Midwesterners transplant.' Patty Dean is doing one of her embroideries. She has a wide face and a blonde page-boy and bangs fluttering on her forehead. And her mouth is an apricot—" She broke off and turned to Carol. "You *did* remember, didn't you? To sign the Guest Book?"

When our waitress came to take our orders, she sniffed the air and asked which one of the two women was wearing "Samsara."

"We *both* are," Carol laughed. "I have a bad habit of raiding my mother's colognes whenever I visit. But how do you know the name?

Mom said it's new this year."

"My daughter told me what it's called, she wore it on *her* visit home last month. Somehow I *knew* you two are mother and daughter. You can see the resemblance." Later, when she served us, she commented that the scent was a little like having her daughter back with her again for a while.

* * *

A "ministering angel," Abby said of the waitress early that autumn. Out of nothing at all, she recalled the waitress and said she was a reader of souls sent to discern the marking on her own and to show her the way. "*That it may be for you a blessing.*" She told me that she had warmed herself in the woman's presence as at a hearth. "The *look* we exchanged, Frank! It's the look that passes between women cherishing at the same moment the memory of hours spent with a beloved child. I don't suppose the rest of you noticed that light. In her eyes. On her face."

I did not reply, but I had seen that light, that radiance on a human countenance. It was in a photograph of a holy man. The look of one cherishing not memory, but hope. Hope of a portion in the next world.

It's the same thing, by the way.

* * *

Workmen were making renovations on the "Makeshift Theatre" we passed on our way to the book shop to buy our tour tickets to the country manor. The turn-of-the-century clapboard house with a two-story portico had been built in the Colonial Revival style. It stands at the top of a hill overlooking the valley. "We opened as a museum in 1947," our guide told us when he welcomed us at the open door to the entrance hall. "Looks as though you folks will have me all to yourselves this afternoon. You may want to stroll around the grounds afterward. There's much to see, because at the turn of the century this was a working farm of well over 200 acres. There were fields and woodlands, vegetable gardens and orchards, meadows fenced for livestock, and many running-feet of stone walls. Today it covers about 150 acres of woodlands and fields. You'll especially want to see the charming sunken garden. There were brick walks and geometric flower beds and grass areas and hedges around the summerhouse, all inside high stone walls—we know this from photographs of the original garden." He told us that the flower beds had been grassed over during World War II because of the labor shortages at the time. "But two garden clubs did the hard work of funding and then reconstructing it, using landscaping and planting designs dated from the Twenties. Well, well, do come in—" He led us into the entrance hall. "There are twenty-four rooms in all, and many treasures to see. The collections of paintings and Chinese porcelains and other decorative pieces." Abby had chosen this site after reading about the feast of art in store for its visitors, French Impressionist works by Degas and Manet and Monet, and their American contemporaries Mary Cassatt and James McVeill Whistler. "In the Ell Room, they have Monet's *'Haystacks'* above the mantel over the fireplace. In the Morning Room they have his *'Boats leaving the Harbor at Le Havre,'* and in the dining room, Whistler's *'Symphony in Violet and Blue'* above the Sheraton sideboard . . . ."

In the beginning, it seemed it was the art Abby recognized. But after a while, I noticed that the furnishings and decorations in the rooms, and in fact the rooms themselves, seemed known to her in a way that her memorizing of the most detailed descriptions in a brochure could not have explained. She greeted some of the pieces as one greets an old friend after a long separation—the brass water clock beside the fireplace in the dining room. The lyre-shaped clock on the mantel in the Parlor Bedroom. The Italian cutwork spread on the Sheraton fruitwood canopy bed in the original Master Bedroom, and the leather travelling case on the closet floor.

As we were leaving that room, she turned and went back to one of the windows on either side of the fireplace. "Come see. This room looks over the sunken garden."

For someone who hadn't toured the grounds yet, Abby was amazingly well oriented, Alan commented to no one in particular.

Our guide was an astute and learned man; his smile said everything. He had long since passed the first moment downstairs when Abby startled him by asking when some of the frames on the paintings had been replaced. Even as we were climbing the staircase, he waited for Abby to answer Carol when she asked if there was a nursery among the many bedrooms we were about to see. And Abby did. "No children were born in this house," she said. When Carol asked if she'd read that somewhere, her mother replied, "I *must* have. But I'd have known it in any case. You can *feel* young life in a house years, *decades* after it's been turned into a museum."

At the end of our tour of the house, our guide invited us to make a return visit to hear one of their concerts or to attend their film and lecture series in the Makeshift Theatre. "Do come back!" he said, and Abby replied, "But I *have*!" As *whom*? he asked, laughing. "As the parlor maid," she quipped. "Their Nora. In those days I wore a lace cap with a white apron over my black dress. I remember dusting the keys of the piano when I was alone in the grand house, and then sitting down and accompanying myself singing one of the old songs." He brought his hands together in a gesture of applause. Carol put her arm around Abby's waist. "My mother's a story writer, can't you tell?" "She's a story-*teller*, too!" he said, "and a most charming one, I might add!"

Abby and Alan and I sat in the summerhouse for a while; Carol wandered about among the flower beds. When she came back, she reported she had seen "*that* pink again. In the 'Apple Blossom' peonies." "*Pearson Pink*," Alan named it. "She's haunting us." Just as she came back to haunt the mansion we visited in the morning, Carol mused. "She stepped out of the past to visit the place again." Alan remarked that Abby had just done the same thing here in the afternoon. "Nora the parlor maid." There was something in the tone of his teasing I had not heard before, a shading just this side of mockery. I announced I wanted a photograph of mother and daughter in the summerhouse. The wind cuffed at them as they clasped one another around the waist in the sororal pose, and just as the eye of the camera was about to blink, it lifted their hair straight up on their heads. "There's a hobgoblin in that contraption!" Abby called. I was too far away to see it, but I could hear in her voice the gleam of challenge in the look she sent Alan.

* * *

That must have been why Alan made the wrong turn. I had thought it would be mother and daughter who'd find some bone to pick before parting the next day. But it was Alan who set the necessary rite of passage into motion, and neither Carol nor I was able to stem the tide of their bickering. Soon after we were on the road again, he took up the lance he had thrown down in the summerhouse. "Enough of the story-teller's past lives and parallel lives, it's Reality time, eh?" *Which* Reality? Abby wanted to know. He bent his head to lecture her eye to eye in the rear-view mirror. "Here's a revelation from the Book of Science, Abby. Nonliving things grow differently from the way living things grow. *Living* things grow from substances unlike themselves. But nonliving things—like crystals, or like your Nora the parlor maid—grow by adding on more and more layers of their own substance." "Where does that leave Tom Moran?" she demanded. "In limbo," I put in. "Where we seem to be, at the moment." We had arrived at our third destination, the Trout Fisheries.

The bumpy dirt road led to a deserted parking lot next to the office building—a little too grand a term for what was no more than a barn with the notice CLOSED posted on the door. "I haven't seen any No Trespassing warnings," Alan said. "Let's round out the day Abby planned for us with a self-conducted tour."

At the edge of the rise overlooking the preserve, Alan commented that Trout Fisheries was too imposing a name for five pools of char and a tall stone boulder down below. The chill winds made our teeth chatter. "Here, Mom," Carol commanded, holding out Abby's shawl. Then she gave Abby a hug, to ask her pardon.

Abby unfolded the knitted cape. Then she shook it out and brought to her lips the part where the band of sacred letters is sewn on the prayer shawl and kissed it, and then draped the garment around her shoulders.

Fee-bee, a bird was calling. *Fee-bee. Fee-bee.*

Then it was quiet, the air throbbing with our stunned silence.

She recovered in a matter of seconds and joked that she was welcoming in the Sabbath about three hours too soon.

That time she would not accept the hand I offered her going down the incline.

"Trusting souls," Carol said. "Remember the guards with their walkie-talkies following us around on our tours?" Alan remarked that's because those places are in private hands, whereas this was a public trust, a state-owned preserve. "Which accounts for the absence of security." Security for what? Carol wanted to know. To protect the fish from crazies who might decide to poison them, Alan replied. "Or crazies who decide to paint a swastika on yon boulder." Abby chided him for casting shadows on our last afternoon together.

But that is exactly what the four of us did; when we came up to the edge, four dark shadow-flames leaped over the pond. And in an instant the fish swarmed away to the other side. We saw the scattering of pennies at the bottom. "Eighteen," Alan counted aloud. "Eighteen," Abby echoed. "The number meaning Life."

We circled the pond and watched as our shadows spread over the char, chasing them back again to their other shore, revealing another sprinkling of pennies at the bottom of the pond. "That copper can't be doing them much good," Alan commented. "People use this place as a wishing-well. Next they'll be bringing their fishing-poles. And then pieces of cardboard and scraps of cloth for lean-to's, when they turn it into a People's Park. Where they can paint messages of hate on yon boulder."

On that note, I laughed, it was high time that we started back. He clapped my shoulder. "Enough of terrorizing the trout, eh, Frank? They'll appreciate our departure." As we turned away, Carol said she had never known they were so tiny. "Like minnows. Minnows the color of mud." Abby linked arms with her as we went up the rise. "Did you see how the pennies gave off fiery reflections from the sunlight? Like jewels. Girasole."

Trout, of course, are not minnows, but game fish. When I was a boy at summer camp, I learned there are two main groups, the black-spotted and the chars. Anglers call the coloring of the brook or speckled trout, the chars, "the bloom of the trout." There are threadings of dark olive and black on their backs, and flame-red spots on their sides. I saw these on some of them before they darted away from our shadows. The dark and orange mottlings on their fins I'd have to take on faith, at that distance.

* * *

"Phrases of music fading," Abby wrote in her last letter to Carol. "Words crumbling, dissolving, melting away. As the white lettering on the screen of my monitor when I lose the thread of my thought and sit staring too long into the void." Abby and Carol both are nurses "by profession," as the phrase goes. Carol would not accept it for months after she heard it, but I think Abby knew the name of her affliction long before that day her doctor made his diagnosis.

She read aloud to me the first page of the last story she tried to write. "Look, it's in my own handwriting. I found it on my desk under the title 'Brief Gallantry': *'It was a day of strong sunlight and blustery winds. Unseasonably chilly, after weeks of suffocating summer heat* . . . . ' I have no memory of having written this, Frank. What was it I meant to say? And what is 'Brief Gallantry?'"

Brief Gallantry. I recognized the words, from Powys's *A Philosophy of Solitude*, a book we had taken turns reading to one another that last summer. In his reflections on the death of passion between former lovers, Powys wrote of the moment "when each can see the other as a tragic skeleton, clothed upon by a brief gallantry of blooming flesh, but in reality as patient, as enduring . . . as the rocks that were blasted to build their house."

She brought me the newspaper in October that year. The headline shouted at me. Not the one on the right-hand side that, I suppose, riveted the attention of most of the *Times*'s readers, PARADE OF WITNESSES SUPPORT HILL'S STORY, THOMAS'S INTEGRITY, but the one over the column on the left, "Washington Voters Weigh If There Is a Right to Die." The article was about Initiative 119, the Death With Dignity proposal. By then, Abby had abandoned her lost character in the Veterans Hospital in Walla Walla for good. She no longer spoke of him, of Tom Moran. Or of possible past lives, or multiple realities where we lead parallel lives. It was the feast of *this* one she wanted to savor.

* * *

In my file of clippings is a news report of a study that was published in *Nature* in the winter of that year. It said that, for the first time, researchers were able to produce genetically modified mice that develop the changes of the brain seen in Alzheimer's disease. A fragment of a human gene for amyloid protein, which is thought to cause Alzheimer's, was inserted into mouse embryos along with genetic instructions for the mice to produce large amounts of this fragment only in their brains and central nervous systems. Eight months later, the amyloid deposits had become the "mature plaques" characteristic of the disease. The mice also developed another hallmark of Alzheimer's, neurofibrillary tangles. These were described as masses shaped like flame inside the dead brain cells. They are formed from coiled, rope-like protein filaments.

Masses shaped like flames. After I read the article, I brought Abby the book on Sargent's paintings by Kate Jennings, and showed her Monet's *"A Woman in a Garden, Springtime."* She looked at the page, then looked up at me. There was no recognition in her eyes. "Remember the Pink Lady?" I persisted. She shook her head, No.

... lunar winds blow eastward in the morning and westward in the evening.

So began my task.

However fragmentary the work of restoration must be, it is a miracle every time it happens. I was witness to this last spring, at evening services, when Abby's eyes were lifted to the Ark as we read one of the prayers responsively. She spoke the words as fluently as though she were reading them:

"*Though we are mortal, we are Creation's crown.*
Flesh and bone, steel and stone.
We dwell in fragile, temporary shelters."

* * *

The evening before that August day, when the four of us were sitting around the table planning our itinerary, Abby said there was no excuse for our never having visited those two historic sites. I joked that was one of the pleasures we were supposed to be saving for our retirement years. "When we're Golden Agers," I laughed. She looked up from the road map. "Frank. Don't you know that the time we're living in *now* is our Golden Age?"

One of the note cards with prints of Monet's paintings the Alzheimer's Association sends to potential donors is the artist's *"White Waterlilies." "Le Bassin aux Nymphéas"*: the hanging willows, the Japanese bridge, the aquatic plants with their floating leaves and showy flowers. I could no more imagine what my perspective would be had I never known her, than imagine what modern art would be had Monet and his second wife never created the gardens of Giverny a century ago.

2000

"God is clever, but not malicious." (Einstein)

Hart Strings

In the dream that was not a dream the small band of Jews were burying his Sarah. Hart stood with his little son in the middle of the gathering, his father-in-law at the child's other side. After Kaddish, the visiting rabbi spoke directly to him: *When a parent leaves a child half-orphaned, the surviving parent is commanded to* replenish. *You must become father-mother to this boy. Country people in Europe called parents the* tateh-mameh. *In any case, where else can our loved ones go when they depart, but into ourselves?*

Riven, he was riven. He remembered Aristophanes' tale in Plato's *Symposium* that there once were three sexes, all of them round like a circle with two faces looking opposite ways—the man, the woman, and the man-woman like himself and his Sarah; and that the gods punished them for their pride by cutting them in two *like a sorbapple halved for pickling.* He had found and now he had lost his other half.

But that was a Greek story, and this was a Jewish graveside.

As he took the shovel, a passage from *Don Quixote* rose up in his soul—the nobler, the more faithful love is love of the inaccessible. That was what his love for Sarah was now. So maybe *Don Quixote* was more a Jewish story, one of loving a presence that cannot be seen.

Hers was the first grave in this portion of the cemetery. Three men had come to him and Sarah's father the night after she died and said they had just purchased a building they were going to convert into a synagogue for the first Jewish congregation in New

Paltz. Also they had purchased a section of the town cemetery and had it consecrated as Jewish burial ground; Sarah could be buried there instead of in Brooklyn.

Sarah's father, also a widower, gripped Hart's arm. *You, a stranger here, you brought my daughter and my grandson here not even a year ago. These three men were sent to us, believe me.*

Hart believed.

On the evening of the last day of the mourning period, Hart left his son with the boy's Zayda and went back to her grave. He lifted up his eyes to the mountains rippling across skyfields of mauve and rose and white-gold in the fierce orange light rimming the tower on the Shawangunk Ridge. When they first came here in midsummer last year Sarah told him that at sundown the tower shows itself to be the figure of a woman. *I'll paint her for you one day*, she promised.

He made a covenant with his Sarah. She would be the guardian spirit of his writing-desk, and he the preserver of her sketchbooks.

My best are the ones I did here, she had said before parting. *The apple orchards, the little iron bridge at the foot of Main Street, the Flatiron building on the corner of Main and Church Street, all the old stone houses in the historic district. Why do I feel so at home here, me, a Brooklyn girl all my life, why is everything in a place founded by French Huguenots in the 17th century so familiar to me, why is the fragrance of the cedar in the loft of Memorial House calling to me from 300 years ago, why does all this feel* bashert?

He swore that for her past life he would say Kaddish in the building on Church Street those three men were converting into a synagogue. And for her future life, he would begin keeping a Journal, he would write her back into life in its pages. For their son's sake, to *replenish*, so he could become the boy's father-mother. Also for his own sake, to put together the man-woman that death had sundered. But mostly for Sarah's, to give her life an afterlife right here on earth. As Chagall gave an afterlife to his dead wife Bella, his beloved, his intended, his *bashert*, in his paintings.

Seven of them were gathered around the table in the study downstairs—Hart and Sarah and the village historian Wolf; a couple with their young son, visitors from the City; and a latecomer, an elderly gentleman. This last had hovered in the doorway asking was this where he could say Kaddish for his wife who was dead thirty-six years now, he happened to see the sign off the Thruway at Exit 18 that said there was this shul on Church Street, so he found his way here, but to say Kaddish you're supposed to have ten adults and they only had six to count in a minyan, should they wait? Wolf's reply was they might as well wait for the Messiah to come, but that if you count the boy anyway, seven is a good Jewish number. Hart let fall that so is the number 18, that 18 is the number for Chai, Life, so 36 means double Life. Then maybe it's *bashert*, their newest arrival decided, and as he pulled out a chair across from the boy he asked him, *You know what bashert means?* and answered his own question that it means something is meant to be.

Hart handed out prayer books from a stack in the middle of the table next to the basket of yarmulkes. There followed a rustling of pages and a capping of heads. He spoke aloud where his train of thought had led him, that we're given an additional soul on the Sabbath, so we are already more than a *minyan*, but maybe we should put four yarmulkes in the middle of the table just to be on the safe side. They did so, and then there was silence, and then Hart invited the two women to light the candles if somebody would clean the dried wax out of the cups of the holder. Wolf got up to perform this service, and Hart told the visitors, "The three men who bought this building promised *If you build it they will come*, so Welcome."

During their service, Hart kept looking at the young boy. He was fascinated because he recognized that the child had the same face as the one in the photograph of his own father as a boy in the family album he inherited when he, an only child, was orphaned for the second time. His eyes cherished the realities the sepia obscured, the strong blue of the boy's own eyes, the feathery tips of his curls. Each time Hart's attention strayed he silently said the Blessing on seeing creatures of striking beauty. It did no good; he kept yielding to the temptation to look again. The child was holding a miniature carving of the one of the old stone houses with a sun porch near the side entrance. Hart recognized that too; it was the miniature model of the 1698 House for sale with its companion models in the Gift Shop of the local Huguenot Historical Society.

When services ended, Hart invited everybody into the adjoining community room. After they said the Blessings over bread and wine, the widower remarked that the place was big enough to hold a seder for a whole congregation. To this Wolf sighed, *But we don't have a whole congregation.* The boy's father asked the age of the building. Wolf replied that in its first former life the upstairs was the little old Methodist-Episcopal Church, built in 1840; and that during the 1880s it was moved from the corner where the Flatiron building now is and raised up and made into a second story on top of this basement. He added that its most recent former life was as a Lutheran house of worship which their benefactors converted to a Jewish one in the 1960s, and asked, *Who wants to see the sanctuary?*

The small band followed Wolf into the hall and up the stairs. At the landing there was a rack with prayer shawls in front of the high windows in the western wall that once were French doors leading to a balcony. *Prayer shawls waiting to enrobe souls,* Hart thought, but did not say. He waited while the others turned east, and Wolf and Sarah led their visitors up the red-carpeted center aisle to the raised platform, the *bimah*. Until only a few weeks ago he'd imagined Sarah and himself under a wedding canopy up there, clasping one another's hands before the red velvet Ark curtains. *My heart is in your heart,/Your heart is in my heart*

His short tour ended, the Wolf led his group back up the aisle, remarking that the hidden Jews of the Southwest had nothing on the hidden Jews of New Paltz, but that the big difference was that the ancestors of the ones in the Southwest had a good excuse for keeping a low profile. Walking backwards to where Hart was waiting, he made known to his audience of four that New Paltz was founded by French Huguenots, refugees of religious persecution. The widower begged his pardon to ask, *What's the connection here?* Wolf replied that the people in a French Huguenot village in the mountains in Vichy France named Le Chambon-sur-Lignon sheltered thousands of Jewish refugees between 1940 and 1944. *And here we Jews are, in a Huguenot village in the mountains. Connection, coincidence, what's the difference?*

No one seemed to have any further questions or comments. Hart flicked off the lights, and they took the hint. *Buildings can have many lives,* Sarah called out as they trooped downstairs, *so maybe people do too.* Behind her their elderly visitor thundered, *Not in* our *tradition!* Hart saw her lips part, then draw tightly together.

The small company disbanded at the street entrance, and Hart stayed behind with Sarah to lock up the building.

They walked past the usual Friday night revelers on Main Street to her apartment in the Queen Anne building students called the Taj Mahal. It would be for the last time; next week she would be moving to New York City to live with her widowed mother while attending graduate school. They had decided to part ways. Art was her consuming passion, she had resolved never to have children. And he wanted above all else in life to become a father.

Sarah broke their silence to say she thought the widower talked as though there were only *one* Jewish tradition. For an answer, Hart asked her if she supposed that in all the galaxies there might be one world, just one, where people love one another for their differences. She asked back how could that be, it was a contradiction in terms.

He took her hand. He was thinking of her conviction that most people are driven to make copies of themselves, of her fierce belief in using the force of your entire being to resist this if you want to make art. He'd had to acknowledge that in writing his stories he had a strong impulse to create characters whose souls mirrored his. "Sing a new song," the Psalm begins, she'd reminded him. He wondered if breathing new life into the old is the highest creativity human beings can aspire to, he wondered if there were universes where people mated and had children out of promptings other than the one to make clones of themselves, he wondered if what you imagined was giving a second life to what you loved, through art in any form, was not that at all, if what you did was bring into being something outside yourself that truly *was* new and therefore destined to become, like grown children become to their parents, beloved strangers. He wondered if it was a reality you were apprehending when you made art, an elsewhere and elsewhen that would prove eternally resistant to your calling it back, that it was fated itself to bring forth new life just as you had, and so on forever and ever in ever-increasing space. He wondered what was coming to him now, and what would happen to the life he and Sarah had begun when they loved, the life that was ending here at her door where they were wishing one another, almost formally. Good Sabbath, Good night, Goodbye.

They kissed without passion, having already parted souls.

The wing dipped so Hart could see the terrain through the small God's-eye port hole. "Those mountains, they have a name?" he asked. *Shawngum,* the answer came, *spelled S-H-A-W-A-N-G-U-N-K.* Hart said that sounds Indian, and the voice said something about the Esopus whose people took the wolf for their totem, and then bade Hart look down as they descended.

The figure of a woman rode the higher of the two tors wavering in the shimmer of silver-blue light beyond the mountains. It seemed to Hart that she was beckoning to him.

Now.

He was loosened on his silver cord.

He alighted on the north end of the curve of the half-moon that was the National Historic Landmark District of Huguenot Street, where a man and a woman were waiting that Saturday afternoon. The guide welcomed them to "the oldest street in America with its original houses." Their tour commenced with the 1694 House on the corner. *If you look in* The World Book Encyclopedia *under "Architecture," you'll find a photo of this one, they call it Dutch Colonial.*

In and out of the six original houses still remaining they followed their guide, Hart growing smaller and smaller between the couple as the three of them were shown vestiges of past lives. By the time they came to the lawn of the 1698 House, Hart had disappeared into the womb of the grieving woman. Her husband lay his hand on her shoulder as the guide pointed to the sun porch near the entrance. They marveled at the beautiful Victorian furnishings of the 1692 House which a descendant had converted into this grand Queen Anne Colonial Revival home during the 1890s. And in the Memorial House loft, the woman breathed deeply of the fragrant cedar, waking the seed nestled within her.

They came to the old churchyard, the stones scattered about, the guide said, *by the Vandal, Time.* Rhododendrons bloomed pink and purple and white along the sides of the replica of The Old

French Church. They entered and saw that the walls were bare save for the lamps with the flame effect; they saw the shadows flickering around them, *spirits of the ancestors,* their guide said. They saw the conch shells used to call people to prayer or meeting, and the ladder the caller climbed to the trap door that opened onto the roof.

After the tour, the couple began the walk back through town to the home of the friends they were visiting. As they passed the new restaurant and brewery at the corner of Huguenot and Main, the wife reminded her husband what the guide had told them, that it had been named after the ship that set sail for New Amsterdam carrying the father-in-law of two of the men who later became the founders of New Paltz. *Is nothing sacred?* she murmured. Her husband replied that buildings have many lives. *Look, Sarah.* He gestured toward the Wallkill River across Huguenot Street. *The riverbank down there would be the perfect place for the Jews to throw bread on the waters at New Year's.* He told her the Jews and the Huguenots led parallel lives for a time in the New World, that there had been resemblances between the two traditions, that sometimes Huguenots blew a horn in place of a conch shell, *a shofar,* for calling people to worship, that both traditions forbade making images of God, that both placed a high value on education, that both studied the Bible on their Sabbath.

After a moment he thought of another. *Both the church of logs and the first stone church of the Huguenots were built before the people had a resident pastor. And according to what the rabbi told us this morning, three men bought that building on Church Street years before they were able to assemble a congregation and hire him.*

She did not reply. She was thinking of what the rabbi had said to them before the others came. She had confided to him their longing for a child; for seven years they had been waiting and hoping. She had said that in her bitterness she sometimes thought God did not want this soul to be born, and if their longing were satisfied one day out of divine exasperation, the child God did not want to be in this world would suffer, and she and her husband would be guilty of that suffering because they had loved him into this world. *What I ought to do, I suppose, rabbi, is have faith that the soul who calls to me will be born somewhere, somewhen, and accept that this ought to be enough, and that we and this child may never meet in this world.*

The rabbi had smiled. For an answer, he had quoted, *"Look now toward heaven, and count the stars, if thou be able to count them."* He had paused, and her husband continued, *"So shall thy seed be."*

Presences filling the sanctuary that in a former life was the Methodist-Episcopal Church, Hart thought at first those were Christian souls among the Jewish ones crowding that chamber upstairs during his son's bar mitzvah. But after the passage of 36 years, he realized that was only the first convocation of all the Sarahs stirring their limbs and breathing the breath of life inside his Journal notebooks. In revisiting the alps of those spiral-bound tablets, he had discovered her multiplicity, her secrets, her darknesses, her variable inner climates. And also his own.

Continuing revelation, she laughed. *Remember Shakespeare? "Now I will believe/that there are unicorns."*

He replied that if that were the only gift from King Death, he'd say it was more than enough.

Another Hart attack coming if you don't calm down, she warned.

He was old, he was tired, he had had more than enough. *Look at you, Sarah, look at me, what are people, God's fruit flies? Somebody should've told the Huguenots what their leader Calvin was getting them into with his predestination, who likes being chosen for multiplication games, our ancestors forgot their lesson, how this started back there in the desert with all that complaining, that murmuring, they had to eat quail until it came out of their ears, that's what you get for murmuring about the arrangements, you get a transfer to another place where you'll find something else to murmur about, some King this Death, a conductor handing out transfers to elsewheres and elsewhens.* Hints, *the Puritans were looking for,* Signs *they called them, the Signs are everywhere you look, but most people don't want to read them,* coincidences *they call them,* mere, *always* mere, *but who can blame them, who wants to hear there are replicas of you swarming all over?* She asked, *All over* what?

The orange Grief-Moon was dissolving. Hart and Sarah and the child were down there on the riverbank with the others, they were tossing their bread crumbs into the Wallkill River. *What are you doing, Zayda?* the child asked, and Hart answered, *Throwing away my sins,* and he lifted the boy up on his shoulders to see how they were floating away, his sins of despair. Happy cries of *Shanah Tovah, a beautiful new year!* rose up over the gathering. Hart climbed the muddy slope with the child riding him piggyback and Sarah close behind them. Then he set him down, and the boy walked between his grandparents, holding each of them by the hand.

Hart pointed across the street. *Up there on that corner is where the Huguenots settled first, they built their cabins and put a palisade around them, logs, maybe, like your Lincoln logs, or maybe mud, like your Play-dough. Listen, I'll tell you the story of some of the lives that spot of land had.* The cabins and the palisade vanished, and the double-storied brick school rose up, and then flames danced in its windows and it crumbled and then rose up again, now three stories high, and then flames danced in the windows as before, and it crumbled once more. Then beyond the rubble railroad tracks appeared, and the little station-house for the trolley rose up. And then all that vanished and the Huguenot Motel rose up in its place. Sarah's father was walking around the corner, saying he was too old to move here to live with them and the boy, he was too old to change, by his age you realize it's hard enough to live with yourself, never mind with other people, he was saying it's good to breathe the country air here, but you'll have to go out of town for the boy's bar mitzvah, *think what would be if instead of Huguenots, the first 23 Jews who came to New Amsterdam in 1654 came here—*

There were 23 in Hart's group that morning, members of a society of descendants of French Huguenots touring the country's oldest Jewish communities for connections to their colonial past. Three of them had been here before; for the others, it was their first visit to the oldest street in America with its original houses. At the end of the tour, one of these three men detained Hart on the porch of the Fort after the others went inside to the gift shop to buy souvenirs. What did Hart make of it, he asked, the correspondence between their numbers that midsummer afternoon and the number of the first Jews who came to these shores 350 years ago?

The man, whose name-tag read Wolf, lifted his yarmulke and set it down firmly again. The gesture was familiar to Hart. When visitors accepted his invitation to take a head covering from the basket on the table inside the old synagogue building on Church Street where his tours commenced, he told them they were not obliged to replace it but could keep it as a souvenir if they so desired. He thought that those who wore it throughout their circuit of the historic district did so as a sign of their feeling of solidarity with a group whose members shared a common history of religious persecution. His reading of the gesture was that Wolf was one of those who wanted to call attention to this fellow-feeling by fiddling with his yarmulke.

In reply to his question, Hart told him of something he'd read about coincidences. In a book of stories by converts about their conversion to Judaism, one of them remembered reading that a coincidence is a miracle for which God chooses to remain anonymous. To his astonishment, the man lifted his palm and pressed it against Hart's name-tag, and blurted out that he was a mixed breed, *half French Huguenot on my mother's side, and half Jewish on my father's; and I'm still two people to this day.*

Embarrassed by this confidence from a stranger, Hart returned to their subject of numbers. *I hadn't thought about 23 until you mentioned it, but isn't there a mystical tradition that there are actually 23 letters to the Hebrew alphabet, not 22, and at the End of Days the Big Shofar sounds and the 23rd is revealed?* Wolf said he didn't know, he was thinking that 12 Jews founded this community, and in the Christian story there are 12 apostles. Hart said he thought ten, not twelve, is a Jewish number; ten is required for a minyan. *And five, there are the Five Books of Moses.* The other observed that six of the ten original stone houses had survived, and that the Star of David has six points, not five.

This reminds me of an elderly gentleman on one of my tours, Hart said, *Let me tell you the story.* The man had held out a dollar bill to him before boarding the chartered bus back to the hotel in the mountains. Thinking it was meant as a tip, Hart said, he had waved it away. But the fellow had insisted, *I'm showing it to you to look! Look how important the Jews are in the story of America, you didn't* mention that! The stars on top of the head of the Eagle on the back of this dollar bill have six points, that's to honor the Jews. Because without Hyam Salomon's asking for donations from Jews in the Americas and in Europe to help the American revolutionaries during that winter at Valley Forge, the British would've won the war. And if anybody wants to know how good that would have been for the Jews who came after, just ask the Irish! It was George Washington's idea to remember how the Jewish people helped the Revolution by putting six-pointed stars over the head of the Eagle. And that's not all. Look what happens when you turn the Eagle upside down, see, you can make out that's a menorah, that's also in honor of us Jews!

His visitor shook his head, marveling at what he said was the *real miracle, the survival of persecuted peoples. I read that John Butler wrote, "Everywhere Huguenots went, they vanished." But maybe that's the secret of survival. We're still here perhaps* because *we intermarried, just as you said the descendants of the first Jewish families did with the Christians,*

The chartered bus pulled up in front of the Fort just as the bells of the Reformed Church began tolling the hour. As the others began streaming out of the gift shop, Hart held out his right hand to his visitor, who extended his and then spread his left hand over their clasped ones. *All my life I've felt like two half-persons. Today, here, I feel whole. Like it was written in my book of life, like it was—what's that word you said about why the first Jews came here?*

Across the street late afternoon sunlight was buttering the fieldstone of the 1698 house. In his reveries their blond waffled walls seemed to Hart like nothing so much as giant matzoh crackers, the bread of affliction for the wanderers in the desert.

Bashert, he said. *That means something's meant to be.*

Hart looked up from the book open on his thigh to see the little arm under his neck raise itself; it was spangled with sticker stars, multicolored six-pointed stars marching elbow to wrist where the straight line turns and makes a diagonal to the index finger, the arrow. The little arrow was pointing upward to mandarin orange skies: gulls coming down, going up, coming down the ladder, sun-limes dangling from the branching foliage of the clouds:

plum-purple gulls caw-cawing an old song without words, their underwings flashing the deep blue of sapphires.

"*Zayda*, see them go down and up and down!" The child's voice trembled with pleasure.

The pair floated over the village, the boy riding him piggyback.

"*Zayda*, from here it looks like a bird with a broken wing!"

"Higher, then!" Hart called, and the boy shouted with wonder that now it had the shape of a bug. So Hart pumped harder still, the breath spiraling out of his body. They hovered up there, Hart and the child, looking down at the shape shaded in at the core of the town nestled at the foot of the mountains.

I'm making where Zayda *and* Bubby *live,* the boy had said that morning, slapping Play-dough between the palms of his hands like his Bubby slapped the dough for her strudel. *I'm an airplane looking down on it.* He had pulled a pinch of his paste out to the right, to the east, and then, lower down, a pinch to the left. But it was too far down, he was changing it, Hart had to tell him the truth, that he was making it into something it wasn't, so it wouldn't work, what they were trying to do, and Hart had said, *That isn't a true letter "a", a true aleph,* and the boy's eyelids had fluttered, his cheek was reddening; Hart had stroked it and whispered *Don't be sad.*

The boy had shaped a curved candleholder with two little candle flames, and the village showed the bug inside the bird, and inside the insect was the letter of the *tzadee*, and Hart said, *You're getting warmer, see how the letter keeps changing as you get closer.*

Then the child had shown him *three* slender candles with their big-headed flames perched on the holder. Reading right to left, the third was dotted, the middle one was tilting like the 1698 House tilts because there's a root cellar underneath the cellar kitchen, and the one on the left was gently curved. He had changed it to the shape of the *sheen*. And then he'd made the dangling squirrel that was the "l," the *lamed*. And lastly the "m," the letter shaped like the flat roofs of the dwellings of the ancient Egyptians that they made this way to protect themselves from the burning sun, the final *mem* that made his word spell *Shalom*,

And now grandfather and grandson floated, drawing the giant letters across the skies above the village.

And now Hart drifted down with the boy on his back, and along the stone wall around the old cemetery he trotted, to the opening; and he bent so the boy could dismount. And then the boy lay the small warm fluttering bird of his hand in Hart's, and they passed by the historical marker and followed the path to the stoop and sat down side by side in the sheltering doorway and watched the play of moonbeams among the headstones, and saw the trembling of small pools of silver become the trumpeted corona of daffodils in the deep yellow of the moonlight. Then Hart put his grandson's hand in his pocket, because that is their agreement, that the child will have the pleasure of finding the sock full of stickers of six-pointed stars in his *Zayda*'s pocket and the pleasure of lifting it out, the sticker stars for the tombstones of the wayfarers of this world, beginning with the one for the stone on the grave in the northeast portion of the burial grounds, and ending with the one for the grave of the artist who never lost his child's heart, the painter of red violins and flying milkmaids who lies buried in a Catholic cemetery in France.

In the dream that was not a dream, Hart was journeying to other *basherts,* to the one where Sarah lives on blessing his memory, and the one where their orphaned son mourns parents who died when he was a child, and the one where he is born of the longing that purifies the heart, and the one where he discovers that the *aleph* of his name is silent that he might hear, and the one where he and Sarah live on to see their children's children, and the one where the pacifist dominie rings the old Jewish song without words on the bells of the Reformed Church, and the one with the village that has a tree-shaded Huguenot Street where father and son are just now walking in midsummer hand in hand on their way to the pool, and the one where he tastes with his light kiss on the forehead of the newborn infant boy the sweetness of newly-baked bread, and the one where Hart's mathematician friend Wolf is laughing like the century-old Sarah laughed when she learned she was pregnant, and teasing him, *For numbers like the ones* I *play with, you at least have to know long division!*

The kingdoms rising up in the opening hand of aloneness, and in the opening hand of desires realized. Recognitions in the God's-eye that sees that the angels descending and ascending the rungs of the ladder are the bodies of the notes of the tiny strings vibrating in the God's-ear. The near Harts he senses in the pull in the curled conch in the middle of the body toward the floating island grazing the one he calls home. And the unpublished writers who have the honor of reading their works to Moses every jubilee year, dreaming of the world at the End of Days where the twenty-third letter of the *aleph-bet* is revealed and the broken-hearted and the half-hearted are made whole, singing the new song, *My Hart is in your heart,/ Your Hart is in my heart*

AFTERWORD

"Storytelling sinks the thing into the life of the storyteller, in order to bring it out of him again. Thus traces of the storyteller cling to the story the way handprints of the potter cling to the dry vessels."

—Walter Benjamin

Afterword

1

Stories have souls, multiple souls, because (although not only because) well-chosen words themselves have souls. A portion of *a people's* Soul is a medley of the souls of all the stories each one tells to oneself or to others along the life-course. Like the life of a people's culture, as Kem in "Evanescence" remembers his professor portrayed it, the essence of every story is ethereal, swift-passing and elusive. It runs on the path ahead of the writer setting it down in words on paper, and thereafter of its readers as they turn its pages. So the essence of those I have written over the past half-century have tantalized me, from the beginning when they were forming in my mind, then through the many sessions when they took form on my pages, and yet again with my every re-reading, to this time of my harvesting of a dozen of them for this volume.

As the jeweled lights of fireflies flickering among the trees on midsummer nights, the possibilities of a story's why and wherefore charm the pursuer who gives chase in reading its pages of print. "The eye sees more than the heart knows," as William Blake said. Every reader's imaginings are as stars falling through meshes of memories and impressions stirred by its words, forming intricate patterns of thought and emotion that are ever-new and evanescent.

Enduring works of the literary imagination have the shimmer of timelessness and everywhereness to which writers of literary fiction aspire. But on this side of that suspension bridge between "real" and imagined worlds, the time-span of the "living present" of any story continually streams forth from its own ceaselessly flowing past toward its ever-ending "ending" in a ceaselessly flowing aftertime. Stories by their very nature happen once-upon-a-time somewhere. Inside every story, its characters breathe in and breathe out the spirit of the times they inhabit as their own. This spirit is an atmosphere infused with the pneuma of any wavering point in the space-time continuum that human beings choose to mark as a particular story's once-and-once-only "moment."

Writers of stories spirit themselves into an elsewhen. They do this to begin their conjuring, and to work the miracle of creation on pages of print of a world beyond or alternate or parallel to the immediate Now of everyday taken-for-granted "reality." All stories begin with four indwelling words, *once upon a time*, inviting the reader to enter the elsewhen of the story-time.

How shall that story-time be measured? What are the writer's and readers' calipers for placing it upon the moving surface in the space-time continuum? How shall the buoys be moored so as to raise the floats of the story's beginning and ending and tell of the "during" between its Before and After? Shall the story unfold in days, or weeks, or seasons, or over years, decades, centuries, or even millennia? Shall the story happen during an era, as the civil rights era, an epoch, as *la belle époque,* an age, as the Age of Discovery? Are story characters to be seen as creatures of a decade we name the Gay Nineties or number as the Forties, the Sixties, the Eighties? Or of a generation someone named Flaming Youth, or of the one someone named the Silent Generation—those born, according to an essay in 1951 in *Time* magazine, between the Depression and World War II? Or of the Greatest Generation, so named by Tom Brokaw in tribute to "the men and women who came out of the Depression, who won great victories and made lasting sacrifices in World War II and then returned home to begin building the world we have today"?

Evanescence is a selection of twelve stories I wrote about life in the United States of America during the second half of the 20th century. In my own studio of literary art, during those fifty years I fashioned stories that in retrospect seem to me to be fiction timepieces with settings as alive as the characters who inhabit them. I arranged twelve of them here in a table of contents that is a timetable unfolding in linear fashion "forward" from the 1950s to the year 2000. This span of time encompasses the course of my fiction writing life from 1950, when I turned twenty, to the end of both the century and the millennium, when I entered my seventies.

Of all my literary estate, my works of fiction and my life writings are the portions I most ardently hope will outlive me and find their way to lovers of literature and cultural historians of future time. Although I have been writing as well as publishing steadily in a variety of genres since the 1960s, and have published a few dozen works of short fiction along the way, *Evanescence* is only my second *published collection* of short stories.

A poet and devotee of the art of letter writing in childhood, I began writing stories and essays in my teens, and continued writing fiction in my twenties, both stories and novels. I published a very few poems and stories during those years. In my thirties, my first book, *Custom: An Essay on Social Codes,* a translation of *Die Sitte* by Ferdinand Tönnies, was published by The Free Press of Glencoe; and I began keeping a Journal, a practice I continue to this day. My book, *One Journal's Life,* a meditation on nearly forty years of Journal-keeping by 2002, was published by Impassio Press that year.

Looking back upon a lifetime of writing, I find that my most productive years of writing essays and academic works were my forties and fifties, and of writing fiction, my forties through my seventies. I believe it was no accident that it was also in midlife that I lost my poet's voice. I did, however, keep the faith with writing fiction and also with life writing, and I serve both the art of letter writing and of Journal-keeping to this day. In my forties, my book of essays, *Redeeming the Sin: Social Science and Literature,* was published by Columbia University Press. In my fifties, *Chimes of Change and Hours,* was published by Fairleigh Dickinson University Press; *Older Women In 20th-Century America: A Selected Annotated Bibliography,* by Garland Publishing; and *Through the Years: A Chronicle of Congregation Ahavath Achim, 5725-5750,* co-authored with my husband, Professor Walter Borenstein, by Franklin Printing in New Paltz, New York.

In my sixties I completed a trilogy of novels, and privately printed fifty copies of one of them, *Simurgh, a novel-in-the-round*. I donated these to libraries with special collections of Judaica and gave them as gifts to friends of my literary estate. In 2009, I published *The Kingdom Where Nobody Dies*, seven tales of life in Louisiana at the time of the civil rights era and the assassination of President Kennedy, through Xlibris. I had completed this fiction collection thirty-two years before, in 1977, with the support of a Fellowship from the National Endowment for the Arts Literature Program awarded me in 1976, and had published two of the seven stories in literary magazines in 1980 and 1981. The Afterword in *The Kingdom Where Nobody Dies* tells the tale of my efforts for nearly 33 years to find a publisher for the collection. To this day, I remain a sometime essayist and a dedicated writer of fiction. The two forms of life writing—Journal-keeping and letter writing—of which I remain a devotee, lead parallel lives with the works of the literary imagination—short stories and novels—taking form at my writing-desk.

Each of the dozen stories I chose for this retrospective of my fiction writing life is a timepiece I fashioned during the second half of the 20th century. Nine of the twelve have been published, and of these, only three were published in the same decade in which they were written—"A Fragment of Glass" (1960s), "Tide of the Unborn" (1970s), and "In a Brief Space" (1980s.") The last three stories in this volume, "After Many Days," "Brief Gallantry," and "Hart Strings," are published here for the first time. I chose these twelve stories for this volume as the ones most telling—with the truth in fiction—of what I witnessed and lived during the last half of "the American century."

How the 20th became known as "the American century" is a tale in itself, one I respectfully leave for historians to tell. That is their calling. The tale I feel compelled to tell here began in my adolescence when I wrote my first essays and stories. I continued to write fiction alongside my life writings, essays and works bridging literature and social science in my middle and later years, to portray my own American experience in stories and novels.

So far as I know, the mode of thinking of personal or historical change in terms of decades can be traced back to the 1890s. Perhaps

I was a census-taker in a former life, as counting in tens "comes naturally" to me. Born in 1930, I apprehended when quite young that I came into the world in a year marking a new decade laden with historical significance in the life of this country, with which my own life would be intertwined. In *A Dictionary of Symbols,* J. E. Cirlot tells us that in decimal systems, the number ten symbolizes the return to unity from multiplicity. Perhaps it is because every new decade marks the beginning of a new multiple series, that birth dates marking the beginning of a new decade and anniversaries in some decimal years are said to be "milestones." A retrospective of selected short stories I wrote from one decade to the next during the second half of the past century accords with the time chart that I would follow in composing a memoir of my writing life and, by way of distillation of my practice of the art of literary portraiture, that could supplant it.

Evanescence is an offering to cultural historians and lovers of literary fiction from a writer who has served both masters since 1950. In reviewing the course of my fiction writing life from youth to my coming-of-age at this, my last season, I wanted to see and mark such changes as I have experienced and rendered in literary art along the journey we Americans may be thought to be taking as a people. I did this in the context of such fields of vision as surrounded my writing-desk, from one space-time period to the next. Because ephemerality is a leitmotif of a great portion of my creative work, as my own life comes to an end I am in quest of a meaning as to why I lived and wrote so much of it during "the American century"—that hundred-year-span that cannot come again.

Like their author, the characters in these stories wrestle with the meaning of what they have lived up to their story-time for the person they feel they have become at that moment. During their story-time they may discover that, "Remembering is harder work than Youth imagines," as the narrator of "After Many Days" recalls having been told forty years before. Her story-time begins on January 11, 1991, four days before the Gulf War, when at sixty she is visited by her Other, the ghost of her younger second self, who asks her if the country is about to wage another Vietnam War.

"I don't know, I'm not a prophet," she replies, "but God forbid we'll have another Vietnam. By my age, one ought to have learned that all wars are alike in too many tragic ways and that every war is different, *also* in too many ways." In the timeshiftings of her reverie, the Biblical "dream that was not a dream," the workings of memory trace the ending of her student days to her time of parting with the Other, the figure she sends forth on a road-not-taken.

2

Human life is storied, and every story has a beginning, a middle and an end. Like that of a triptych, its design may be apprehended when the leaves or panels at either side are unfolded to reveal the one at the center, and also the interconnections between the three. So it may be with the meaning of a life as a whole: its secret, as Frost's poem says, "sits in the middle and knows." As three generations of a family may succeed one another during the span of threescore years and ten, one "reads" the passage of time from left to right, the one in the middle succeeding its elders and preceding its progeny, thus serving as a bridge between them.

The youngest characters in this volume are at some point on the threshold of adulthood. For George, in "The Natural History of a Friendship," the passage from youth to maturity seems as protracted and critical as that from middle age to old age to the narrator of "Rites of Separation." George says at thirty-one, "Half my life's over. And I'm like a kid who's having such a good time in the playground, he won't go home." At the same age, the narrator Martin says, "My limitations were clear to me, and my awareness of them still raw; I had yet to really accept my falling sky." Of his friendship with George which began in their student days, Martin reflects, "we both had the great moral flaw of youth—we were more anxious to be understood than to understand." It is after Martin's wife becomes pregnant that George says to him morosely, "We're not kids anymore."

After forty, the lengthening distance from youth is undeniable. The narrator of "Rites of Separation" says of her three daughters,

"They are almost grown; they are so young." Gallagher, in "Tide of the Unborn" regards his daughter's college classmates with a gimlet eye: "Most of them looked so raggle-tag, smelled so gamey. This the result of years of vitamins, orthodontics, music lessons, private rooms and telephones, and expensive summer camps." His cohorts had "brought up a generation of eternal children, they had!" In turn, young people can be as disdainful of their parents' generation. "Like, I don't care for the way you teach. Like, we don't have to take notes, to spit this stuff back at you on exams," Peg's student tells her in the story "In a Brief Space." "We know so much more than your generation ever knew. We've been places you never heard of. Kant said this? Well, Kant was stupid."

At sixty, the narrator of "After Many Days," an anthropologist, says, "Half a lifetime in academe has taught me that when the young turn to you for guidance, they're quick to translate any counsel of prudence into rejection. Youth has that keenness. And that pride." She remembers with rue that forty years before, middle-aged Harriet had rebuked her flippancy by observing that maturity "is a coat of mail," that "a captive turtlet has to grow a strong shell if it wants to survive to adulthood. Ever notice how strong an adult turtle shell is? That's what protects you from rough treatment by the young of the species." Yet the narrator also remembers with gratitude that Harriet had taught her some vital differences between youth and maturity. Once, Harriet had crossed a threshold ahead of her, and then cautioned, "Careful, there's a step up."

Middle age is the bridge between the first and last of life. As the sociologist George Simmel wrote, "Although a bridge connects two banks, it also makes the distance between them measurable." In midlife, the aging parental figure in the image in the third panel may become ever more distinct and all too familiar to the one in the center, emerging as one's mirrored reflection. The narrator of "Rites of Separation" says that it must have seemed to her mother "that we would always be with her. She did not grasp the equation: growing up is growing away. I am only beginning to understand it as my own children draw nearer the threshold."

In "The Cameo," Miriam finds that her mother-daughter talks with thirty-two-year-old Caro "belonged to another era," that "the closing era had begun . . . the era of observing the proprieties between parent and grown child who in the fullness of time, ineluctably become beloved strangers to one another." Bernie in "A Time For Goodbye Forevers" strives to accept what the long moment of truth that the gaze into the central panel discloses. In the throes of a bitter divorce, his wife had accused him of being responsible for their son's alienation from them. "When did you ever put your children or your wife first?" she demanded. "You, you failed as a father. Because all you ever knew was how to be a son!"

For Laura in "Evanescence," an unexpected discovery after marrying for a second time in midlife is the longing for solitude: "How could she have known when she married Frank that there would soon come a time when she would outgrow the need for human company? Since his retirement he could not have enough of hers. Wherever she took herself he stalked her." A bleak future spreads out before her. In 1984, she thinks of how few are the years before the end of the century, when she will find herself "with all the somedays spent."

In "Tide of the Unborn," Gallagher wants to warn his college-age daughter, "there's not much in these few years you're living now that you can use later on. And that later on is so long, so long." He himself "did not know when this happened," that "a new sense of things had come to him, an understanding of things passing. And he had grown silent." In "A Time For Goodbye Forevers," Bernie prays to the ghost of his dead friend, "Briskin, tell me why life is so long."

Age-mates seek one another's company as sharers of their common prospects seen from the middle distance. In "The Visions," the doomed physician turns to his friend and colleague for an understanding he cannot hope to find elsewhere. In "The Cameo," Miriam cries to her sister-in-law Dorrie, "I can't stand it that they call Mama by her first name! It robs you of your last semblance of human dignity!" Dorrie reminds her of the common fate awaiting the middle-aged, that this is what old age does, "old age is a thief, you want to be spared, pray you'll die before you meet up with him." "Brief Gallantry" is the *beau geste* the narrator makes of completing his wife's last work for her when she is afflicted with Alzheimer's.

Joseph in "A Fragment of Glass" has a transformative vision of the bond between all people around the world and of the common fate of all humanity when his mirror image appears to him in a shard of glass embedded in his navel and speaks his name and calls him *hermano*, brother.

In the second half of life, the middle-aged seek mentors among their elders. The narrator of "Rites of Separation" says that her mother-in-law "is in need of a confessor, now, of one who will listen in silence to her," and that the old woman "does not begin to know how much she is teaching me, and how magnificent she can sometimes be." When "In a Time For Goodbye Forevers," Bernie pleads for Briskin's ghost to tell him that his lost son will come back, the wraith of his old friend sing-songs, "I'll say it, he'll come back. Nobody goes away for good anymore. But maybe he won't come back like you expect. Maybe he'll have a little boy by the hand. And maybe the love of that boy you'll have." The whimsical humor and far-sightedness of the old can ease the pain of the generation in the middle. In "The Cameo," Mr. Becker asks Miriam if she'd ever noticed how elderly one becomes at the age of thirty. When Miriam confides to him of her grief that there are no grandchildren on her horizon, he says gently, "Everybody in the whole world is family . . . all the children are our grandchildren, look at it that way."

The spirit of the early Fifties, as the shadows began to fall over the crest of the American century, rustles the pages of two stories of friendship between two men. In "The Visions," a story of two physicians in their forties, Carl has just learned he has a terminal illness and asks Thaddeus for a favor his friend is loath to grant. In "The Natural History of a Friendship," the narrator retraces the history of his friendship with George, an emigré from Czechoslovakia, beginning with their post-World War II student days and ending when they go their separate ways—when "now the women correspond."

In "The Visions," the friend of the doomed man "saw with love and pity" how Carl "held his head high going down" in the prime of life ("thought I had *time!*"), and was reminded of having "warned him off" years before of "tearing up his life" for a woman who had "quickened something" in him—"the mad dream of immortality maybe, eternal youth." In "The Natural History of a Friendship," the narrator winnows the fading youthful dreams of adventure and bright expectancy and the era's growing existential angst from the threshing of his friend's harsh censure of the privatism of "the Eisenhower years." Yeats envisioned the years as black oxen treading the world. In this volume, the essence of the *Zeitgeist* during the second half of the American century—waking from the dream of invincibility—bodies forth in the twelve stories in *Evanescence* as the five decades succeed one another.

As one grows older, the play of memory seems to favor decades as nesting dolls. In "The Cameo," Miriam sees the end of World War II from the perspective of the 1980s as a time when both her mother's life and the life of the country were at their peak: "Gemini was in her prime in 1945, when the lights were going on all over the world . . . the whole world had seemed in its prime that year." The late Forties are a touchstone of the Fata Morgana of his ill-fated marriage for Gallagher in "Tide of the Unborn." He remembers how, "to 'A small café/Mam'selle' and 'Red Sails in the Sunset,' he and his ex-wife had "swept one another off their feet and away on the Roof Garden of downtown Milwaukee."

In the story "In a Brief Space," Peg remembers the lunch in 1969 when she last saw her late Professor Moberg. He had reminisced then about the postwar years when Parade Ground units mushroomed on the campus. He told her of one night when engineering students wired the entire football field, and a fireworks display controlled by timing devices went on until dawn. "One of the last communal pranks of the innocents," she had remarked. "Today they smash windows, slash couches and draperies and oil portraits of the emeriti." In 1981, she recognizes that it was not her last but her first sight of Moberg when she was his student that was indelibly imprinted on her memory. He was "smiling, grasping both sides of the lectern with his huge and shapely hands, a STEVENSON button bright-blooming on his lapel." When she tells his ghost that his manuscript could circulate forever and ever, he chides her, "Margaret, you said long, long ago that you were choosing Life; here, take it then."

A feeling of the times emanates from sounds and scents and phrases as memory unfolds its tapestry of sensoria: for Bernie, on Washington Avenue in South Miami Beach, the novelty shops with the souvenirs, the key chains with sea horses dangling from them, the underpants for the grandchildren with "Grandma loves me" stamped on them, the tiny crates stuffed with orange gumballs . . . for Gallagher, his daughter's "blather about seven arrows and the nuclear family," her lecturing him about overpopulation . . . for Peg, the People's Mural, a Great Dove of Peace, flowering on the stone face of the building across the street from the restaurant where Moberg asked what she thought of his manuscript, the 800-page tome on the folly of war he had bequeathed her as her burden . . . for Laura, the twin peaks of the Shawangunks in the calm sea of sky over the Mid-Hudson Valley, a shimmering cascade of light auguring the sunset, Kem's whisper, "It is so beautiful a planet" . . . for the narrator of "After Many Days," the whitened sky of the raw, windy winter day in Illinois in 1950, Harriet asking "Where are you going?" the "rust-colored babushka she was tying under her chin with mittened fingers aging the heart-shaped eager face inside." Remembering Harriet forty years later, the narrator recalls that a co-worker Mary Ellen had been seven months' pregnant in June of 1951. It occurs to her that Mary Ellen gave birth to a baby boy later that summer—"born at the right time to come of draft age during the Vietnam War."

Cross-currents flow between these stories: the palindromic year of 1991 is the story-time of "After Many Days" and also of "Brief Gallantry." A village in the Mid-Hudson Valley is a living presence in the elsewhere of "Evanescence," "The Cameo," "After Many Days" and "Hart Strings." There are time travels in "Brief Gallantry" and "Hart Strings." Animism pervades three stories: The narrator of "Rites of Separation" imagines what old age is for her mother-in-law: "In this very old book her grandfather breathes; in this bit of cloth her father stirs. Her mother looks out from this mirror; that is why its face is turned to the wall." And, "Aging is a diminishing. Whatever you still cling to, that will bind you to life." And, "The cameo is sick with an old passion that all but only children come to know." In "Evanescence," Kem counsels Laura that only way to put an end to the recurrent dream that pursues her is to appease the spirit of whatever it was that she abandoned, by bringing it back into her life. The cameo in the story of that title speaks to Miriam of "The covenant between the generations: the promise of continuance upheld by honoring the sacred trust. Replenishment. The lessons of the mind and spirit and heart fully received only by passing them on."

3

Works of the literary imagination bear witness to their authors' fascinations. Readers of these stories will encounter variations on universal themes: jealousy and rivalry—between friends (in "The Natural History of a Friendship"), siblings (in "Rites of Separation," the narrator's cautionary tale of the refusal to bury old swords in the shadowed playground of childhood; and also in "The Cameo"— "No, no, dolink," Bubby used to say, "Jealousy kills, jealousy kills"), and spouses (in "A Time For Goodbye Forevers," "Tide of the Unborn,"—and for the Mobergs "In a Brief Space," Laura and Jerry in "Evanescence," and Miriam and Hugh in "The Cameo," the recurrent thrust and parry in the contest for recognition between two talented and ambitious people who happen to be married to one another.)

In writing this retrospective, I recognize some of my own signature haunts: the Other, the second self, parallel lives (in "A Fragment of Glass," "After Many Days," "Brief Gallantry," and "Hart Strings".) Readers will also find that the characters in these tales are wrestling with matters compelling to writers from *both* the worlds of the social sciences and literature. Among these are abortion, feminism, interfaith marriage, and war, about which bones of contention still rattle in public forums as well as in their own private lives. "In a Brief Space" is a story of a woman's keenly felt responsibility to fulfill a mission impossible—to find a publisher for her late Professor Moberg's tome on the folly of war. With the Supreme Court ruling on draft registration handed down just days before she is sent on this mission she despairs of ever accomplishing, she remembers one of her students, "Nineteen years old, and his heart was as dead as the moon." The traces of the storyteller that cling to this story are made by the tracks of my shuttling back and forth between two lives, the one in academe teaching courses in sociology and anthropology, and the other at my writing-desk, conjuring stories of what I learned and taught in classrooms at the University of Illinois, Louisiana State University, Cornell College in Mount Vernon, Iowa, and the State University College of New York at New Paltz.

I have gone to and fro between two studios throughout my worklife. In faithfulness to my understanding of storytelling as a transmutation of what I experience and witness into art, I am ever attentive to the differences between the parallel worlds of fact and fiction, of documentation and portrayal, and to the subtle ways they can shade into one another. As my imagination gives rise to shapes that become characters calling to me with their thoughts and feelings and circumstances, I seek to portray the texture of life in my characters' space-times in the rhythms and with the poetic immediacy of their own language. The timepieces in this volume were fashioned by one writer at work in her studio of literary art, practicing portraiture of figures in three dimensions, weaving the texture of their lived experiences into whole cloth, and imbuing their narratives with the distinctive flavors of a time and place.

Stories tell of the parallel lives of the people who write them and also of the people who read them. One who enters the story as a first-time reader may willingly become a creature of its story-time and therefore a changed person from having read it. Enhanced by the encounter, one is offered an afterlife, perhaps even an ever-afterlife, as it ripens within the mind and heart. The act of reading a story may endow the reader with a heightened sense of transport to another world, perhaps one that turns out to be amazingly close at hand, where one also lives. A work of art has this possibility of transforming past, present or future experience powerfully as it opens new paths between them.

In reading literature, as in gazing at a painting, or listening to a musical composition, we experience art directly: there is no one between ourselves and the composition. Granted, there may be this subtle difference between literature and fine art on the one hand and music on the other, that one may have the feeling that the spirit of the performer who plays the musical instrument is infused with that of the one who composed it so that one may "forget" they are not one and the same in applauding the performance. But just as what one apprehends from experiencing a work of art depends in part on what one brings to it, so what one brings *from* it always has this possibility of transformation. Reading is a transformative art.

Reading also can be one of the most intense experiences of a person's life. It can happen that a reader unwittingly transforms something in the work to bring it nearer to "this" reality. Caught in the trance of deep reading, one may *hear* a character's voice or know what the character will say, before turning the page on which the words appear. As words on a page of the forth-and-back call-and-response between two intimates engaged in exchanging letters, a story may "come to life" in the mind of a reader who then converses in the inner forum with this or that character, or with its author, about what is going on. This happens more often than not after a period of ripening of the words in one's mind, one's heart, one's soul. Sparks of life in the reader's dreams or imagined worlds may be ignited. Words in a story read long ago and "forgotten" can irrupt in consciousness, as the words of a prayer return to Abby in my story "Brief Gallantry." It has been said that no voice is ever wholly lost.

The stories in this volume are laden with my time-haunted thoughts of the evanescence of all things. The historical memory of a culture is storied. Since I was a child, I have longed to rescue what I love and value from oblivion, to rush to write down what I saw and heard lest it perish. I recognized the redemptive power of stories, that stories are our medicine animals, our dinihowi, as the narrator of "After Many Days" says. Telling our stories and listening to the stories of others are a joy to us, a celebration of our common humanity. What Hawthorne wrote of his five-year-old son Julian is true of all storytellers and listeners: "It is his desire of sympathy that lies at the bottom of the great heap of his babblement. He wants to enrich all his enjoyments by steeping them in the heart of some friend."

It has been said that living well is our best revenge. So is reading well and deeply. Stories are our consolation. Hart of "Hart Strings" keeps a Journal of his beloved late wife Sarah; by writing its pages, he writes her back into life. To replenish. To give her an afterlife here. Time, even as one utters the word *time*, ever becomes past-time. Writing stories is as close an approximation as a literary artist may ever hope to achieve to work the miracle of the resurrection of the dead.

Hart wonders if there is a reality you were apprehending when you made Art—an elsewhere, an elsewhen. Proust too wondered if there are other worlds more real than this one. Perhaps a new world is created with every story; perhaps there are infinite worlds created in every newly created story. Years before I knew the concept of a culture, I knew that a people's history is storied, that a human being is an archive of stories, and that fiction writers are born to tell the stories of those who for whatever reason are not able to write them down. For pilgrims journeying on the long road of a lifetime's memory, the spirit of a time they call theirs inhabits a span of years and then vanishes to hide in their stories. I hear the words from the wrestling-match with the angel in Bethel as I sit down at my writing-desk to begin with the words, *once upon a time:* "I will not let thee go except thou bless me." So does the story-writer pray the story will find readers to preserve its life, that it may live in another clime, in another soul, becoming part of the story of humanity.

A people who cease to tell and write stories extinguish the light of their Soul. That is because a story contains multitudes. Stories beget stories. A written story whose author declares it completed and releases it into the world is a work of art fashioned by its maker once and once only at the moment the author says Amen to it. Left unpublished, or published but left unread, the light of its soul fades and disappears. But if its author recalls it later and rewrites it, the old story changes, "yielding place to new." Because stories have as many lives as they have people who read and re-read them, and because a story ripens within the mind of its reader, stories can multiply exceedingly, each bequeathing new souls to readers, with successive writings and readings *unto the generations.*

The spirit of this Afterword is a play upon The Many Worlds Interpretation of Quantum Mechanics: there are as many imagined worlds as there are stories. This is also why every story, thanks to the possibility of begettings beyond number of its infinite varieties across space-times, is an ancient tale inside myriad wrappings of atmosphere and happenings. The soul of every story that is written or read aspires to immortality. Our fecund powers of imagination are our most precious endowment. The transformative arts of writing and reading stories reveal that we may indeed be made in the divine image. We must live as if all things are possible.

The words *Once upon a time,* opening the door to an elsewhere and elsewhen in that space-time, invite the reader to enter, offering the possibility of discovering that the tale running ahead on the path, ethereal and swift-passing, has *a local habitation and a name.* It is thought that if parallel worlds collide, that will mean the destruction of everything. But if they graze one another in passing, by grace of the imagination, that promises us the joys of continuous creation.

Audrey Borenstein
9 November 2009

www.ingramcontent.com/pod-product-compliance
Lightning Source LLC
LaVergne TN
LVHW091535060526
838200LV00036B/621